A WARRIOR'S HEART

A WARRIOR'S HEART

MISTY M. BELLER

THORNDIKE PRESS
A part of Gale, a Cengage Company

**LIBRARY OF CONGRESS CIP DATA ON FILE.
CATALOGUING IN PUBLICATION FOR THIS BOOK
IS AVAILABLE FROM THE LIBRARY OF CONGRESS.**

ISBN-13: 978-1-4328-9223-4 (hardcover alk. paper)

Published in 2021 by arrangement with Bethany House Publishers, a division of Baker Publishing Group

Printed in Mexico
Print Number: 01   Print Year: 2022

To my mother.
My first reader, proofreader,
endless babysitter, and
primary moral support.
I couldn't do this book thing
without you!

The LORD is my rock, and my fortress, and my deliverer; my God, my strength, in whom I will trust; my buckler, and the horn of my salvation, and my high tower.

Psalm 18:2

1

September 1814
Rocky Mountains, Rupert's Land (Canada)
Another ten paces and she'd have to shoot.

Brielle Durand steadied the arrow fletching against her cheek, then pushed her body farther into the bow to draw the cord tighter.

The man in her sights rode calmly forward, his breath blowing white in the early morning air. The mount beneath him snorted, releasing its own cloud as it bobbed against the bit. The animal must sense the nearing danger.

In truth, the beast had more intelligence than its rider. As was usual in the ways of animals. Especially when compared to an Englishman like this fellow appeared to be.

Five more strides.

She narrowed her gaze, focusing on the point of aim so her arrow would hit his midsection. Should she give him warning?

9

Perhaps the cry of a mountain lion would plant fear in his chest. She caught her breath, preparing to make the fierce scream she'd practiced so oft.

But the man spurred his horse faster, as though eager to charge through the opening in the rock. Surely he couldn't see the sheltered courtyard just beyond. The place forbidden to outsiders — especially Englishmen.

She locked her jaw to steady herself. Since her eighteenth birthday, when she'd finally been allowed to fight with the warriors, she swore an oath each morning to protect their village. Never again would an Englishman enter their inner circle unhindered. Her people had learned the terrible lesson well the last time. Memory of her mother's lifeless eyes tried to surface, but she pushed the distraction away.

Pressing against the bow, she took a final breath to aim, then let the arrow fly. *Guide its path, Lord.*

A roar broke the morning quiet, radiating from the rocky cliffs like the bellow of a wounded bear. The man doubled over, wrapping his arms around his middle. The long slender shaft of her arrow extended from the leathers that clothed him.

She inhaled a steadying breath, then

released it. She'd done what she must to protect her people. Now came the time to uncover his reason for approaching the circle. Her home.

The safety of her people.

Evan MacManus gripped the arrow shaft with both hands, forcing his body to draw in air despite the agony in his gut.

He'd not even heard the Indians' approach. Not noticed any quieting of the forest creatures. He must be losing his instincts, and this arrow served as grave proof of that fact.

He reined Granite into a cluster of trees, where the trunks might shield him from another arrow. Precious little time remained to extract the point before the Indians would be upon him. His hammering pulse only made each breath harder to inhale. He had to push aside the pain and focus on what must be done.

Feeling for the solid thickness of the arrowhead to make sure the iron hadn't sunk completely beneath his skin, he clenched his jaw at the cramping in his gut. Best to get this over with.

The arrow pulled loose from his flesh in a clean motion — maybe it hadn't sunk deep enough to damage any organs. The tip snagged on his buckskin tunic, and he wiggled it loose but stopped himself before hurling the wicked thing into the woods. With a hand pressing his undershirt against the wound to staunch the bleeding, he tucked the arrow in his musket scabbard and peered around the trunk of the tree nearest him. He could investigate which tribe had made the weapon later. If he survived this attack. At the moment, he had to find a way to ensure he didn't get a more personal introduction to whoever shot him.

No movement flashed in the morning light beyond the trees. Only a cluster of scraggly bushes marked the other side of the trail. But the warrior had likely been shooting from farther ahead, maybe even from the bend in the path, where the bases of two mountains met to form a narrow opening between them. The gap created a natural gateway where an enemy could find cover and wait.

A spasm seized Evan, doubling him over as he fought to stifle a groan. He had to keep breathing, or this lightness in his head would take over.

"To the ground. Now," barked a voice behind him. The tone held an accent, but not any Indian tongue he'd ever heard.

Evan twisted, biting back a grunt as he

12

tried to focus his wavering vision on the figure standing not five strides behind his horse, bow and arrow at the ready. He had no doubt that second arrow would find its way into his flesh if he didn't obey the order.

Pressing a hand tight against his wound, he clutched his saddle horn with the other and eased himself to the ground. He didn't release his hold on either the saddle or his gut as he tried to settle the spinning in his head. Had he lost so much blood already? The warm liquid coated his hand, which meant he wasn't staunching the flow. Yet he shouldn't be this lightheaded so quickly.

Ignoring the thought, he squinted at the bundle of furs before him.

"To the ground, I said. Or it's another arrow you'll meet."

That was no Indian's speech. Certainly not broken English, but the words contained a lilt only a Frenchman could master.

Blast. How had he stumbled upon the enemy all the way out here? He'd hoped — prayed — this territory was too far west for him to meet one of the Canadians they were fighting.

"Who are you?" He knew better than to argue with a man pointing a weapon, but the cramping in his gut made his thoughts swim in a disjointed flow.

A growl emanated from his adversary. Guttural, but not so deep as he would have expected. Still, the tone made it clear the fellow's patience was fast waning.

Evan released the saddle horn, lowered his arm, and sank to his knees on the frozen ground. Snow hadn't yet fallen in this part of the territory, but if the cold stinging his exposed skin was any indicator, an icy torrent would be upon them soon.

The Indian — or whoever was cloaked in the animal skins — circled around him, never dropping the aim of his arrow. The faint crackle of leaves bespoke an approach from behind. Would the man bind his wrists or pierce him with a knife and end his life?

Evan would have to turn and topple the stranger if he were to have any chance of getting the upper hand. He could do it, even with the arrow wound, certainly. He'd fought tougher opponents in battle after having received more than one slice from a saber. A Frenchman would be an easy match — if only he could keep his swirling wits about him.

Footsteps padded behind him, and Evan tensed to spin and strike.

"Lower your —"

He whirled and shot his fist forward, praying his aim would be true, even though his target blurred into three shapes. His arm struck something — fur? — and the man issued a high-pitched gasp. Was this a boy?

But Evan had no time to ponder as something grabbed his wrist and a force slammed into his back, shoving him down, almost to the ground.

He writhed, jerking his arm to get away from the man's grasp. Evan brought his free hand around to strike a blow. The effort sent a knife of pain through his gut, but he clamped his jaw tight and fought harder.

His opponent moved too quickly, out of striking distance before Evan could land a blow. His dizziness must be slowing his movements, but he had to overcome that. The man had Evan's arm pinned behind him now, and a boot in his back, pressing him toward the dirt.

He resisted the pressure, his stomach hovering about a foot above the forest floor. But the effort stole his strength more every second. He'd have enough energy left for one more counterattack, and this time he had to overcome his enemy or he'd never complete his mission. He'd already spotted signs that he might have reached his goal.

This mountain he'd been riding around possessed the orange striations usually found near pitchblende. Now, he had to

15

locate that mineral itself so the army's scientists could create the blast that would finally end this brutal war. This work was all he had left, and he'd carry out his assignment no matter what it took.

Somehow, he had to make restitution for last time.

With a mighty effort, he twisted around, reaching for the ankle that held him low. The attacker must have been prepared for his movement and grabbed Evan's free wrist, jerking his hand upward so his arms burned at the joint of his shoulders — effectively stealing the last of his strength and gaining the upper hand. Literally.

Were these his final moments? They couldn't be. *God, help me.*

Evan knelt there, struggling for breath. Even when he sucked in air, the wind didn't seem to satisfy the craving in his chest. Perhaps the arrow had punctured his breathing vessel.

His captor worked quickly with his wrists, wrapping a rough cord around them. Despite the unsteadiness in his head, Evan strained to look around, to keep his ears aware of any sound that might give notice of more enemies approaching. Perhaps help, even, as unlikely as that was. But one could hope.

No unnatural noises greeted him. Only a pheasant's call broke the cold silence.

At last, the man behind him gave a final jerk on the binding, then released Evan's hands. The immediate relief in his upper arms seemed to sap a little more of his strength as his body sagged.

"You will walk." The man's voice had such an unusual accent, making it hard to place either his age or nationality. Definitely young, though.

How humbling. Here he was, Evan Mac-Manus, former captain in the American army and now a trusted spy commissioned by President Madison himself, brought down by a lad with a bow and arrow.

Evan struggled to his feet, spreading them wide to keep from toppling over as his vision swam. Even with his eyes squeezed tight, his body wobbled more than he could control. He shouldn't be this affected by a simple wound, even with the blood loss. Had the arrowhead been tainted? He'd heard tales of Indians dipping the tips in poison before battle.

A hand gripped his arm, giving him something to brace against — until it yanked him forward. Still, the hold kept him upright as he forced one foot in front of the other. The grip felt small, even through the layers of his coat.

Evan forced his eyes open, but the sunlight made the dizziness more intense. He tried squinting, which helped. He had to stay alert, watch his surroundings if he was going to get out of this alive. So far, they appeared to be walking the same path north he'd been riding. Toward the opening between the mountains.

When they reached the spot, his captor loosed a piercing whistle. Evan fought to keep from cringing at the surprise blast so near his ear, but a fresh blade of pain pierced his middle anyway. When a second shrill whistle came, he almost jabbed the lad with his elbow.

But the reply that sounded from the other side of the rock grabbed his focus. They wove around a boulder to proceed through the opening, and Evan squinted again now that he could see bright daylight on the other side.

The place looked to be a meadow of sorts. With figures darting through the winter brown grass. Voices called, or maybe laughed. Children's voices? The pain and blood loss must be making him daft. Or maybe he was being taken to an Indian village. He had to stay awake and watch for a chance to escape.

His captor pushed him forward as other figures approached. These, too, were wrapped in animal skins, but their bulk proved them to be full-grown men. His vision blurred further, even when he tried to focus. He couldn't make out much more than dark or light hair.

Low murmurings sounded around him, yet they seemed to come from so far away. Or maybe it was he who had moved. He had to recover his strength. Squinting again, he tried to straighten. "Who are you?"

The talking around him ceased, and a figure stepped in front of him. He blinked to focus, and the fur cloaking the person began to look familiar. His captor.

The man reached up and pushed the hood off his head, revealing dark hair and a smooth face.

Evan blinked. He must be dafter than he realized, although with the person less than a stride away, it was hard to miss what his eyes took in.

A woman?

Even through his shadowy vision, he could make out the delicate angles of her face. Those piercing dark eyes.

"You have come to Laurent. Now you will tell us why." The lilt in her voice sounded different now that he could see her. With her tone so melodic, how could he not have recognized her as female?

A fresh wave of dizziness washed over him, and he braced his feet. A hand gripped his arm, that same small hand as before.

"Your purpose, monsieur. Before you swoon, if you please."

Even if he wanted to tell her, his mouth had turned to cotton. Blackness circled the edge of his vision, increasing until he could only see her blurry form through a small hole, like he was looking through a field glass. This lightness in his head almost took over completely. His body sank like it weighed twice as much as usual.

Lord, don't let them kill me. Not yet.

He had too much to make up for. Too much left to fix before he faced the final judgment.

2

Brielle knelt beside the crumpled form on the ground, a knife in her hand. His collapse was most likely due to the sleeping potion she'd coated the arrowhead with, but she couldn't be too cautious with an outsider. She worked two fingers under the collar of his coat, then stilled as she felt the flow of his life blood. Not a strong surge, but steady.

She allowed her gaze to roam his face. Strength resonated from the tanned skin around his eyes, although most of his lower features were covered with a close-cut beard. Its shortness almost made him look like a vain popinjay that spent hours on his appearance, except for the untrimmed edges. Perhaps a fresh growth for the winter months, as a few of her villagers allowed.

The man's lips parted slightly, his steady breaths tinged with a ragged sound. She glanced down at the blood spotting his middle. The patch had grown to cover most of his midsection. He should be moved inside, where Audrey could attend him.

Straightening, she looked at the four men forming a semicircle near the stranger's feet, awaiting her instructions. "Leonard, fetch his horse. Philip, Geoffrey, take him to the holding chamber. I'll get the healer and follow soon."

She pushed to her feet and stepped back, clearing the way for the others to carry him inside. The man's clothing wasn't much different than her own people's, although she'd never seen that style of foot covering.

From where had he come? And for what purpose? They'd worked so hard to keep their village hidden from the outside world. Even a hundred years ago, when the grandfathers had left New France to settle here, they'd traveled months to find an area this far from civilization. The mountain caves had provided the perfect place to build their community.

But now a stranger invaded their privacy. The only other time Englishmen had entered their circle had been . . . awful.

That day had changed Laurent forever.

But at least those murdering Englishmen hadn't escaped to tell of the hidden French village. Perhaps this man had heard of their

22

people from the Dinee natives and come to see for himself. But whether he meant ill or was only curious would have to be determined before he could be released.

Turning, she scooped up her bow and strode toward the mountain that curved to form two sides of the open courtyard. The other two walls were made of stone. Some of them had been placed there by God, but the gaps had been carefully filled in by former generations to make the courtyard secure and not obvious from the outside.

She aimed her steps toward Audrey's quarters. Her sister, Charlotte, would be irked that Brielle wasn't coming straight-away with news of the stranger, but a healer was of greater import just now. And besides, the girl would be safest away from the stranger until they understood his purpose.

She couldn't risk losing her sister the same way their mother had been taken.

The burning in Evan's gut pierced deep, yanking him from the haze of sleep. Scuffling sounded near his head, and he forced his body to remain still as he cracked his eyes. A figure stood over him, and he tensed, preparing for a fight. The person moved in a graceful rhythm, like that of a female.

He opened his eyes wider to make out her

23

features in the dim light. The woman seemed to be working on something. Then, an icy substance touched his middle. He inhaled a sharp breath before he could stop himself.

She glanced at his face, and the light illuminated part of her features. "I'm sorry, but we must clean it." Glancing up, she nodded at someone across the room, then returned to her work.

The cold spread across his belly as she scrubbed, probably at dried blood. At least, he hoped the stuff had dried and the wound wasn't seeping still. Each pass of her cloth tugged on his injury with an aching jolt. He forced his focus away from the pain of her movements and looked over to see what she had glanced at.

Another person stood against the far wall. A familiar form with an animal-skin cloak still draped over her shoulders, yet the hood no longer shrouding her face. A single black braid hung down her shoulder, light from a torch flickering off the ebony strands, turning them golden.

He focused on her face, this woman who had so ruthlessly shot him in the gut, then bound him and marched him like a prize turkey back to her tribe — or whatever these people called themselves. In his experience, women were a bit daintier than she'd acted so far. Even the sturdy pioneer stock wore dresses to their ankles and knew their place was cooking and caring for the home. His eyes skimmed unbidden to where her cloak ended, not much past her knees. In the shadows of the room, he could only make out the outline of her lower limbs, which gave his mind just enough leeway to fill in the details.

He jerked his eyes back up to her face, catching her gaze as she studied him with a hostility he'd certainly not earned. *He* was the one who'd been shot, by saints. It was high time he regain the upper hand, even if his own were still bound. At least they were now tied in front of him instead of behind.

He swallowed to remove the cotton from his mouth, then forced his clammy mouth to work. "Who are you?" His voice came out more gravely than it should, so he cleared his throat.

She raised her chin, those dark brows arching in a look of calculated amusement. "That's a better question for you, I think. From where do you hail, monsieur?"

With the lilting accent and the occasional foreign word, she must be French. Was everyone else from the Canadas, too? What kind of enemy hotbed had he ridden into?

The French weren't currently attacking his home country, although they'd been troublesome at the start of the war. The British were the primary enemies, but the French certainly hadn't proved allies. And where did the loyalties of this little settlement lie?

The question she'd asked wasn't one he was willing to answer, so he motioned toward the woman working over him. "Is she finishing me off?"

He meant it half in jest, and the smile that touched the corner of her mouth said she caught the humor. "If I wanted that done, I would have accomplished the task myself."

The brunette woman who dabbed at his wound with a thick paste glanced up at his captor, and they shared a smile.

That was all well and good, but he couldn't have been brought here merely as sport for a gaggle of women. He pulled his elbows back and lifted his chest in an attempt to sit up, but the fire in his gut seared hot.

"Lie still. You'll start the bleeding anew." The woman working on his injury pushed on his shoulder, but he ignored the pressure.

He shifted his bound wrists so he could press one hand to his wound, trying not to react when he touched a wet mass of something. His shirt still covered his upper half, but they'd pulled up the bottom to tend the wound. At least they hadn't stripped him bare.

"Lie still." This bark came from the black-haired archer, but he paid no heed to the command as he fought through the pain to sit up.

A flurry of motion whirled around him, even as his head spun from the change in position. A sharp jab was the first sensation that gave him pause. He looked up into the sparking glare of his captor. The lady warrior.

Another pair of eyes glared from just behind her, these decidedly belonging to a man. Two more men hovered on his other side, the one in front holding a hatchet poised to strike Evan as though he were a piece of firewood to be split down the center.

His chest clenched so tight he couldn't draw air. He hated being in confined spaces, especially with his hands bound. But he couldn't react. Couldn't show the irrational fear that hammered in his chest — not so much from the hatchet as from so many people hovering over him like a smothering blanket.

He eased his hands up to show he meant

no harm. "I'll not hurt anyone. Just give me a moment to sit." *And back away from me.*

Wary gazes studied him all around, and that hatchet still poised high above him. Apparently, his words hadn't convinced them. He couldn't promise he wouldn't try to escape, but his mission was a peaceable one. Unless he had to fight for his life, he'd not cause injury.

"I swear it on my honor. You've nothing to fear from me." He met each gaze in turn, ending with Miss Archer, who still had the point of her knife poked into his chest. She was probably making a good-sized hole in his shirt.

Of course, her arrow had already done that once.

He met her hard glare with a look of his own, trying to keep his gaze as neutral as he could. In truth, if he made it out of this place alive, the accomplishment would be by the mercy of God alone.

She studied him for another long moment, then pulled the knife away from his chest and straightened. She flicked a glance to the man with the hatchet and spoke something, but this time it was loud enough that he could tell for sure the words weren't English. Definitely French. The man's quick response came in the same language. Evan had picked up a few French words in his work as a spy, but these two spoke so rapidly he couldn't decipher much.

All four of them took a collective step back, but the woman returned her glare to him. "Audrey will finish tending your wound. But if you give her trouble, I shall slit your throat."

Although her tone was quiet, the words seemed to echo off the walls when she paused for effect. Part of him wanted to scoff at the idea of a woman doing him in, yet he was no fool. She'd already disarmed him, leaving him lying on his back — wounded, hands bound, and surrounded. He would need to overcome at least a few of those obstacles before he had any hope of escape.

He glanced at the brunette female standing by the stone wall, behind the man with the hatchet. "I'll not give her trouble." He could only pray she planned to apply a healing salve, not a poisonous concoction.

The men appeared to be pacified by his answer, for they all stepped away. At a word from the hatchet-wielder, the other two left the room through a wooden door tucked in the corner.

The remaining man propped himself against the wall near the door, and the lady warrior moved back to her position on the other side of the chamber. The young woman, Audrey, returned with a basket that must contain her supplies.

As she worked, Evan sent a glance around the room. His chest clenched again, and he struggled for slow, steady breaths. This space was large, but the walls were made of solid stone, as though he was in a cave. He wouldn't be able to get out except through the single door.

Three torches lit the area from their various mounts along the walls. With the dimness of the room, a fourth would have been welcome. Maybe more light would ease the hammering in his chest. *Settle yourself, MacManus.*

Pressure at his wound brought a blessed distraction, and he turned his focus to Audrey, the only name he knew among these people.

She looked at him. "I need to wrap the bandage in place. Can you lean up?"

He nodded, then worked his elbows under him again and bit back a groan as he strained to a sitting position. He'd not show weakness to these people, no matter that his belly felt as if a searing knife twisted deep.

When she finished, she touched his shoulder. "Lie back now."

He did so, more to make them complacent by his obedience than anything. But the instant relief in his muscles made it hard not to ease out a long breath. This way he could save his strength.

Audrey looked over at the lady warrior. "He needs to rest now."

The other woman nodded. Even the bob of her chin bespoke an aura of fierceness. For one so young, she appeared to hold a position of importance in the group. And a woman, no less.

She pushed away from the wall and sauntered over to him, the bottom of her animal-skin cloak swaying with each step. She stopped less than a stride away and dropped to one knee.

He could raise his hands and touch her if he wanted. Try to grab her wrist and overpower her. Though he had a feeling gaining the upper hand against this she-warrior would be no small feat. Especially with his wrists still tied.

"What is your name?" Her accent barely came through this time, just enough to give her an air of mystery.

"Evan." He met her dark gaze squarely. "What is yours?"

Her eyes gave away none of her thoughts. "I am called Brielle."

The name suited her. Unusual, yet strong. "And from where do you hail, Evan?"

Hearing his given name in her voice, with that light accent, captured his attention in a way that distracted him. He forced the thought aside and focused on her question. "I'm from the mountain country, but not this area." Hopefully she would accept that answer. He couldn't say he was from America. That would likely raise suspicion about his reason for being so far north and so near the British colonies, while the war raged between the two countries.

And he wouldn't lie. He'd done enough things he wasn't proud of in his time as a spy, he didn't need to compound his sins by building a web of deceit. Usually silence or only a snippet of the truth would suffice.

She studied him, and with the shadows, it was impossible to read her thoughts. She looked to be weighing the truth in his words. Did she realize he'd avoided the question?

Perhaps it was time to ask some questions of his own. He tossed a casual glance around the room. "Where are we?"

She followed his gaze, lingering on the man by the door, then on the brown-haired woman who had risen and returned to her position beside the wall. "This is where we hold our prisoners." She looked back at him, and he could have sworn her eyes held a glimmer of mirth. "You might call it a dungeon."

3

Brielle studied the man's response to her quip. They'd not kept a prisoner here since the Dinee lad they'd caught stealing from one of the supply caves several years back.

From the interest this Englishman tried to mask with a wary gaze, he didn't seem to know what to make of them. The feeling was mutual, to be sure.

"A dungeon, you say? Have I stumbled upon an ancient castle?" He raised dark brows.

"Not a castle." How had she let the questioning turn to her people? She had much to discover about this stranger. "I don't believe you finished telling me of your purpose here."

"Had I begun to tell you?" A glimmer of concern touched his eyes, as though he might be afraid he'd spoken too much. Either he was hiding something or the effects of the sleeping tincture still muddled his brain.

It was amazing how much power was contained in that combination of herbs Audrey had discovered. Dipping their arrows in the potion had been an act of genius. Of course, the coating typically only helped bring down caribou or deer, in case her arrow didn't accomplish the task. This was the first time she'd had opportunity to see how it worked on a human.

If he truly didn't remember the scene, perhaps a bit of help would jog his memory. "*Oui.* You said you'd been looking for a hidden village, then just as you opened your mouth to reveal why, you swooned like a young girl."

The confusion washing his face cleared within seconds, replaced with a stoic look that didn't conceal the mirth in his eyes. "You must be mistaken, mademoiselle. I've never swooned in my life, nor have I done *anything* like a young girl."

She had to bite back a chuckle. In truth, she should be affronted by the distaste with which he spoke the final words. Yet he wasn't jesting. This strapping fellow seemed as far from a female as night from day. And she'd not missed the muscle rippling across his midsection before Audrey finished the bandage and readjusted his tunic.

But enough of that line of thought. "Please, finish what you began to tell us before."

His right eye twitched. "I can't imagine what that might have been. Your arrow had quite an effect on me." Then both his eyes narrowed. "More effect than simple blood loss. Could it be you added some sort of poison to the tip?"

She worked hard not to show surprise. This man was no simpleton, apparently. Either that, or he was merely drawing from his own past deceptions.

She let a smile touch her mouth. "Very good, monsieur. Not poison, though. Merely a tonic to help our visitors relax."

He snorted.

Audrey shifted from her nearby perch, and Brielle looked over at her. The woman's eyes spoke very clearly the reprimand that would soon leave her lips if Brielle didn't allow this man to rest. She glared at her friend, then used their native French tongue so their prisoner didn't understand. "I must seek out his purpose for invading our village."

Audrey rolled her eyes, then responded in the same language. "You said he wandered too near the entrance of the circle. He's likely a hapless stranger who knew nothing of us before you pierced him with your arrow. Let the man rest and recover, then we'll send him on his way."

A surge of anger washed through Brielle. She'd be drawn and quartered before she released an Englishman, not until they knew full well he meant the village no harm. The last time they'd trusted such, her mother and five others had paid the price with their lives. Never again.

The man had been following the exchange with his eyes, as though trying to pick out words he knew. Maybe he understood French. Perhaps she and Audrey should switch to Italian. All of the villagers were trained in the three languages from their infancy, but mayhap this man also spoke all three tongues. Best not to discuss such things in front of him at all.

She rose and stalked to her position against the far wall. Then she turned to face Audrey and Philip. "You may both go. I'll take the first watch."

Philip straightened and turned to the door, then they both filed out. Over her shoulder, Audrey threw her a final warning look. "I'll keep my door cracked in case you whistle." By *whistle,* her friend meant the bird call they used when either one of them needed the other. A low twitter traveled perfectly down the stone corridor that linked each family's apartment.

As the door closed behind her friends, Brielle's heart begged to follow them. She much preferred to be out roaming the mountains instead of caged in these caves. If only she could have finished the hunting excursion she'd begun when she spotted this man. Yet her work was here just now. As *Le Commandant,* leader of the guards and hunters for the village of Laurent, her people depended upon her diligence.

This stranger would not go free until they uncovered his secrets.

Evan jolted from the murky depths of sleep and blinked to focus his eyes in the dim room. Had he been snoring? Hopefully not. Sophia had never liked his snoring and always prodded him awake. That too-familiar wave of remorse settled in his chest. If only snoring had been the worst of his errors where she had been concerned.

A rustle sounded across the room, and he looked over to see Brielle sitting propped against the wall. Watching him. Had she seen a man sleep before? Surely a warrior such as her would have spent time around men. In fact . . . might she be married?

The thought planted a sour taste in his

gut. Or perhaps that was the pain still lingering from her arrow wound. Maybe the man with the hatchet earlier had been her husband.

He swallowed the cobwebs in his mouth so he could ask, but a knock at the door sounded first.

"Enter." Brielle stood as the door opened, and a familiar sweet smile poked in.

"I have stew for our guest, and for you." Audrey spoke to Brielle but smiled at Evan, as though apologizing for whatever he'd had to suffer in her absence.

Brielle took the tray from her as Audrey entered and closed the door, then came to kneel beside him. "How are you feeling? Did my friend allow you rest?" Her smile reminded him of a peaceful, sunny day, lying on his back beside a creek and guessing shapes from the clouds. If he'd had a sister, he'd want her to have a pleasant smile like Audrey's.

"She did." He cleared his throat to smooth away the gravel, then worked to sit up so he could eat. He could stand a bite or two.

"Don't move." The smile cleared from her expression. "You'll reopen your wound."

He froze, but only because she looked so stricken. He eased back down. "It'll be hard to eat like this." And though the wound

39

ached, it didn't feel like his insides would burst. The arrow must not have gone deep enough to damage anything important.

"I'll feed you." Audrey scooped a spoonful from the bowl.

All brotherly affection fled his mind at the thought, and he glared at her. "I'll feed myself." Letting her handle the task would make him appear weak, a status he couldn't stand for since they were holding him prisoner.

The woman glanced at Brielle, as though summoning support for her cause.

The lady warrior turned those piercing eyes on him. "I care not whether you live or die, but you will not cause trouble for my friend, nor any of our people. If she wishes to feed you, you will consent."

She looked so fierce in that moment, like a mother bear defending her cubs, he couldn't help but soften his response. "As you wish." Maybe staying on her good side would benefit him most in his escape.

He settled in, then Audrey raised a scoop of stew to his lips. *Lord, don't let it be poison.* He was at their mercy, which was not a position he preferred. Perhaps they would at least untie his hands. He'd ask after the meal.

A second trencher of stew rested on the

tray, yet Brielle didn't eat while he did. Just knelt nearby, watching his every move.

He turned his attention to Audrey as he swallowed a bite. She might be more open to casual conversation. "Your friend said this is a village, and I thought I heard children before I succumbed to her sleeping potion." He allowed his mouth to tip into a smile, although he was still a tad bitter about that trick. "Are there many people in this area?" He opened his mouth to accept the next bite she ladled in.

"Our numbers have grown through the years, but we are a small group. Each member is like family." Her eyes shone.

"How long have you lived here?" He still couldn't quite fathom that an entire community resided in the heart of these icy mountains, so far from civilization. And he was getting the feeling they were quite content keeping to themselves.

"For many generations."

"No more questions." Brielle's sharp tone broke through the relaxed conversation, drawing both their gazes. She had her mouth pursed, and her eyes sparked enough to light a campfire. Yet something about the look made her seem vulnerable, like she was barely more than a girl. Which might, in fact, be close to the truth. She couldn't be more than two or three and twenty.

Turning to Audrey, he let a grin play at his mouth. "Is she always this pleasant and talkative?"

Audrey seemed to understand the jest, for her face lit in a matching smile as she slid a glance at her friend. "Brielle may be a warrior, but she's not always as fierce as she appears. In fact, I've found her kindness and good will to be almost without end."

A sound like a combination of a *humph* and a *pshaw* issued from the lady warrior, and she threw up a hand. "I see I'm to be bested by you both." She turned to her friend. "Perhaps you should focus on feeding your guest."

Audrey offered a gentle smile, as though she knew a secret, then she raised another bite of stew to Evan's mouth.

Brielle stood and carried her trencher back to her position at the wall, then placed it on the ground beside her. But she didn't eat. Or even sit. Just stood with her arms crossed, staring at him as if the strength of her gaze could keep him pinned to the ground.

But it wasn't fear that kept him in place. Nor the pain, if he were honest. As long as he was to be held prisoner here, having a captor like Brielle might be a pleasant diversion.

An hour later, that one thought proved more correct than Evan could have imagined. Not long after he'd filled the empty places in his belly with stew, the hatchet-wielding guard returned. Brielle exchanged a few words with the man, then shifted back into her fierce warrior personality as she picked up her bow and quiver and escorted Audrey out the door.

The room seemed to darken after the women left, and Evan forced himself to breathe steadily in order to keep the walls from closing in on him. The guard didn't give him a second's notice as he lumbered over to the position against the wall, where Brielle had kept her vigil.

"Will you untie my hands if I give my word not to move?" Evan raised his bound wrists, ignoring the rawness already burning his skin.

The man grunted, then heaved himself down to sit on the floor. "Brielle meets with the elders now. We'll wait for their judgment."

With that, the fellow propped his arms on his knees and fiddled with the leather strap wrapping the hilt of his knife. As he sat, the minutes crawled by like the breaths of a hibernating bear. In fact, this man reminded him of a big sluggish bear. His glassy gaze never wavered from that leather piece.

It wasn't sharp and fierce like Brielle's gaze. No wonder she'd earned a place as a leader among them. Not many women could shoot an arrow with her accuracy, nor command respect from a group of warriors as their leader.

In fact, he'd never met such a woman.

And now, what would she and the elders decide about his fate? The idea of his future being in another's hands rankled. Only God held his life in hand, and the Almighty expected him to use his head to get out of this mess.

With an eye on the oaf guarding him, Evan tested the strength of the rope binding his wrists. His fingers had almost lost their feeling, and the tie certainly felt strong. If he could knock the man senseless, he could use one of the torches to burn through the rope and release his arms. Or maybe the guard would fall asleep.

The fellow appeared bored as he idly studied the knife, but he didn't show any signs of weariness. Waiting for him to slumber would be an uncertain option and might take far too long.

Force would be necessary, then. Evan scanned the dark recesses of the room. If only he had one of those arrows dipped in the sleeping tonic.

And then the seed of an idea formed in his mind. A plan that just might work.

Turning to the guard, he made his voice as agreeable as possible. "Have you a chamber pot or privy I might use?"

4

Brielle strode through the dim hallway, turning toward the outer exit more by memory than sight. She pushed through the heavy wooden door into the bright glare of the sun. Without a moment's slowing of her stride, she inhaled the nip in the air, soaking in the remnants of smoke from the cook fires. If only she could remain out here.

Maybe she should sprint through the hidden rock gateway and out into the forest — leave the English stranger and her jumble of emotions far behind.

But that escape couldn't happen. Not yet. *Give me strength, Lord.*

Locking her jaw in place, she kept her march pointed toward the rock wall opposite her. More specifically, toward the cluster of at least a dozen men gathered at its base.

The council. A man from every single family in the village would be represented there, and none would miss this urgent meeting. The Englishman in their midst would cause quite a stir.

"Brielle." A high-pitched male voice broke her focus, slowing her stride.

She forced herself to pause and turn to the kind face approaching. "Marcellus. I can't speak now." She allowed him to clasp her elbow in greeting. "The leaders are meeting. The chief has asked me to come."

"Then I can meet him?" Marcellus's boyish face looked so hopeful.

"The chief? My father?" Why would Marcellus think he needed to reserve time to see her father when he would sit beside the stewpot with them that very night? It was a wonder Marcellus hadn't charged into the middle of the council meeting already. But maybe he had, and one of the elders sent him away.

The overgrown lad shook his head. "The visitor. Audrey said you might let me meet him."

The visitor. She bit back a grimace, as the expression would hurt Marcellus's tender feelings. But she did look him square in the eyes as she gripped his arms. "Marcellus. Stay far away from the storage chamber. He might hurt you, so do *not* approach him unless I give you leave. Do you understand?"

His eager face crumpled, and his chin dipped. "Oui."

The look pierced her chest with a stab of guilt, but she didn't have time to smooth things over just now. The council waited for her, and Marcellus had to steer clear of the stranger for his own safety. And maybe that of the entire village. She wouldn't let another poor child grow up motherless.

"Good man." She patted his shoulder and turned away.

When she reached the gathering of men, they parted to allow her into their midst. She aimed her focus at the two figures in the center. The pair stopped speaking as she halted before them, and she met the weary gaze of her father.

She dipped her chin to them both. "Papa. Erik."

Her father acknowledged her with an answering nod, then motioned toward the crowd around them. "What can you tell us of the stranger?"

She had her answer ready. The long walk through the tunnel passages had allowed plenty of time to prepare. She detailed her actions with the man in succinct order. How she'd given him time to turn aside from the gateway before resorting to violence. The manner in which she'd apprehended him.

The few words he'd spoken when he awoke in the chamber.

"Did he give any sign of his business here?" Despite the concern in his eyes, her father's patient tone was the one he used when considering all sides of a matter.

"Only that he was not from this area."

"You think he knew of our village?" This from a voice in the crowd. Bisset, if she wasn't mistaken.

She turned to find the man. "I can't be sure. He never spoke clearly on the matter." In fact, his words had been more like riddles, bending each question she asked in a way she'd not meant it to go.

He'd been intriguing at the time, but now her neck heated at the lack of detail she'd been able to ascertain from him. She straightened her shoulders. "I will use stronger means to learn his purpose here."

Her father motioned for her to pause, then looked to the other man in the circle's middle. "What say you, Erik? What states the law on the subject?"

The tall man's brow puckered, no doubt because his mind sifted through all the laws he'd memorized throughout the years. "He has not violated any laws, save that of secrecy. We are to keep the presence of Laurent secret from all except the Dinee people,

49

who have proven to be friends and welcome partners in trade."

Her father turned back to her. "Do you believe he will keep silent about what he has seen if we send him away?"

She struggled to keep her expression poised. "I do not." Had Papa taken leave of his senses? Had he not also endured the awful repercussions from the last visit of Englishmen to their village? He of all people . . .

She'd sooner spend a winter with no furs than turn the man loose with only a simple warning. "Unless one of our healers can create a potion to make him lose his memories, I strongly advise against freeing him until we are certain of his purpose here. Even then, I'm not sure we can trust him."

Papa gave her one of his looks that contained so many layers that she would need a lifetime to wade through them. The sadness she recognized. And perhaps a wistfulness? And resignation.

He'd endured too much through the years, raising not only his three motherless children but an entire village. He shouldn't have to face this stranger who resurrected so many painful memories.

"We should kill him. The risk he brings is too great." Audrey's father spoke with a bitterness that tightened Brielle's middle. Surely he hadn't imbibed so early in the day.

She didn't turn to look at the man, but Papa's gaze honed that direction. "Death is not something to be taken lightly. Especially when he hasn't broken any of our laws."

Silence settled in the wake of his words. Papa's voice usually had that effect, especially when he used his wise chieftain tone. Usually Brielle agreed with him. But in this case, her thoughts churned in such chaos and his statement struck a sour note in her belly.

Papa straightened and turned his focus to the circle of men. "I propose that we keep this stranger — Evan — under guard. We need time to pray for God's guidance to help us discover his purpose and whether he's trustworthy. In a few weeks, we'll meet again to vote on what to do with him. Speak with your families and make sure you represent all those in your clans for the final vote, not only your own opinion. Do any oppose this plan?"

Murmurs of assent rumbled all around her. Not even Martin, Audrey's father, raised an objection. These council members would have their work cut out for them, finding a decision everyone approved.

Especially those from families who didn't always agree amongst themselves.

Papa turned to meet her gaze again. "Brielle, I am trusting you to oversee his guard and find out his purpose here. The people depend on you to oversee the protection of Laurent. I leave you to discover everything you can about him and report back to us."

Brielle inhaled a steadying breath, released it, and then nodded. This meant they'd have to assign guards for night and day. One less warrior would be available to protect the village or hunt food. But she'd rather have control over the stranger's whereabouts than allow someone else the responsibility of keeping the people safe.

With that, Papa nodded, effectively ending the meeting. As voices resumed their normal volume around them, he started toward her. Except someone else called out to him, pulling away Papa's attention.

Good. She wasn't quite ready to face the voice of reason her father always tried to be. Peace and forgiveness had been so ingrained in him, maybe by his own father, or maybe when he became the village leader, replacing the previous chieftain.

Peace was an excellent notion, but the concept didn't unite well with safety. Keeping the village from danger required wariness and keen senses. Not to mention the ability to make quick decisions and strike hard before the prey attacked first. She'd learned that lesson well at the hands of a bear on her fourteenth birthday. And lest she forget, the scar on her cheek served as a daily reminder.

Evan struggled to sit up as his guard stood. The man grunted with the action, as though his joints ached with rheumatism.

Evan's body hummed with impatience, but he forced himself not to show eagerness. He couldn't let this man think he had anything planned but a simple trip to the privy.

But instead of coming nearer to loose the binds around Evan's ankles, the guard motioned toward the dark corner. "There's dirt in the corner. Just hobble over."

Disappointment sank through him as he peered toward the spot. Did they truly plan to never let him out of this tiny closet? He would go mad trapped within these rock walls. Even now they closed in around him. He squeezed his eyes shut against the sensation, drawing in labored breaths.

"Go, if you plan to." The guard motioned toward the corner again, impatience thickening his accent.

Evan opened his eyes and steadied his breathing, forcing his mind to think rationally. He should use this opportunity to relieve himself, for he certainly wouldn't be doing so if either of the women came back. And maybe he should start showing these people he meant them no harm. A friendly conversation would be a good start.

Rolling to his hands and knees proved no easy feat with pain twisting its blade in his stomach. By the time he worked his way up to standing, he could only take in tiny gasps of air. He stood motionless to let his body adjust and focused on thin inhales to keep away the darkness threatening the edges of his vision.

When his body finally settled, he sent a glance at the guard.

The man watched him with the corners of his mouth tipped, even as his nose squinted in a knowing look. "Brielle's arrow leaves a lasting mark, eh? I always wondered what that potion would do to a man. The concoction knocks caribou into sound sleep."

Evan had too little control of himself to stop his glare. Did the man mean to say they never tested the poison on a human? The she-warrior really hadn't cared if he lived or died. He'd better not depend on her female sensibilities. Mayhap she wasn't really a female at all. What woman had the nerve to shoot a deer, much less a fellow human being? Certainly none he'd ever met.

"Will you cut my legs free so I can walk?"

The man shook his head. "You can shuffle to the corner."

Evan bit back a retort and started across the span. It shouldn't bother him so much to be degraded in front of this man. Something about him seemed like he could be friendly if he wanted to. Maybe Evan's goal for now should be to make the man amiable toward him.

When he reached the dark corner, he searched for a topic that wouldn't arouse suspicion. "I hear a bit of French in your accent, but I'm amazed at how well all of you speak the American tongue." Maybe he should have said *British* tongue so they wouldn't know where his allegiance lay, but the word slipped out before he thought about it. Did this village know of the war in the east? If so, did they side with Britain? This place was secluded, though, far west of the Canadas.

He slid a glance toward the man to see his reaction.

The guard's brow furrowed. "You are from the American colonies then?"

Evan barely caught his confusion before it

showed on his face. The only colonies in the New World were the British colonies of Canada. Except for the French ones far to the south. But American colonies . . . ?

Had these people really been so isolated that they didn't know America had fought fiercely to gain their independence nearly forty years before? And the United States had been fighting again to keep that independence these last three years. What question could he ask to test the man's knowledge without raising suspicion?

He replayed the guard's last statement in his mind. He'd have to betray his allegiances. But then, maybe he'd already done so. Better to be clear than make the man think he was hedging or had something to hide. "I'm from the American states."

The man's brows lifted. "States? Britain allowed the colonies to become states?" His surprise couldn't be feigned. And he must assume they were still under Britain's rule, as if the great people of America wouldn't have the ability to break free of Britain's domineering thumb. He'd often heard of that attitude prevalent amongst Tories during the days of the revolution.

How much should Evan tell? Would these people even believe him? The war had been fought. America firmly secured its independence. All they need do to confirm his news would be to send a scout down east to learn the truth. This part was no secret. Nor should it endanger his life. Hopefully.

Readjusting his tunic, he turned to face the man, propping his hand against the stone wall to keep from swaying each time a wave of vertigo passed through him. "The American colonies fought and won their independence from Britain back in 1776. We're a free country, made up of thirteen states." Better to stop there.

The man's dropped jaw seemed to indicate that what little Evan had shared was plenty enough for him to take in.

"You can't mean it." The guard snapped his mouth shut, apparently realizing he shouldn't reveal his shock so plainly.

Evan nodded, but the blackness flooding his vision made him regret the movement. "It's true."

The man's tone turned almost wistful. "I'll bet there have been lots of changes we don't know about."

Evan worked to form a question that might help him understand more about these people. But a new bout of spinning forced him to squeeze his eyes shut.

When he opened them, the man was studying him. He motioned to the fur Evan had been laying on. "You better lay back down before you fall."

Evan shuffled forward. The man was more right than he wanted to admit.

When he reached the fur, he dropped his hands down first, then lowered himself to his knees. He'd just started to ease down onto his side when a single tap on the door sounded. The wood panel opened, and Brielle stepped in.

He paused in his motion, then shifted to a sitting position so he could see her better.

Her expression gave no sign of the tidings she brought. She could rival any Indian brave with her expressionless mask.

But what news did she carry underneath that stoic look? She must have brought the council's decision, and their verdict had the power to set him free . . . or take his life.

5

Evan held his breath as Brielle paused a few steps into the room and surveyed him, then shifted her focus to the guard.

He readied himself to interpret her French, but she spoke to the man in English. Maybe she used that language so Evan would understand, too.

"We continue the guard. The council will vote on his fate in a few weeks' time." She motioned the man toward her. "I'll take over. Go. Eat. Send Philip when night falls."

Evan's chest tightened at her words. *A few weeks.* He'd been ordered to return before the new year. To meet that deadline, he'd need to head back to the States in three weeks at the most. A winter storm could blast through at any time and slow his travels, so he needed to give an extra window for that possibility.

And before he could return, he had to find pitchblende.

The guard studied Brielle even as he stepped forward to obey her command. He seemed to see something in her gaze that eased his concern. With a nod and a salute, he strode out the door. Had she murmured something under her breath only he heard?

When the door closed behind the man, Brielle swept her gaze over Evan. He couldn't help straightening under her scrutiny. Did she see a man who was weak and injured? Or only a potential threat to her people? Both possibilities soured his gut.

Whatever she saw, her face gave no hint of her opinion. She turned and strode to her former place against the wall. But this time she slid down to sit, as she hadn't before. She sat cross-legged, settling as though she planned to be there a while.

Her gaze hovered on him, but from the faint lines between her brows, her thoughts seemed to be far away. If he asked, would she tell him what was said at the meeting? She clearly didn't plan to explain on her own.

He reached for a strip of rawhide that had split from the hide underneath him and fingered the piece with both hands, a gesture that should appear relaxed. His screaming belly told him he would need to lie down again soon, but he hated being in that

60

vulnerable position. Especially in front of this woman.

He inhaled a steadying breath. "Do you plan to keep me locked up until the council's vote?"

She gave only a single nod. Not even a word of response.

He tamped down his rising frustration. "Is there a reason your people don't trust me? Or are you this unfriendly to all outsiders?" Perhaps he should have been more subtle, but she didn't strike him as the kind of person who enjoyed cat-and-mouse games. She'd already proven she shot straight for the gut.

Again, her face revealed no sign of her thoughts. Nor surprise at his bold questions. She sharpened her gaze on him. "Why have you come here?"

Yup, straight through the ribs. Too bad he couldn't be as forthcoming. But he needed to make her think he was.

He kept his expression relaxed and laced his tone with a hint of earnestness, but not so much as to sound feigned. He'd learned the skill well in his years as a spy. "I'm exploring. Little is known of this area." Should he say anything about the government sending him? That would be as much truth as he could give, but it also might raise

61

concerns. These people clearly wanted to remain hidden away. They wouldn't be pleased to think a large country wanted to take control of their unusual village.

Better they think he was exploring for the sake of adventure. Although, if she asked directly, he wouldn't lie. Not anymore. He may not answer, he may come up with a creative way to respond without giving away his mission, but he would only speak the absolute truth.

"What is it you seek in your exploration? What do you hope to find?"

Of all the focus her questions could've taken, how did she know to hone in on that specific detail? She didn't ask why he came alone. Why he'd wandered so far north. Only what he sought.

He shrugged. "I suspect I'll know it when I find it." Then he forced a casual grin. "At least I hope so."

Her mouth pinched, sealing away her very appealing lips. Good. He shouldn't be thinking about them anyway, and the more she kept her questions to herself, the better.

Brielle swung the front legs of the caribou carcass off her left shoulder, then slipped out from under the load as it thunked to the ground in front of Marcellus's mother,

Jeanette. "I'm sorry I haven't removed the skin. I'm to take my turn with the prisoner at dawn."

"No apologies, dear." The woman reached a hand to rest on Brielle's arm. "I'm just grateful for the meat. And the other parts, of course. Most of them anyway." A gentle smile wreathed her mouth, sinking deep in the lines around her eyes. As much as this woman had been through in the past dozen years, she still possessed a sweet spirit that Brielle herself had never been able to master.

Brielle nodded, then backed away from the fire the woman had been tending. "I need to go."

"Brielle?" Jeanette's expression had shifted to a pensive look. "The stranger . . . is he dangerous, do you think?"

A lump burned up Brielle's throat. Was she remembering the last Englishmen who'd come into these walls? That day had changed both of their lives forever. Losing her mother had been the worst thing Brielle could imagine.

But Jeanette's husband had been shot, too, rendering his body useless from the waist down. Jeanette had been left with his care, along with full responsibility for providing for their family, including Marcellus.

The boy's tender heart made him incapable of killing an animal, even if it meant he and his parents would starve to death. His simple mind and fumbling fingers wouldn't allow him proficiency with a bow or knife anyway.

Those long-ago days when Brielle had attempted to teach him had helped her to hone her own skills, and ever since then, she'd been providing enough meat for both their families. At least Jeanette didn't have that worry weighing on her sloped shoulders.

But now, what should Brielle say about the man locked away in their storage room? "I don't know, Jeanette. But I'll make sure he doesn't go free until we're certain of his intentions." At least he didn't have a means of escape, as his horse had broken free from the young man assigned to watch him. They had Evan's packs, gun, and saddle still, but the animal had run far out of sight.

All the better. No matter what, she wouldn't allow this dear friend, or anyone else in this village, to suffer more pain and hardship than they already had — especially not at the hands of an Englishman, not when she was in a position to stop it.

Jeanette nodded, her face relaxing. "I know you will, Brielle. I never worry when you're involved." She waved her off. "Go, do your duty. And make sure Audrey is bringing you and the prisoner meals. I'll send some of this meat to her for that purpose."

Brielle turned and strode across the open area, Jeanette's words echoing in her mind. *"I never worry when you're involved."*

At least one of them didn't.

She'd not made much progress in discovering the man's purpose here. His answers had been so vague, but she was fairly certain he'd not attempted a falsehood. She might get more details from him during the course of simple conversation than direct questioning. Although he seemed careful with his words, even when chatting with Audrey. It was more likely he'd gather information from them than that he'd let details slip he didn't want to share.

Not with her, though.

She'd always hated speaking just for the sake of filling the air with words, but she'd force herself if idle talk helped her learn the truth.

She stepped through the main door into the corridor and breathed in. Leaving the crisp outside air for the dark interior of the

65

caves always sobered her spirit, but the dank richness of the tunnels held its own comfort. Papa told stories that had been handed down to him of villages not carved into a mountainside but made up of individual structures built of stacked trees and rocks. Surely they didn't last as long as these caves had.

When she reached the entrance to the storage room, she tapped once on the door before removing the bar and stepping inside.

Philip sat on the far wall, hands propped on his knees, head resting against the stone behind him. He sat straighter when she entered but didn't look like he'd been asleep before. Good man. He was one of the few she could trust on the night watch. Steady and solid. Did whatever necessary to ensure the job was done right.

Thankfully, he also didn't mind the chore. She would take his place some nights, though. She would never ask any of her guards to do a job she wasn't willing to handle herself.

She slid a glance at their prisoner. He lay flat on his pallet, hands resting atop his midsection. He didn't sleep. Those intense eyes watched her.

She greeted them both with a nod, then turned her attention to Philip as she strode to him. "Thank you, my friend." She spoke in Italian, since she didn't believe they had used that language in front of the prisoner the day before.

The entire village made an effort to speak all three languages regularly so they could stay fluent. She didn't have reason to hide her greeting from their captive, but this would keep him guessing if he'd understood their French words.

Philip lumbered to his feet and wiped his hands on his tunic as he responded in Italian. "He slept soundly. Didn't talk much, just slept."

She nodded. "You'll come again at dark? I'll take the next night."

He shrugged. "Or I can do both. I have no difficulty sleeping through the day."

Maybe she should allow him all the nights so he could keep a regular pattern with his sleeping. But it seemed a horrible punishment to deny a person sunlight, at least every few days. Her gaze slid to the prisoner. He wouldn't be seeing the light of day, either. A twinge of guilt twisted her belly, but she pressed it away. She couldn't risk the people's safety until she knew more about him.

She refocused on Philip and smiled her thanks. "I'll stay here tomorrow night. Take your Rona for a walk outside the walls while the children are occupied."

His white teeth flashed, and he ducked his head as he turned toward the door. With a farewell wave to Evan, he closed the wood partition behind him, the slight clink of the bar sounding from the hall.

Brielle scanned the room. All seemed as she'd left it the night before. She let her gaze settle on the man. He still lay flat, his fingers playing a pattern on his stomach as he watched her.

Even lying prone like that, the man still exuded strength. Maybe it was the wide set of his shoulders or the rough leather of his tunic and leggings. Of course, the thick scruff covering his jaw only added to the look.

What all had he discovered in his travels? How much vast country had he uncovered? A surge of excitement slipped through her. What would it be like to ride on a horse for days . . . weeks . . . ? What would it be like to live and travel in a land that didn't dip and rise in an endless landscape of mountains?

It took everything within her not to settle herself beside him right now and beg to hear everything he'd seen. Maybe he would tell her, but she needed to maintain a bit of propriety in the asking.

She walked the few steps between them. Dried blood still covered his tunic. Audrey would likely bring him a shirt while she laundered his. "Your wound is better?"

Evan dipped his chin. "That poison makes for a decent sleeping potion. It's about out of me now, I expect." The corners of his mouth twitched in what he might have meant for a smile, but his eyes belied the expression.

She ignored the barb and moved back to her place against the wall. She should sit if she planned to make relaxed conversation. Although sitting in the presence of a possible enemy certainly wouldn't relax her.

But the challenge of appearing nonchalant would give her something to work at. No matter what, she had to learn more about this stranger.

6

After Brielle settled herself across from her prisoner, silence sank over the room. What meaningless bit of chatter could she offer to set the man at ease? "Audrey should be here soon with your morning meal. Have you need of anything else?"

Her mind sped ahead to what he might ask for, but the first possibility made heat rise up her neck. Hopefully, Philip had shown him where he could take care of *that* personal concern. Although she'd probably have to be around for the need at some point if she took part in regular guard duty.

Blessedly, Evan shook his head. "Food sounds good. I still have a bit of water from what she left last night." He motioned to a wooden cup beside his pallet.

Good. "If you have need of anything, let your guard know." That sounded friendly enough.

"It'd sure be nice to see daylight again."

He raised his brows and one corner of his mouth tipped in a hopeful half-smile.

Her own mouth twitched. "Dawn is just breaking over the eastern mountains." She couldn't tell him when he might get to see the sun rise again. That would depend on him. And how willing he was to speak of his business here. She needed to pull every detail she could before council's vote. But hopefully her answer would suffice.

His gaze dipped down to her feet. "You've been for a walk already?"

He must be seeing the wetness of her moccasins. She'd expected him to be observant, and she'd been right. Of course, he'd been staring at the same dark walls for more than half a day now. It made sense he would notice any new details in the space.

"A short hunting trip."

His brows lifted. "Did you get anything?"

"A caribou. You might be eating the meat in one of your meals soon."

He pressed his lips together, and his head dropped flat against the fur. "Sounds great. It's been a while since I've had fresh meat. Not sure I've ever tasted caribou."

"The herds are plentiful around here," she said slowly. He must have seen them if he'd been exploring as he said. Did his gun not work?

No one would dare travel without a weapon capable of bringing down food. She'd not tested his musket, only placed the weapon with his packs and saddle in a corner of their quarters. In truth, she hated guns. Their people only possessed the few they'd obtained from the English party who wrought so much damage the last time.

A bow accomplished her purpose well without so much torment for her prey, especially with the concoction she dipped the arrowheads in.

She made a note to check his belongings, though. They might give her more insight into the man and his purposes.

He'd turned to watch her again, so she refocused her attention on him. "I saw a couple herds the day before you took me captive, but I still had plenty of roasted meat. I've been eating food cold for a while now."

This was her opening for a few casual questions. "Where did you explore before you came to this land?" She kept her voice lightly curious.

He matched her easy tone. "I've been traveling northwest. I'd heard the mountains are different the farther north you go, so I was curious to see how. I didn't expect them to have built-in tunnels and caves with people living inside them." This time the grin twinkled in his eyes.

"Yes, well. I doubt you'll find that in many of the other mountains around. What other changes have you seen?" She didn't have to feign curiosity with this question. Only had to keep herself from leaning in for his answer.

"The ice, for one. It looks like entire parts of some of these mountains are made up simply of ice. Farther south, many of the peaks stay covered in snow, but it's only a layer over the rock. Not the entire structure."

Interesting. "Why do you think that is?"

"The cold, I'm guessing." He shrugged, as though shaking off the chill. "We don't have to wear furs in the winter back home. We can even walk around in shirtsleeves during the summer months."

As that idea turned in her mind, he spoke again. "The sun isn't as bright here, either, and darkness seems to last much longer, even into daylight hours."

She propped her hands on her knees. "How much longer? Our summer days are brighter, perhaps more like you're accustomed to."

His brows lowered and he grew silent, probably trying to make sense of her words.

He could do his thinking later, though. Now that she had him talking, maybe he would tell her more. "What other differences have you noticed?"

Another smile lit his eyes. "The caribou. I'd heard of them, but never saw them until those two herds I mentioned."

Maybe he really had recently come into their country. That gave her a better sense of timing. "What else?"

"We have other animals where I come from that I haven't seen in these parts."

"Like what?"

As he spoke of bright red birds and tiny cougars he called house cats, she could almost picture the animals. Her chest tightened as an old longing rose up within her. She loved her home here, but how wonderful it must be to see distant lands. These things he described were probably only a small taste of other wonders to be seen.

As her mind spun with images, she finally realized quiet had settled over them. She blinked to pull herself back to the present.

He looked at her with his head tipped as if trying to decipher something about her. "So you've really lived in this place your entire life? You never traveled elsewhere?"

She shrugged, pulling back to lean against

the wall. Perhaps she'd shown too much eagerness. "We have all we need here." She'd always believed that before anyway. They had safety and food and clothing and companionship. What more could they require?

Silence settled again, but not an awkward quiet. He appeared as deep in his thoughts as she was.

But she should probably keep him talking. He seemed open to speaking of the place he came from.

"With so many differences in animals and mountains, and even the length of the day, your home must be far away. How long did you travel to reach this place?"

He raised his gaze to the ceiling, as though calculating the time.

But before he could answer, the scuff of footsteps sounded outside the door. Then a tap so light it must be Audrey's.

"Enter." Brielle pushed to her feet and moved toward the door as the clang of the bar sounded, then the wood pushed open.

Audrey's sweet smile glowed in the light of the torches as she stepped into the room carrying a large tray. "I come with *Breton galette* to break your fast. And also fresh torches."

Thoughtful Audrey.

Audrey's smile brightened even more as she turned to their prisoner. "And how are you feeling this morning, good sir?"

Brielle had to hold in a snort. If Audrey had her way, she would send the man off with a fortnight's provisions, including sweet meats and all manner of pastries. That is, if she couldn't talk him into staying so she could continue to ply him with her hospitality. The woman truly saw the best in everyone and lived to bring pleasure, especially through the stomach.

"I'll be doing even better when I taste whatever's under that cloth that smells so good." The earnest appreciation in Evan's eyes pressed a twinge in Brielle's chest. Maybe she should try kindness, too. Real kindness, not feigned to get what she wanted. Perhaps Audrey was right in her claim that a kind word or act always brought out the best in people.

While Audrey fussed over the man, rolling part of his furs to prop his head up, Brielle took her portion of the meal from the tray. The aroma from Audrey's meat pastry filled the room, raising her empty belly to life.

Audrey worked with her back to Brielle, setting out platters she'd brought. "I'm going to free his hands so he can eat. A good meal will help his wounds heal, and there's no reason he shouldn't feed himself." She spoke in French without looking back at Brielle, but her tone and the switch in language made it clear the words were meant for her.

Frustration surged through Brielle, and she changed to Italian for her response, just in case the man could understand French. "Don't do it, Audrey. He might be dangerous."

Her friend didn't answer, simply sent raised brows over her shoulder that meant she would do what she wanted — or felt was necessary. She probably also meant the look as her opinion on Brielle's lack of trust in the goodness of humankind, but she wouldn't ponder that line of thought any longer.

She sighed and put down her bite of galette, then reached to make sure her blade sat at the ready. The man probably wouldn't do anything to endanger Audrey — truly, how could anyone hurt someone so innately good? Especially when she was offering with such tasty fare.

But Brielle's duty was to make sure her people stayed safe.

Audrey's body blocked her view of what she was doing, but when Evan's eyes slid shut and he released a long groan of pleasure, Brielle was fairly certain his hands had been unbound.

Audrey sat back, pushing the tray closer. "There. Now you can eat at your leisure." She clasped her hands around her knees and settled in to watch the man enjoy what she'd brought him.

Brielle shifted her focus back to Evan to watch for any plan of escape he might be crafting.

But running away seemed far from his thoughts as he took his first bite of Audrey's honey-drizzled pastry. His eyes drifted shut as his mouth worked the bite, and for once, she could see why Audrey loved to watch the delight of others.

Before, Brielle had been able to ignore his striking features, but the joy lighting his entire face raised a yearning inside her. What was she doing, feeling this way toward a stranger? An Englishman, at that.

She forced her focus away from his face, dropping it down to his tunic. Maybe the bloodstain there would provide enough distraction. But the pleasure in his expression was forefront in her thoughts and she imagined each nuance of his joy as it played across his features.

Thankfully, Audrey came to the rescue from Brielle's wild imaginings. "So,

Evan . . . Should we call you Evan? Have you a surname we should use?"

Brielle's gaze dared to creep to his face again, in time to see him shake his head as he swallowed down his bite. The Adam's apple at his throat bobbed, a manly action she'd never appreciated in the males around her before. At least not the way the simple motion drew her fascination now.

"Evan MacManus. But call me Evan." His teeth sank into the pastry again, and she couldn't blame him for preferring the treat over conversation.

Nor could she allow herself to ogle him again.

"So, Evan, have you a favorite food?" Audrey took up her former questioning. "I could make *tourtière* or a *ragoût* for the midday meal. Or tell me if you prefer something heartier."

His eyes had closed in apparent appreciation for the bite he ate, but he opened the lids partway. "Miss Audrey, you could make corn gruel and I think it would taste like heaven. Whatever you cook will be much appreciated, I promise."

Audrey's face dipped with a sheepish look, but her widening smile was impossible to miss. What woman wouldn't melt under such appreciation from a man this handsome?

Still, the time had come to remind her friend he'd not proven trustworthy yet.

She cleared her throat and gave Audrey a pointed look. "Jeanette will bring you caribou meat to use in feeding our *prisoner.*" Hopefully she'd pick up on that last word.

"Good." Her eyes brightened. "I'll prepare tourtière, then." She turned to Evan. "I'll make sure to include the parts of the meat that are best for healing." She glanced back at Brielle. "Marcellus came by this morning. He wanted to come with me to deliver the food." Her friend's gaze took on a sweet sadness. "I told him I would ask you."

Brielle sighed. Marcellus took too much interest in this man. How many times would she have to tell him before he ceased pressing her? She switched to Italian. "Tell him he may not come near this room, not even to the corridor tunnel until I personally give him leave. It's very important for his safety."

Audrey's smile was sad as she nodded. "I'll tell him."

The light atmosphere in the room evaporated after that, and not even Audrey's sweet spirit raised the shroud of worry weighing Brielle's shoulders.

When her friend left them, Brielle turned

to the prisoner and leveled a piercing gaze on him. "I won't tie your hands again now, but if you even think of moving off that fur without your guard's approval, you'll be bound hand and foot."

His brows rose, but he nodded, his gaze respectful — mostly. "I'll stay on the fur."

That was the best she could ask for now, though time would tell how well his word could be trusted.

She moved to her place by the wall and lowered to sit, then pulled out her knife and one of the sticks she'd brought to whittle arrows. She always needed more, so this would be a good task to keep her hands busy during the long hours she stayed in here. Too bad the man twiddling his thumbs across from her couldn't be put to work, also. But she couldn't allow him a blade, nor could she trust that he wouldn't sabotage whatever she set him to. Her Bible might have been better to pass the hours, but she'd not thought to grab it. *Sorry, Lord.*

"So, French, English, and Italian? Any other languages I haven't heard?" Evan's voice made her tense as she jerked her gaze up to him.

Or maybe it was his words that startled her. He recognized all three languages. Did that mean he spoke them also? She probably shouldn't have assumed him ignorant.

"I know enough of the Dinee tongue to trade with them. But that's all. And what of you? Which languages do you speak?"

"Only English fluently. I can pick out a few words of French, Italian, and Spanish. Enough to know which language they are anyway." His tone sounded truthful, but he could easily be feigning.

From now on, she'd have to leave this room if she had something private to say to one of the others. No matter what, she couldn't underestimate Evan MacManus.

7

Lying around like this should make Evan feel better, not worse. He flinched as another knife of pain plunged through his gut. His insides gurgled loudly enough for the guard across the room to hear.

Gerald, a man he'd not yet seen over the past two days, scowled at Evan. "Food will be here soon." This fellow didn't seem as amiable as the other guards. "Not that we should be wasting a meal on a good-for-nothing like you. Don't know why the council didn't put you out of your misery first thing. They'll see your real colors soon enough, though."

Evan clamped hard on his jaw, but the guard's words were merely buzzing gnats compared to the chaos within him. His insides wielded bayonets and clubs, plunging and hacking until he could think of nothing except the agony. He rolled onto his side, curling his legs to ease the pressure within. Had they fed him something tainted? This guard might have led the effort.

Maybe they were poisoning him to make him tell his secrets. Surely she wasn't lacing her delectables with arsenic. Audrey's food tasted better than anything he'd eaten since Sophia had employed a cook. He played through the symptoms he'd learned during his training to be a spy. Stomach pain, muscle cramping, vomiting. He had the first two, but not the latter.

Yet.

Should he refuse to eat? The way he felt, his body would refuse the meal for him.

Another pain plunged in, and this time the bile rose up into his throat. His stomach convulsed. He was going to lose his insides. There was no way to hold it back this time.

He pushed up to his hands and knees, but as he worked to gain his feet, another spasm struck, and he stumbled down to his knees again. He tried to crawl forward, but the leather binding his ankles kept him from moving more than a handbreadth. They'd left his hands unbound after Audrey cut him free, but no one had loosed his feet.

His stomach revolted, and the meat pie from his midday meal spewed up his throat and out his mouth.

He barely heard the guard's yelp through

the rushing in his ears. Wave after wave of regurgitated food forced its way out of him. Maybe now his belly would finally settle.

The guard was murmuring something in French as Evan finally sank back to sit on the fur. "Sorry," he mumbled. The word graveled out through his raw throat. He'd made a mess of the place. Would they make him clean it?

Probably not, for they didn't seem inclined to let him leave the fur, except to occasionally shuffle to the patch of dirt in the corner. Even the dogs must be given more freedom than this. The night guard had replaced that pile of dirt a couple times now, and Evan hated watching the man clean up after him. If only he could be free to take care of things like that himself, he could lighten the work for them all.

But just now, his limbs barely had the strength to hold him in a sitting position. He sank down to lay on the hide as the guard stepped around the mess to reach the wooden door.

The man bellowed down the hallway, and the way his voice echoed off the walls, the corridor must be long and made of stone the entire way. How deep into the mountain were they?

The guard stood still, silence hanging in

the air as he waited for a response. The man murmured more things under his breath, and Evan didn't even try to translate. With the stench rising in the room, the words were probably just as foul.

The man sent him a glare, then stepped into the hallway, closing the door behind him. The clank of what must be a metal or stone bar blocking the door shut was the only sound. Then quiet.

Evan's pulse leapt. This was his chance. The first time he'd been left alone since the moment he'd been struck with Brielle's arrow.

He pushed himself up to sitting and eyed the door. He'd studied every inch of the walls, floor, and ceiling these past two days, and that partition was the only way out. The hinge must be on the outside, so if that truly was a metal bar he'd heard slipping into place, his only option would be to break the wood.

Did he have time? He strained for the sound of footsteps, but he'd not even heard the guard walk away. Was the man outside, even now, listening? Testing Evan? The fellow had looked rattled. Surely he'd gone for help.

But even if Evan made his way into the hall, he had no idea how he would get out of this compound of caves. The guards would know every dark corner to find him. He couldn't risk losing their trust after he was working so hard to gain it.

And he was so weak. He perhaps could muster the strength to sneak out, but if forced into a match of fists with one of these brawny men, he wasn't sure he could win. He'd better wait for a more opportune chance.

He'd likely only have one shot at escape.

Voices outside the door made his heart skip a beat, and he smoothed his face into a bland expression. That same clang sounded again, then the partition opened. Brielle was the first to enter, followed by Audrey, then the other guard whose name he still didn't know.

Brielle paused inside the doorway and scanned the mess. Something about her seemed different . . . softer. As her head turned, the light from a torch glimmered off the dark of her hair, revealing the kind of muss that came from leaning back against something — like a bed. Had they awakened her? How late was it, anyway? He'd been trying to keep track of time by the meals they served and the changing of their guard, and he was fairly certain this was late after-noon.

Brielle was speaking to Audrey in a low voice, her melodious French much more pleasing to the ear than what the guard had bellowed down the hall.

Audrey nodded and spoke back to her, pointing at the far edges of the room. Then Audrey turned her kind eyes on Evan and sympathy warmed them even more than usual. "You're ill? Has my food done this to you?"

As much as he hated to dim the kindness in her gaze, he had to speak the truth. "I don't know."

Brielle turned to the guard. "Go with Audrey and bring whatever she needs. I'll begin my watch." She'd switched back to English. Was it her goal to keep him on his toes with the language shifts? Or maybe she meant to always speak English and forgot at times. That seemed highly unlikely. As far as he could tell, this woman never did anything without a purpose. At first, he'd assumed the things they said in the other languages were intended to be kept from him.

Now he didn't know what to think. His head ached from the force of the convulsions. His muscles had regained some of their strength, but his belly roiled again. He had a feeling that might not be the only time he cast up his accounts.

As Audrey turned to go with the man, Evan raised a hand to catch her attention. "It might be good to bring a bucket or bowl or something." She was looking at him with her head cocked, and heat flooded his ears. "Just in case."

Understanding shifted her expression, and she nodded. "Oui."

When the two closed the door behind them, Brielle made her way to the guard's place against the wall, then turned to survey the mess from the new angle. Her brow furrowed, a look he didn't often see on her stoic features. "You're feeling better?" She swung her focus to him.

The part of him where his ego resided wanted to say yes. Of course, he was better. He was strong and strapping and every bit the capable man he'd been before she shot him in the gut. He hated to appear a weakling in front of anyone, especially this tough woman. But if he used bravado here, he had a feeling his body would prove him a liar. Perhaps it would be best to give them a little warning so they could prepare.

And if this sickness was a result of their poison, what did it matter if they knew their potion was working?

He pressed a hand to his stomach and

scrunched his nose. "A little better than before." Maybe that wasn't completely honest. She would read between the lines and plan for the worst.

For a long moment, she studied him.

At first, he didn't respond. Didn't meet her gaze. But the longer she stood immobile, her focus penetrating, the more her stare raised his hackles. He finally turned to meet her look.

Her eyes were dark. "We're not poisoning you."

As much as he tried, he couldn't keep from raising his brows. She was blunt, especially for a woman.

One side of her mouth twitched, the only hint that she noticed his reaction. "I'm sure that question crossed your mind."

He let his smile ease out, although the effort reminded him he still wasn't as strong as he should be. "I had wondered."

Her brow lowered again, as though debating whether to say whatever was pressing in her mind. At this point, he couldn't even imagine what that might be.

"We don't intend to hurt you. As long as you don't intend to hurt us." Her eyes bore into him. "We're keeping you until we can be certain of your intentions."

Now they were coming down to the bedrock, the core of the matter, unencumbered by casual conversation or bushes to beat around.

He didn't shirk from the intensity of her gaze, letting her see deep inside him to the truth in his words. "I mean no harm to you or your people. You have my word." He couldn't confirm that the United States government wouldn't do them harm if he found what he sought here. And with the markings he'd seen on the southern side of this mountain, he had a feeling he'd find pitchblende somewhere nearby — likely deep inside a mountain, according to the army's source.

"Then what is your reason for being here?" Her stare had lost none of its intensity.

Letting her see so far inside him was starting to burn his chest now, especially with this question. "Like I said, I'm exploring. Few from the east have ever been to this land, and very few descriptions of the area are recorded."

Except for the journal entries he'd memorized, ones written by a trapper over a century ago. Those few pages where he'd remarked on the curious copper stone that sparked a small explosion in his fire had been the catalyst to the army's research. The

91

man had been intrigued by the rock enough to save a sample with his journals. And the army had been able to reproduce the explosion with the tiny stone. Thus the purpose for his mission.

"Why are you interested in our land?"

Please, Lord. Make her stop asking questions. Was God testing him? Had the Almighty decided his time had come and planned to take him out at the hands of this she-warrior?

He wouldn't lie, but he'd also sworn an oath on a Bible that he would keep the details of this mission secret at any cost. If she pressed harder, he'd have to hedge.

But her intuition would probably realize he wasn't being forthright. What would she do then? Kill him outright, or let him die a slow wasting death in this cell?

He pushed back the thoughts and focused on his answer. "I'm looking for things I've never seen before."

"Like what?"

Was she trying to benefit from his weakness by pushing so hard? Maybe they really had poisoned him, and she was pressing the advantage. Twisting the blade, so to speak.

He could only die with honor. And truth. He forced his muddled mind to find an answer that would be both honest and hide his mission. "Things I've never seen before. Things that can't be found where I live. Like caribou." He tried for a smile, but it had no effect on her. As he knew it wouldn't.

"Anything in particular you're looking for?"

It was as though she knew of his mission and was trying to force his confession. Could that be possible? Did they have another spy in the war department? The way General Benedict Arnold had turned, anything was possible.

Maybe someone from the States had heard of his mission and ridden ahead to find the mineral first.

He studied Brielle from that new perspective, trying to align what little she'd said and done with that possibility. If a stranger had come to this village ahead of him, the man likely would have received the same treatment, would have been locked away in this dungeon for days.

Unless . . . they were only doing this to Evan because they knew what he sought and were trying to hold him back.

Perhaps it was time to turn the questioning on her. "Do you treat all your visitors as you have me?" He nodded toward the door. "Lock them away and assault them with endless questions and no daylight until they nearly lose their senses? Poison them until they're so weak they'll admit to any crime, no matter whether they performed the act or not?"

Her eyes flared and her back stiffened. "We did *not* poison you. Not other than the sleeping potion on the arrowhead. And if you committed a crime, or plan to commit one here, you can be certain I will hold you responsible. No Englishman will enter Laurent and hurt my people. Never again."

Never again? The lethal tone of her voice spoke even more than her revealing words.

8

Brielle hated feeling out of control. But watching Evan cast up his accounts all through the night smothered her with the sensation.

Audrey had stayed with them for a while, soothing his brow with wet cloths after each episode, then coaxing sips of cool water down his throat.

The man looked truly miserable, his face pale and tinged with green, and each vomit seemed to leave him lifeless. Watching him brought back memories of the last time she'd been overtaken by a similar ailment. She'd nearly wished for the relief of death. Maybe not quite, but that time had been the most miserable sickness in her recollection. Her sister, Charlotte, had succumbed to the vomiting, too. Brielle had been too weak to help, and Audrey had come to nurse them both. Her tender touch and sweet demeanor had been more healing than the tonic she administered. Thankfully, Audrey hadn't succumbed to the illness, though she'd stayed with them through the worst of it.

Brielle glanced at Evan. Was his malady catching? Or was this truly an effect of the sleeping potion? *Lord, don't let Audrey take sick because of caring for him.* Her kindness shouldn't be repaid with misery.

Somewhere around midnight, Evan finally dozed off. Audrey's weary eyes were lined with exhaustion, and her shoulders drooped, so Brielle motioned for her to go on to her family's apartment.

Audrey stood and gathered a tray of cups and bowls. "Have him drink water anytime he awakes."

Brielle motioned her on. "I'll see to him."

Audrey turned and shuffled out. She rose early each morning, so she'd likely been on her feet for nearly a full day. With the close of the door, silence settled, broken only by Evan's steady breathing.

Brielle settled against the cool stone wall to make arrows again. She'd have a dozen quivers full by the time they decided what to do with this man.

For a long moment, she allowed herself to pause and study him. He lay curled on his side facing her, a shock of hair lying across his brow. In the torchlight, the strands shone bright amber, but she remembered it as almost black that day she'd watched him approach the entrance to Laurent.

His face appeared earnest in sleep, his brow puckered, as though concerned about something. Did he relive their conversation in his dreams? She'd already replayed the words many times herself.

He wasn't telling all about his journey, of that she was certain. When Papa went through his packs, he'd found a paper with the letterhead of the United States Army. Was he a soldier? Or a spy?

If he'd come looking for their village, how had he known they were there? The Dinee natives might have spread the word about Laurent's existence. But what did he want? Merely to find out if the rumor was true? Had his country sent him to spy out her people's strengths and weaknesses while they planned an attack?

If they let him go, where would he return to? Whom would he tell? Would they send back men with guns? Or were they only curious? So much they needed to know, and she needed to learn answers before the council's vote.

But even if Evan told all, would she be able to trust that he was speaking the truth?

She had to find a way to make him talk. Torture wasn't an option, despite the fact he thought they poisoned him for that purpose. Her people were peace-loving. They only wanted to remain completely on their own, invisible to the world except for the natives they traded with.

A moan drifted across the space between them, and the wrinkles in his brow grew deeper, scrunching into a look of pain.

Not the sickness again.

Should she do something to help him? She'd tried to tend her brother and sister during their childhood sickness, but Audrey always seemed to know when to show up to help. And the children always preferred her gentle touch over Brielle's fumbling.

If this man needed another arrow in his gut, she could do the job well, hitting exactly where she aimed. She could hunt meat, decipher the tracks of every animal in the area. She could distinguish between the calls of all the birds. Could even know a herd of caribou or elk simply by the actions of the birds around them.

But nursing was Audrey's specialty.

Another groan sounded, this one filling the room and knotting her own insides with its agony.

Evan clutched his belly and rolled, squeezing his eyes shut and tucking his knees up to his middle.

Maybe she should put a damp cloth over his forehead like Audrey had done. Or was that only after the man vomited? He'd cast up his accounts so many times, there couldn't be anything left inside to spew. Except maybe the few sips of water Audrey had coaxed down him.

She pushed to her feet, but as she started toward him, he fumbled for the bowl and heaved himself upright. With a grunt that echoed through the little stone room, his body convulsed. He pressed his face over the bowl, but despite the spasms, nothing came out.

Brielle hovered two strides away as another surge hit him. This wave seemed to come up from his deepest core and thrust his face down into the bowl. The third time, a moan accompanied the convulsion. The sound ripped through her, drawing her closer to him.

In truth, he sounded as though he might be dying. For a long moment, he sat hunched over the container, drawing in deep rasping breaths. He couldn't seem to get enough air, and each gulp gurgled, like the breath was half water. What was wrong with him? This must be more than a simple stomach ailment. Was it a delayed reaction to the potion from her arrow? The tip had entered his midsection, so maybe the poison had finally spread into his gut, and his body now tried to rid itself of the toxic substance. *Don't die, Evan.*

She'd never killed a man, but if she'd caused his death in defense of her people, would it be justified? The thought of losing him, of snuffing out the kindness in his eyes, twisted in her chest like a knife blade.

At last, Evan pushed the bowl aside and turned back to slump down on his pallet. This time he faced away from her, his shoulders still heaving with every breath.

She forced herself to close the final step between them and drop to her knees by his side. He seemed in so much pain; the last thing she wanted was for her efforts to make his suffering worse. But she took up the bowl of cool water and rag, then wrung out some of the liquid and lifted the cloth to his face.

She could only reach his temple the way he'd positioned himself, but as she dabbed the rag on the sweat gathered there, his breathing slowed. His shoulders no longer heaved. Instead, they rose and fell in a steady rhythm. His body slowly relaxed.

She stroked the cloth over his face, every

part she could reach. Then drew it back to dip in the water again. He turned his head toward her, his eyes still shut. His lips parted in a single word. "Please."

The ache inside her pulled so tight that she could barely breathe. She quickly wrung out the cloth and laid it over the part of his brow she hadn't been able to reach before. "I'm here."

The words seemed to soothe him as much as the cool cloth, although she wouldn't have thought he'd want her presence, of all people. Maybe he simply didn't want to be alone during his misery.

Alone as he died.

The idea of his death pierced her own midsection. *Lord, please. I was only protecting my people.*

She soothed the cloth over his face until the fabric grew warm again, but this time she warned him before drawing away. "I'm going to make it cool again."

His mouth parted as though he would speak, but then his lips simply worked like he was struggling to moisten them.

Water. Audrey said he needed to drink lots of water.

She reached for the cup. "See if you can take a sip. I'll lift your head."

As she slipped her hand into the thick hair

at the back of his head, she tried not to let herself dwell on being so near this man. Even ill, he wore a kind of virile manliness like a layer over his skin. The warmth of his body under her fingers stirred her too much. She pressed the thought aside and focused on not spilling the water as she raised the cup to his mouth. When the smooth wood touched his lips, his eyelids raised. He watched the cup as he swallowed once, then lifted his gaze to her while he swallowed a second time.

They were half an arm's length apart, and she could see every golden fleck scattered through the brown of his eyes. His lips — full lips for a man — were dry and chapped.

His lashes lowered again . . . long lashes. How had she not noticed them before? They framed his eyes, probably adding to the intensity of his gaze.

After a third sip, he laid back, and she eased her hand from behind his head.

Her nerves hummed from being so near him. Had he felt a stirring, too? He must be too miserable to feel pleasure of any kind. She needed to escape back to her wall so she could bring order to the churning inside her, but she should cool him more with the wet cloth first. That seemed to settle his pain more than anything.

Her fear of his proximity gnawed at her. She was a warrior. She could sit here and cool the man's brow if that's what was needed.

Three more times she wrung the dripping water from the cloth and soothed it over his face until the fabric grew hot. He wasn't feverish exactly. At least, not that she could tell. His warmth might have come from the exertion of vomiting. The act seemed to have stripped all the strength from him.

At last, his breathing grew even again, so she dropped the rag back into the water and simply sat beside him. Her eyes roamed his features, but sitting here staring at him would do her no good. While he slept, she should retreat to her wall and work on her arrows. She should.

But another length of time passed before she finally made herself push to her feet. By then, every line of his face was imprinted in her mind's eye.

Now, she wouldn't be able to forget him, even if she wanted to.

"Brielle, he needs to spend some time in the sunlight." Audrey had pulled Brielle to the side as Evan ate his midday meal. Nibbled at the meal, anyway. This was the first bit of food he'd attempted since his sickness started the night before. "He should be strong enough to walk now, and I can't imagine he's a danger, not as bad as he feels."

Brielle studied the man, still pale from the illness. Still handsome, despite his dire situation.

He glanced up to meet her look, raising his brows in question.

Did her nonsensical thoughts betray her? She schooled her features. She'd not allow him to think her weak. Especially in that way.

He probably knew they were speaking about him. Audrey spoke in French, but not so loud that he could hear and understand the words if he knew the language.

She shifted her focus back to her friend. "Are you certain he's strong enough?" He'd vomited only once more after that first time she tended him alone, but the final time had seemed to strip the remainder of his strength. The rest of the night he lay almost lifeless, the gentle rise and fall of his chest the only sign he still breathed.

When Gerald arrived that morning to begin his shift as guard, she left for a little while to take care of her responsibilities in their quarters. When she'd arrived back in this room, Evan had been awake. Audrey had propped his head up and was helping him drink from the water cup.

He seemed exhausted, but his eyes had offered a weary greeting as they tracked her across the room. Awareness of him tightened her insides, but she worked to focus on her duties. Audrey had cared for him in her pleasant, thorough way, and Brielle had to push down the surge of whatever it was that made her want — only for a moment — to take her friend's place.

The memory rose up completely unbidden from the night before, of the warm strands of his hair sliding across her fingers. It was then that she turned away from Evan to speak to Gerald again.

As much as she should have taken herself far away from the storage chamber, she told Gerald his shift was over. She would watch Evan for the day, and Philip would relieve her at nightfall when his shift started.

Thankfully, Evan had slept the remainder of the morning, and the slumber must have done him good, as evidenced by the way he now sat up and nibbled the pastry.

"Can I ask him? I'm sure he's strong enough." Audrey's voice tugged her back to the question at hand.

A bit of sunlight might do them all good. At least the visit outdoors would keep her from being alone with the man all after-noon, with only the work on her arrows to keep her from staring at him. She'd done enough of that to last a lifetime.

When Brielle nodded, Audrey spun, and pleasure rang from her voice as she switched to English. "Evan, are you up for a stroll outside? It's a warm day, and I think the sunshine will do you good."

He straightened and lowered the pastry, his gaze pivoting to Brielle.

She nodded her consent, although he'd surely seen her make the same motion to Audrey. He must have thought he'd never see daylight again.

She wasn't such an ogre that she would deny a man sunshine forever, although perhaps it was best he thought of her that way. The twist in her belly said otherwise, but she pressed the feeling down.

Audrey reached to help him up, but he shook his head. "I can do it better if I go slowly." His voice had taken on a gentle tone that seemed more than weariness. Perhaps the sickness had brought out a softer side.

With Audrey hovering near his right arm, Brielle stationed herself at his left — near enough she could step close if he appeared unstable, but far enough he couldn't grab one of her weapons. She kept her hand near her blade, just in case. Yet she was fairly certain his exhaustion wasn't feigned.

And her intuition told her he wouldn't attempt an escape during this particular outing. He seemed pleased with the prospect of sunlight.

He made it to his feet and paused, his breathing heavy. Was he also dizzy? She readied herself to step close enough to catch him if he started to topple.

But then he looked steadier and started a steady shuffle to the door.

They moved down the long corridor that extended along the rear of each family's abode. She could still remember when this hallway had been hacked out of the mountain after the English massacre. Before that, each home only opened to the main courtyard. But the elders decided they should have a way to connect the people if they were ever forced to hide from intruders inside the rock walls.

"We can go through here." Audrey motioned to the rear door of her family's chamber.

Although that cut through would be quicker than walking all the way down to the only door leading directly from the hallway to outside, Brielle shook her head. "The main door."

Better not to let him see inside any of their homes. Maybe he would find something he liked and plan to take it with him if they ever let him leave — perhaps that *something* he'd alluded to when they were talking. Something he'd never seen before that he'd come searching for.

When they finally reached the main entrance, Brielle gave the door a hard nudge with her shoulder. The cold tended to make the wood swell and scrape the stone around the frame. Better a snug fit than to allow the icy wind and snow into the cave, though.

As sunlight poured in, she blinked against the brightness. Evan slapped a hand over his eyes and tucked his chin. Poor man. The brilliance must be nearly blinding to him. She could only imagine how miserable he'd been locked inside for days. Bringing him out would be helpful, if only for a few minutes.

Across the yard, some of the children were tossing a short rope between them, and their laughter floated across the breeze. The giggling sounded like one of the Mignot twins, or maybe Philip's youngest. A boy shouted that he was open to receive the throw, then a flurry of voices rose as the leather cord was tossed high into the air.

The cacophony increased in pitch as the

object landed, and they all dove for it. Someone howled, maybe in delight, but another cry rose along with the sound. One of the youngest must have been caught in the midst of the melee.

Widow Cameron waded through the youngsters, soothing as she went. When Monsieur Cameron had died in a snowstorm, she became the unofficial nursemaid of the youngsters. In exchange, the families around her helped supply food, firewood, and anything else she might need.

Brielle glanced at Evan, who was staring at the children. He seemed caught by the drama, more than she would've expected. Had he planned some ill deed toward the youngsters? But the expression on his face held no malice. In truth, he looked even more pale than before, although that could be attributed to exhaustion, sickness, or simply the brightness of the sunlight. Yet, he looked almost stricken.

He blinked and seemed to come back to himself. After glancing around the yard, he pointed toward the gateway. "There. That's where I first realized you were a woman." One side of his mouth tipped as he slid a glance toward her.

She bit her lip to keep in her grin but didn't do a very good job of it. "You thought me a man?"

His brows rose. "When your arrow struck me, yes. Then I heard you speak and wondered how in the world a lad had bested me."

She stiffened. He'd thought she was a young boy? That was even worse than if he'd realized immediately that she was a woman.

Maybe he realized he'd offended her, for his next words came softer. "Then when I saw your face, there" — he pointed to the place just inside the gateway where he'd collapsed — "I knew nothing was as I'd thought."

The words slipped inside her, circling as they settled in her mind. What had he thought he'd find here? If he'd been sent by his country to scout their village before they planned an assault, was he now having second thoughts?

9

Sitting on this pallet for days on end was making Evan lose his senses. The guards required him to stay on the fur mat, except when he had to make a trip to the loose dirt they'd piled in the corner. He did as much movement as he could manage while staying on the hide — running in place and all manner of agility and strengthening movements — anything to restore his body now that he'd recovered from the sickness three days before.

He had to find a way to search for pitch-blende. He had only had a few weeks to locate a substantial grouping of the mineral. He'd been keeping careful count of the passing days, and the deadline loomed heavy on his chest.

He had to find a way to escape from his guard so he could search for the mineral. Most of the time, they kept him locked in this room with someone always watching.

But now they allowed him a few moments outside, always accompanied by Brielle and at least one other person. That quarter hour was precious, and he'd never take sunshine for granted again. Even though the sun here held much less potency than it did farther south.

Maybe he could find a chance to break free during one of those outings. Yet how would he manage without his supplies? No knife or gun. No furs to stay warm when the weather turned blustery. If he had even one type of weapon, he might be able to hunt enough to fill his stomach and guard against cold weather. But that would slow him down. Finding pitchblende and returning to the States by the end of the year might be impossible under those conditions.

He would have to convince these people he didn't mean them harm. They would release him once they came to trust him. He could soon be on his way in search of a mountain containing the mineral he *had* to find.

He picked at the line of dark hair that marked the edge of the hide, where it had wrapped around the animal's belly. He'd memorized every nuance of the fur underneath him — a caribou pelt, Philip had said. He'd imagined the animal's entire lifespan, from where it must have been born, how it must have frolicked with the other young caribou, how it had fought with the other males as it came of age. How it might have split off with a few cows to form its own small band, then been struck down by one of the hunters here. Maybe by Brielle herself.

He asked every person who entered the room if there was anything he could do to be helpful. He'd offered to whittle arrows as Brielle did or stitch moccasins like Philip, the night guard. He'd be willing to braid rope if they would only give him something to occupy his mind and hands.

A few of the men had been open to conversation — in small bits, anyway. Philip had told of his wife, Rona, and their two children.

Leonard, the man watching him now, spoke of the woman he was betrothed to marry in the spring. He seemed a few years younger than the other guards and was eager both to do his job well and to be generally pleasant. Evan had asked about Brielle and when the man mentioned she still lived in her father's home, a bit of relief wound through him. She must not be married. But when he asked how she'd come to be head of the guard, Leonard had clamped his mouth shut and shrugged.

The door opened, and a man poked his head in. At his place against the far wall, Leonard scrambled to his feet. "Marcellus. You're not supposed to be in here."

Marcellus. He'd heard that name before. Was he the one Brielle and Audrey had spoken of? Brielle had been adamant he wasn't to see Evan.

Of course, she'd been adamant about all of Evan's restrictions. If only he could make her see he hadn't come to hurt her people. The image of the children playing outside slipped through his mind. He would *not* hurt these people, especially not the children.

His last assignment had been to help sneak a wagon of explosives into a Canadian fort. He'd not realized how many women and children the place contained until their cries rose with the smoke. He could still hear their screams. He could never let that happen again on one of his missions.

Marcellus lumbered into the room and closed the door behind him, pulling Evan from the awful memories. The fellow gave Leonard a grin that flashed both rows of teeth. "I only came to say hello." He spoke French, but his S sounds carried a slight lisp that made his words even harder to translate. Hearing the language these last few days had brought back what Evan had learned in the past, and his understanding of what he heard was growing better each day. But he had to think hard to process what Marcellus was saying.

Evan looked closer at the fellow. He was big, but probably not much older than himself. Yet something in his face gave him a boyish look.

Leonard let out a sigh. "Say hello, then, and get it over with."

Marcellus turned his wide grin on Evan and walked right up to him with his hand extended. Evan reached out to clasp it in greeting, but the man moved past his outstretched palm and clapped Evan on the shoulder. "I'm Marcellus. I'm really happy to meet you. Your name is Evan?"

The man's jubilance was hard not to appreciate, and Evan reached up to pat Marcellus's shoulder in the same way. "It's a pleasure to meet you. I'm happy you came to say hello. It gets a little quiet here." He sent a sideways grin to Leonard. Though he'd shared a little, he seemed just as pleased to maintain silence.

Marcellus leaned in as he spoke. "Brielle told me she had to find out if you could be trusted before I came to visit, but it's been five whole days and I'm sure she's decided by now. I can see right off you can be trusted, so if she doesn't know it, I'll tell her. Where did you come from anyway? Mama said it was far away. She said your people are bad sometimes. You're not bad, though, are you? I told her I didn't think you would be bad. I'm bad sometimes, but I try hard not to be."

Evan had to work to hold back his chuckle, both at the man's words and the way they poured out of him. This one certainly didn't value silence.

The fellow finally seemed to be waiting for him to speak, but there was so much to respond to. Evan picked the easiest and most recent comment. "I'm sure you try hard, Marcellus. I try hard not to be bad, too. And your mama is right, I'm from a place far away. I had no idea you and your village were up here."

"Really?" The lad — for it was hard not to think of him as a lad with some of the boyish expressions that crossed his face — tipped his head in curiosity. "Because I heard Papa Durand talking to my papa and they were saying they thought you came to see what we were doing up here. They thought you would go back and tell an army, and they would come take over our

116

homes."

The words stung as their possibility sank through him. If he did find pitchblende in their mountain, the miners would cause great damage to the homes in Laurent. But pitchblende wouldn't be *here*. What were the odds that this was the specific location?

Yet, even if he found the mineral in a nearby mountain, the work would still cause a disruption to Laurent's way of life. Outsiders would learn of them, and probably intermingle with them. There would be competition for hunting while the work was being done. And Laurent might be exposed to diseases and other threats they'd not faced in their protected village.

"That's enough, Marcellus." Leonard marched forward and ushered the fellow toward the door.

Marcellus turned back to Evan with a wave. "I'll come back and see you soon."

Evan forced a smile. "Anytime. I'd like the company."

As the guard murmured quiet words to Marcellus at the door, Evan sank into his spinning thoughts, focusing on a different part of the lad's words.

Was there something here in Laurent that needed to be protected? Something an army would be willing to march for months to obtain? It couldn't be pitchblende, for its explosive properties were only a recent discovery, only known by a few chemists. Even if the people knew they had that mineral, they couldn't know its value.

So, what could these people or this location have that would be so precious to an entire country?

It was time he had a heart-to-heart with Brielle.

If she forced herself to admit the truth, Brielle had been avoiding Evan MacManus.

But why should she take on guard duty every day when they had so many capable guards? She'd stayed with him for almost a full night and day when he was sick and stopped in to see him each day since then, albeit, making sure someone else was always there, too.

Each time she attempted to start a casual conversation with the man, she was reminded how incapable she was at small talk. Combined with the way his handsome features drew her gaze like a magnet tugged a compass north, she was better off avoiding him.

She made sure she stayed long enough to allow him a bit of time outside, though. Every human being deserved such, and his spirits always seemed lighter after a few minutes in the sunlight.

Maybe the outings also allowed him a chance to study his surroundings, to examine the best route of escape. But he wouldn't be allowed the opportunity to flee, so that possibility mattered little.

She tapped once on the storage room door before entering. Perhaps they should call it the holding room now, since all storage had been removed when they first brought Evan here. Or perhaps they should name the area the dungeon, as he had done more than once, sometimes with a glare and sometimes with a humorous tip to his lips.

As she pushed open the door, her gaze immediately found the owner of those lips. His eyes had already landed on her, and their power flowed through her like water in a hot spring, both scalding and soothing at the same time.

She had to work to pull her gaze from his, shifting into her warrior mindset as she turned to Leonard. "I'll take over for the night." She spoke in English, as she'd long stopped trying to hide anything she said around Evan.

Leonard nodded and stepped forward, making his way around her to the door. But then he hesitated.

Tension gripped her chest, but she forced her tone to stay casual. "Did anything happen today?" Surely someone would have come to find her if there had been cause for alarm.

A guilty expression crossed Leonard's face. The knot inside her tightened. The man scratched his nose, as though hating to tell her what he had to. "Marcellus came by. I let him speak to Evan for a short time. Thought it might settle his eagerness. Then I sent him away and told him not to come back until you said he could."

Anger washed through her, but she swallowed down the emotion to keep control of herself. "I told him not to come at all. I made sure he understood. Over and over, I said no." She had to clench her teeth with those last words to keep more from spewing out.

Leonard nodded sympathetically. "I know you did. But you know Marcellus." He switched to Italian. "He said you'd had enough time to decide whether the stranger could be trusted. In fact, he said if you weren't sure yet, he'd be happy to tell you Evan was a good man."

A laugh slipped out before she could stop it, and she shook her head, then switched back to English for her answer. "If you see

Marcellus, tell him I want a word with him in the morning."

Leonard saluted. "Oui, Commandant." Then he headed out the door with a jaunt in his step.

Her mind churned with the impact of Marcellus's visit as she took her place against the wall. Perhaps Marcellus, with all his innocence, might have pulled information from the man she hadn't. She should have asked Leonard what they'd spoken of. Had Marcellus said anything that could endanger the village? There wasn't really anything the lad could share. The people of Laurent had no secrets.

It was Evan who withheld details they needed to know.

10

Brielle held her focus on their prisoner. Evan watched her as he sat on the fur, legs crossed at the ankles. His look was more than a casual glance. No, he seemed to be searching her expression for something. Intensity marked his gaze. What was he looking for?

Why hadn't she asked Leonard what Evan and Marcellus spoke of? She would simply have to inquire of this man. She could always check with Leonard later to confirm what Evan said. He looked like he had something to ask her anyway.

She worked for a smile, or at least a softer expression. "Have you already eaten your evening meal?"

He nodded, a slow calculating dip of his chin. "Audrey's food tasted as good as ever. And no more poisoning, it seems." His lips tipped, as if to prove he didn't mean the comment. "I assume the fresh elk meat was your doing?"

Although the question couldn't really be considered a compliment, the way his voice softened made it feel like one.

She gave a single nod. "We have many who hunt, though." And maybe she had pictured Evan's delight at the fresh game when she brought the bull elk to Audrey, but she certainly didn't want credit for thoughtfulness. This man didn't need to know how often his image entered her thoughts. He should think he disappeared from her mind the moment she left this room.

She turned her focus back to more productive matters. "Have you need of anything for the night?"

Evan shook his head. "Not unless you have something I can do to pass the time. I'm happy to braid rugs or rope — anything at all that'll keep my hands, and hopefully my mind, busy." Again, there was a tip of his lips that could've been a smile, but without a sparkle in his eye, the look turned wry.

Maybe it was his words, or maybe it was the thought of how she would feel being locked away in this little room for day upon day, but something compressed inside her. "I'll see what I can find in the morning.

Maybe Marcellus's mother will have something you can do to help."

A light slipped into his gaze, reminding her of the discussion they would need to have. She hadn't intended such a perfect segue but best to grasp hold of it.

She dropped to sit on the stone floor, wrapping her arms around her knees in front of her. She was about to open her mouth to start the discussion, but Evan beat her to it.

"I met Marcellus today." He nodded in the direction Leonard had gone. "I guess the other guard told you."

She offered a grim smile. "Marcellus is . . . eager. It's been hard to keep him from coming to see you."

Evan's gaze softened. "I'm glad he came. He was a pleasure." A grin tickled the corners of his mouth. "I'm not much for talking usually. But I have to say, after all these days of quiet, it was nice to hear so many words come at me so quickly."

She almost chuckled at how the conversation had probably gone.

Then Evan's face sobered. "There was one thing he said that helped me understand why you're holding me."

She stilled, then worked to keep herself from stiffening too much as her chest tightened. Marcellus *had* said something. She wanted to pull the words from Evan's mouth but forced herself to not appear too eager. "Oh?"

"He said you thought I was here as a spy, that my country wanted to send an army to take over Laurent." His gaze turned questioning. "I'm curious why you would think that. I've made it clear I was only on an exploring trip. I didn't know your village was here at all. I might have never discovered Laurent if you hadn't dragged me inside the rock wall."

She took her time answering him. His face seemed earnest, and his voice held nothing that raised an internal warning.

Should she mention the paper Papa found? Her father had told her not to speak of it, so she'd better not. But maybe she could tell the deeper reason they were all cautious. Perhaps if she revealed that part, he would tell more about himself.

She studied him once more. Maybe it was the way his eyes always drew her in. Maybe it was how handsome he was, even with how his beard thickened a little more each day, hiding the strong jawline she knew lay underneath. Something in her chest tightened. She yearned . . . but for what?

Pushing the question aside, she dropped

her gaze and focused on that day a decade ago. "I was twelve years old when the last Englishmen came to our village. We still don't know how they found us, but they rode right through the gate. My mother was the first to spot them. When she called out that we had visitors, three other women were nearby with their children. Most of the men had gone on a hunting trip, but Marcellus's father was one of the few who stayed behind. He came running when he heard one of the strangers shout." A knot thickened her throat, drying her mouth and making it hard to speak. That day had been so long ago; she'd been able to speak of it without emotion for years now. Why did this retelling threaten to choke out her voice?

Maybe because Evan's presence resurrected the memories in such vivid detail. She could see the faces of those strangers. Hear her mother's voice rise in greeting to them. She blinked to clear the image. Only the basic elements of the story were sufficient to share right now. Not details.

"Since my father is chief of our village, my mother approached to greet them in his stead. She made me sit with my younger brother and sister. She wanted them to stay back until we knew who the strangers were. She'd barely lifted her hand in greeting when one of the men . . . shot her." Her voice trembled on that life-changing word. She clenched her fists to pull herself back under control.

"Louis — Marcellus's father — arrived and had the foresight to bring his sword, just as my mother fell to her knees. Others came with weapons, and by the time the fighting ended, six of our people had fallen and two more were badly injured." She was shaking now, and every part of her stretched tight as she worked to still herself. "All ten of their men died. None of them made it out of our walls."

But they'd wreaked enough devastation to impact the life of every person in this village. Laurent had learned an important lesson that day. *She* had learned an important lesson. Her people's safety couldn't be left to chance. And now that she'd earned the right to protect them, she couldn't fail those she loved.

With that reminder, her body finally stopped trembling. She raised her gaze to meet Evan's. "Now you understand why we don't trust outsiders. Especially Englishmen."

Evan's face didn't show the worry her words might have inspired. Nor apprehension that they would take their fury out on

127

him, nor fear that the last time had made them strengthen themselves so much an attack wouldn't be successful.

Nor was there sympathy, as she'd half expected since she'd come to know this man.

No, the look in his eyes was . . . hard to read. If she'd had to name it, she would have said his gaze had turned haunted. As though he could see the courtyard as it had stood twelve years before, bloodied bodies strewn about. Children and wives and husbands weeping over their lost. Women scurrying to tend the wounds of the two who yet lived.

As though he could see the little girl Brielle had been, crying over her mother. Brushing the hair away from Mama's familiar face, away from the lifeless eyes that had regarded her so tenderly. The love they'd always held no longer shimmering in their glassy depths.

She wrenched her mind away from that image. She'd unravel if she stayed there much longer.

Evan's throat worked, and she focused on the dip of his Adam's apple, letting it bring her back to the present.

"I wish I knew what to say." His voice came out rough, almost hoarse, yet laced with a tenderness that made her want to curl inside his arms and take refuge.

Her gaze drifted to those arms. What would it be like to be held within their strength? For a tiny moment, she longed to close the distance between them and let herself be protected. As much as she wanted this position as provider and protector of Laurent, the job she'd worked so hard to earn, sometimes she hated always being the strong one. If only there was someone who could carry the weight of responsibility for her every once in a while.

She straightened, shoving the thought aside. She alone didn't bear the entire responsibility for Laurent's well-being. The council took on most of the decisions, and the other guards and hunters helped with protection and provision. They all worked together. She certainly didn't need an outsider to help her.

Evan's mouth formed a curve so weighed with sadness, it couldn't be called a smile. "I'm sorry, Brielle. Thank you for trusting me with your story."

So often, this man seemed capable of seeing deep inside her. Of reading her thoughts in a way no one else could. Maybe it was that ability that made her want to connect with him. It was certainly that ability that made her *afraid* of connecting with him.

She acknowledged his words with a nod.

His brow creased, and his gaze shifted in what appeared to be deep thought, and alarm rose in Brielle. He must be planning his next actions based on the story she'd told. Maybe she'd been a fool to share so much. She could try to distract him from whatever scheme he was working out, but there was no way she could keep him from thinking all day and all night indefinitely. She couldn't retract the words now, so she'd have to trust that her instincts hadn't led her astray in telling him.

He seemed to realize he'd been quiet, for he met her gaze again and the lines at the corners of his eyes deepened. "I guess I do understand better why you're keeping me locked in this hole." Then his mouth formed a wry look. "Takes a bit of the punch out of my anger."

He'd been remarkably in control of his anger, a fact that hadn't escaped her. She couldn't imagine what some of the other guards who struggled with their tempers would do if forced to stay locked away in the dark, night and day, without end. If Evan really was as innocent as he claimed, he was being held somewhat unjustly.

But something in her said the situation

was not exactly as it seemed. Why wouldn't
he tell the truth?

11

A fresh wave of determination rose inside Brielle, and she leveled a firm look on Evan. "Now you understand why it's so important that we not let you leave until we know what you came for. In the past, we allowed outsiders in, but that trust took the lives of my mother and five other women. One man's arm had to be removed to save the rest of him. Marcellus's father has no feeling below his waist." She pressed a hand to her own belly to mark the spot.

Then she squared her shoulders. "Tell me. Why have you come? What is it you want from us?"

A flash of uncertainty slid through his gaze — there and gone so fast, maybe she imagined it. But she spent far too much time watching for the flick of a deer's ear to tell her it had caught her scent, or a flash of movement in the brush to signal a rabbit attempting to flee. During the longer winters,

132

even a rabbit was a precious commodity to fill their hungry bellies. She'd honed her eyes and instincts to see the smallest flash of movement and act in an instant.

His gaze had shuttered now, leaving her to ponder what that uncertainty had meant. He must be deciding how much to reveal.

She waited. If he wouldn't speak at all, she could prompt him by asking exactly where he came from. She knew so little about the American colonies, or rather *states,* as Evan had told Leonard. But she would press for details until she had a clear picture of where he was from and what that government was like now.

But Evan spoke before she had to decide how to begin. "I suppose the first thing you should know is that I'm not an Englishman."

The words were so far from what she expected, she had to blink to take in what he meant. But even then, his statement wasn't clear. Was he French, then? Why did he not have a French accent?

"I'm an American. We fought a war decades ago to be free from England's tyranny. We're the United States of America now, not colonies. American citizens, not English."

Now his meaning made sense, but she

133

strained to remember about the group that had attacked them all those years ago. Had they known for sure those men were from England? Or could they have been Americans? A dozen years before, the war Evan spoke of had already taken place. America had already been states, a country of their own. Her father and the others in Laurent hadn't known of those changes back then.

She studied him. "If what you say is true, I'm not sure whether those who attacked us were from England or from your American states. You all speak the same language?"

He nodded. "But most of us speak it a little different than the fellows in England."

He reached for a strand of hair on the fur underneath him. "England still has control of the Canadian colonies. And they've been itching to move down on us again. These last three years, America's been at war with England for a second time. They've riled the Indians and have some of the tribes fighting on their side."

She squinted. "Indians? You mean the Dinee?"

Now it was his turn to scratch his brow in confusion. "The natives. The bronze-skinned people who were on the land before the colonies were settled. We have lots of different tribes in the States and the territories to the west. You might have other tribes up here."

She nodded. That made sense. But there were a few other pieces missing in the picture he painted. "What of the French? Do they not have colonies in New France anymore?"

"France had to give most of its lands to England when they lost the Seven Years' War." He tipped his head as he eyed her. "Maybe it would be easier if you tell me when your people were cut off from civilization. I can do my best to fill in the gaps of what's happened since then. What's the last thing you know about?"

She'd already said so much; this last detail wouldn't give him further knowledge that he could use to harm them. Of course, he could tell her anything about the world beyond and she wouldn't know whether he spoke the truth. She'd have to keep that in mind and weigh his words and actions as he spoke.

"We've been here just over a century. My great-great-grandfather helped cut our homes from the original caves. What I've always been told was that New France lies to the east and the British colonies south of that. Thirteen of them. France holds more colonies somewhere below them."

He nodded, and his brow wrinkled. "Well, then. I've told you most of the big changes. Those French colonies to the south of the states were actually sold to America about a decade ago. President Jefferson bought them as part of the Louisiana Purchase. As for New France, as you call it, the British own it now. The land is split between Upper Canada and Lower Canada along the Ottawa River, although Upper Canada's actually a bit south and west, but it's the way the river runs."

She sorted through the facts, trying to cipher out her questions. Could all this be true? None of it seemed like something he would fabricate.

And none of it seemed to have any bearing on why he'd come here.

He was giving so much detail that he must realize she was trying to determine whether she could trust him or not. She should press on now that she had him talking. Better to learn more about his government. "What of your land? How far away did you say it was?"

"Over three months on horseback. From my home, that is. I went west until I passed Missouri, then northwest through the territories until I left the lands owned by America."

"And how long did you travel after you left those lands?"

He squinted. "About . . . a month and a half, I think." He gave her a wry look. "These last few days have made everything blur together."

A month and a half. That wasn't too far for an army to travel. She'd known other people lived in the world, but the reality of them being so near washed through her with painful clarity. The people of Laurent — her people — were in more danger than she'd allowed herself to believe.

She worked for a casual tone. "And there are many of your countrymen who live at the edge of your American lands?"

He raised his brows in surprise. "You mean the edge of the territories? Not at all. Mostly Indians, and a few trappers, although most of those are French.

"Most are tied up with skirmish and battles related to the war." His voice grew weary. "It's been hard. With the British fighting on one side, and the Indians attacking on the other, we've lost so many men. And not just men." His voice caught on those last words.

She homed in on his face. Who had he lost, specifically? Dare she ask? The need to know pressed her. "You've lost friends?"

He didn't shy away from her gaze. A depth of pain flashed in his eyes. "The war has taken many people I would call acquaintances, a few friends, too. And my wife."

Like a punch to the gut, his words slammed into her, knocking the breath from her lungs. He'd been married? How had the war taken her? Surely not in battle.

Every part of her ached to ask more, but this time she didn't dare. What he'd revealed already felt like too much. More than she wanted to know.

A new awareness hummed through her, and she couldn't see him as she had before. Not as a man who'd possibly come to take over Laurent, to see many of her people killed, and even more devastation brought on those who lived.

No. Evan was simply a man. One who'd lost someone very dear to him.

As she had.

Except he'd lost his *wife.* Something deep inside her stabbed with a blade that tasted faintly of jealousy.

A woman had known this man well enough to share his life and his bed — maybe even his heart. She knew well enough every marriage wasn't a love match.

In a small village such as Laurent, when male and female came of age, unions had to form for the simple matter of procreation. Of course, there were many other reasons, but the village would die away if no one married.

Evan's face gave no indication of whether he and his wife had been blissfully happy before her passing or only carrying on the duties of each day.

Children. Did he have a son or daughter waiting for him back in America?

A whole host of new worries turned inside her. If Evan didn't return to them, would a precious child become both fatherless and motherless? A fist clenched her heart, squeezing until she could bear it no longer.

She swallowed to summon moisture into her mouth. "Did you . . . do you . . . have . . . children?" Her chest wouldn't allow in air as she watched his face for an answer.

He shook his head, a new flash of pain clouding his eyes. "Sophia wanted them, but . . . we didn't have any."

A wash of thoughts and emotions swirled inside her. Sophia. What an elegant name. French, too, just like the people of Laurent.

Her mind churned with questions, but only one burned to be answered. "How long ago did she . . . ?" What word would be appropriate to mark the passing of a loved one? She struggled with the same question about her mother.

Passing seemed so flimsy, as though the awful day that Brielle's heart had been forever shredded was only a flimsy blade of grass that could blow off in the wind. Not the marking of the day a young woman was a girl no longer. Not marking the day she became mistress of the home, mother to two hurting children, one who would never hold a memory of the woman who bore them.

Evan's answer pierced through her thoughts. "Two years ago. While I was —" his voice broke, then he looked to be forcing out the rest of his words — "gone. A fever took her life. She'd been helping in one of the soldiers' hospitals when she took ill. Some might not blame the war for her death, but the war was also what kept me from being with her at the end." A hard grunt slipped out that might have been a chuckle. "It was another five months before I came home and learned she was gone."

She could understand the tinge of bitterness that laced his tone. "You were a soldier?" Maybe she shouldn't have pressed with that question, but now she wanted to know more about this man. He drew her like no man ever had before.

He dipped his chin. "I worked for the army."

"You . . . don't work for the army any longer?"

A slight hesitation. Just barely a pause, but enough to make her carefully consider his next words. "After Sophia was gone, I had nothing left to hold me to Maryland. I dove into my work with everything I had, trying to lose myself in becoming the best. I worked hard."

The cords in his throat flexed. "I did everything asked of me. But things didn't always turn out well." His voice took on a raw edge, like the memories were almost too much. "I couldn't do it anymore. I couldn't handle the horrors of war." He inhaled a breath, and his voice leveled out. "So, I began exploring. First I went west, and found I liked the freedom. On my second trip, I came northwest." He held out a palm. "And here I am."

Brielle nodded, but her mind was turning with so many thoughts, she needed time to sort through everything. She laid her head back against the stone wall behind her. "You must be tired. I'll not bother you with any more questions."

Maybe Evan's thoughts were as cluttered as her own, for he stretched out on his side.

141

But it was a long time before his eyes closed, and even longer before his breathing settled into the steady rhythm of sleep.

Good thing she would be staying awake as his guard, for the longer she dwelt on their conversation, the more questions she had. But they weren't questions about his whereabouts and intentions here in Laurent. Her mind struggled to fill the gaps in the picture that was his life before he came.

Now that she knew a little about him as a person, her heart craved to know so much more. What of his parents? Were they still alive? Had they been loving? Where had he grown up? Village or farm? When had he married?

And that question that burned every time it raised its nagging head — Had he loved his wife? Did he love her still?

Evan sat by Audrey's outside cook fire, relishing the warmth of the mild sun caressing his face. He would never again take sunlight for granted, not as long as he lived.

"So, then, have you any brothers or sisters?" Audrey's voice held its usual chipper note, and she offered him a smile as she kneaded some kind of dough in her wooden mixing bowl. Everything these people used seemed to be wooden, at least for eating and drinking. Their ancestors must not have brought pewter or tin dishware with them, or else those metals had worn out long ago.

"I had a brother, but he died back in Scotland. My parents died there, too." He could feel Brielle's awareness on him, but he didn't look at her. When she turned that penetrating gaze on him, she made him want to let her see him — the real him. He'd told her far too much the night before, and he didn't plan to continue making himself so vulnerable.

At least their conversation had seemed to earn a little more of her trust. Enough that she'd allowed him to stay outside for a good hour so far. The three of them sat around Audrey's cook fire while she worked her magic with food.

He labored to keep his attention on Audrey, the gentle sympathy in her eyes a balm for any man.

"I'm so sorry. I didn't realize you were from Scotland. I guess I assumed you were born in America." She slid a glance at Brielle. "We've learned of Scotland, of course, but I confess I don't know much about the place. The lessons never stuck as well with me as they did Brielle."

So, the children of Laurent were taught geography? And three languages, besides. They certainly weren't wasting their minds in this little mountain haven.

Audrey focused on him again. "You were born in Scotland, then? What was it like there? I don't suppose any of us will ever see it, so tell us all you can." Her voice held an eagerness hard to miss. Did she wish she could leave this place and explore the world?

He nodded. "Born in Scotland, but I came to America when I was ten and six."

Before he could describe the land, she

tipped her head at him. "Do they speak English in Scotland?"

"And Gaelic. The English has a distinct accent, though." He adjusted his mouth so he could slip into the brogue he hadn't used in years. "Dinna kin, the words cum out soundin' a bit lazy, like this."

Audrey paused in her work to raise her brows at him, and even Brielle sat straighter, no longer concealing her interest.

"Say something else." Audrey's eagerness had the innocence of a child, making the request impossible to decline.

For years, he'd worked hard to lose the brogue, but it was easy enough to slip back into it. "I dinna think it would hurt n'thin'." He laid the accent thick in the words and was rewarded with a beaming grin.

"You should speak that way always. It's much more interesting than plain English." Audrey turned to Brielle. "We should have the children learn a Scottish accent, too. It would be a good stretch for their minds, and they'd have such fun with it."

Brielle raised her brows and pressed her lips in a look that showed interest without committing. "I'm sure they would. Perhaps Gerald could learn it first, then teach the little ones. He's good at languages — and you could help them."

145

Audrey's expression shifted, her chin ducking as red splotched her cheeks. "Perhaps."

One of Evan's guards had been named Gerald. The man who always slipped in a snide remark or two about his dislike toward Evan. Most of the guards were fairly quiet and respectful, but Gerald didn't disguise his anger. Evan had spent more time on his back with his eyes closed those days, and it hadn't been from pain in his gut.

But the man seemed important to Audrey, if her flustered silence meant something. Anyone who could capture the attention of this kindhearted woman deserved a second chance. At least so Evan could make sure the man was good enough for Audrey.

She reminded him just a little of his mother, always doing for others and taking pleasure in the happiness she brought. Mum hadn't deserved the pain her final years had laid on her, but perhaps he could spare Audrey from an equally difficult fate.

He readjusted his tongue position to settle back into the American accent that finally felt familiar. "When Gerald is guarding me again, I'll offer to teach him some." He directed the next part to Brielle. "If that's acceptable."

She nodded. "He's scheduled for tomorrow. I'll let him know." Then with a gleam in her gaze, she slid her focus to Audrey. "But if you see him first, feel free to tell him your idea. He might be more amenable to the job if he hears it from you."

Audrey didn't look up at either of them, just kept her focus on the dough she rolled. From the looks of it, she was making those delicious rolls again. Although the way she strangled the dough, it didn't seem possible the loaves would be as light and fluffy as the last batch she'd brought him. She mumbled to Brielle in French.

He probably wasn't supposed to know what she said, but he still strained to pick out the words. He was pretty certain he caught "evening meal," but Brielle saved him from having to guess the rest.

"Good then." She switched the conversation back to English, loud enough she clearly meant for all three of them to hear. "You can discuss the plan when he comes to eat the evening meal with your family." Her cheeks tugged in a smile that would captivate even a grizzly bear.

There was no way he could resist his own grin, no matter whether he approved of this particular match or not. The look on his face was probably half besotted, for being

147

in Brielle's presence made him feel exactly that.

Her striking beauty was one thing. A man could eventually steel himself against her appearance. Maybe.

But combined with her impressive abilities and the depth of her loyalty and caring for those in her inner circle, he'd never met a woman so remarkable. He should probably do better at keeping his emotions distant. He had a job to do, after all.

It was high time he focus on finding pitchblende as his mission required.

Philip's steady snores filled the small room, echoing off the stone walls. Evan laid on his back, hands resting atop his stomach in an all-too-familiar position. At least Brielle had begun to loosen his restrictions. Not only had he spent well over an hour in the courtyard with her and Audrey the day before, now his night guard actually slept.

He could easily imagine that the sleeping was accidental. Philip was usually so vigilant, bringing books and carving projects to keep himself awake while Evan slept.

Last night had started out the same, but when Evan awoke partway through, the snoring had been bad enough to reverberate through his shoulders. That awful sound was probably what woke him again tonight, for he'd not slept well since.

Maybe this was God's way of getting him back on track with his mission.

He'd not found any pitchblende laced through the rock walls in this room, but he should make certain the mineral didn't exist anywhere else in Laurent before he left.

A knot tightened in his chest. Maybe he should forget about looking inside this peaceful haven. If he found the mineral the American government needed so badly to win the war, they would bring soldiers and excavators who would upend this quiet village as much as these peaceful people feared his presence would. Not that the soldiers would come to kill, but they would certainly change the heart of the place, at least for a time.

But he had to do his diligence. He'd sworn an oath before setting out on this mission. Pitchblende was the only mineral still needed to finalize the blasting powder able to create an explosion significant enough to end this war.

He couldn't dwell on the fact that the explosion would take countless lives. It was not much different than on a battlefield, although he'd never been directly responsible for the ravages of what happened on the front line.

Only for the annihilation of a fort full of women and children.

He clenched his fists as their desperate cries rose up to cut off his breathing. That nightmare was in the past. He couldn't go back and change things. And it was why he'd requested this mission. Searching for a mineral in the icy north should hurt no one.

But he'd never expected to find a village like this.

The snoring broke off in a snort, and Philip licked his lips as he raised a hand to wipe the sleep from his eyes. He pushed himself up to a sitting position and eyed Evan with a sleep-clouded gaze. A spike of hair rose up on his head, which meant he probably had a flat spot at the back.

The man cleared his throat. "Must be morning, but it's hard to tell without daylight showing under the door."

Evan sat up, too, and spread his shoulders to stretch the tightness from them. "It is hard to tell night from day." If he hadn't been keeping such careful count, he would have completely lost track of what day it was. He pressed a hand to his middle. "My belly is the only thing that keeps the mornings and evenings straight."

Philip nodded and flashed a grin. "Audrey's meals are what make night duty worth the effort."

Evan nodded his agreement. "Not sure I've had such good cooking in years. I don't know how she does it without a cookstove." The man might not know what that was, so he added, "That's a kind of big fireplace we have back home, with a cooking surface built on top to hold pots and such. It helps cook things more evenly."

Philip raised his bushy brows and curiosity brightened his eyes. "I've wondered what inventions the rest of the world has been coming up with. This cookstove sounds like something we should build for Audrey. You'll have to sketch it out for us."

Now there was a good idea — a way he could actually help these people, especially the one who'd done an awful lot of good for him, between her nursing skills and her food three times a day.

Evan nodded toward the cloak still wadded on the ground where Philip had laid his head. "Was your bed too hard? If I'd known you planned to sleep, I could've shared my fur." He offered a friendly grin. The fur was barely large enough for him, so if the man wanted one, he should bring his own. But maybe the offer would be kindly received.

Philip reached up to rub his neck, tilting his head sideways with a grimace. "I'll bring something softer tonight. Didn't expect to sleep, but Brielle stopped me on my way in here the other night and said I could." He straightened and sent Evan another grin. "Guess she's starting to trust you a little more."

Then the man's expression grew into a look so stern it almost made Evan chuckle. "But I'm a light sleeper, so don't think you can sneak out." As his face relaxed, a bit of a twinkle slipped back into his eye.

Philip was a good man. Maybe they could become friends by the end of this debacle. In truth, most of these people seemed like the kind he'd enjoy living among. Working alongside. Sharing meals together.

Most of them. Gerald hadn't passed muster yet, but maybe today would change that opinion.

Evan stood to perform his morning ritual and had just returned to his mat when Audrey's step sounded in the hall. He'd know that soft scuffle anywhere. It was not as hushed as Brielle's stealthy tread, which was the most silent of anyone's. Brielle's lighter stature probably helped her walk quietly, along with the way she'd honed the ability to move without sound.

Audrey entered, and a delicious aroma followed her a breath later. He soaked in the spicy scent of some kind of sausage and couldn't help a teasing grin. "Do I get your pastries with my meal this morning? Or did Gerald eat them all last night?"

She ducked as a blush flooded her face, but he suspected it was more from his words than the wink he included with them. "I brought Breton galette again. I hope you're not growing weary of it." She lifted the cover, and a fresh burst of the rich aroma nearly made him lunge forward and take the plate from her hands.

He controlled himself, though. But as he took his first bite, he closed his eyes and let his body fully relish the pleasure. When he'd absorbed the very last taste, he opened his eyes and grinned. "That was almost worth being held under guard for."

Her face bloomed again as she turned to hand Philip his own plate. "I brought fresh torches, too." As she moved around the room, replacing the pitch-covered logs that had burned to nubs, another footstep sounded in the corridor.

The door opened and Gerald stepped in, a scowl darkening his face. When his gaze caught on Audrey, though, his expression shifted completely.

Still, something in it didn't sit right with Evan. The look wasn't the way a gentleman appreciated the lady. There was something . . . lustful . . . in the gaze.

Every one of Evan's protective instincts rose up within him. Audrey needed to leave this room. She shouldn't be subjected to attentions like that from any man, and she certainly shouldn't be alone with the cad.

But she turned and — the epitome of kindness that she was — gave the man a brilliant smile. "Gerald. Have you eaten yet? I brought extras for you and Evan to snack on through the morning. You can eat it now and I'll bring more."

His grin deepened a little. Too self-confident by far. "That would please me a great deal."

Audrey dipped her chin as shyness captured her features. Apparently, she was entirely charmed. Evan would've expected her to see through the man, but maybe she simply saw the good in everyone.

In less than a minute, Audrey and Philip had gone, with Audrey promising to return posthaste with more food.

Gerald marched around the room, examining each corner as though Evan might have hidden a weapon there. Every step grated more tightly on his nerves.

At last, the man settled himself against the wall, resting his plate in his lap. He gripped a meat pastry between grubby fingers and raised it to his nose. He closed his eyes as he inhaled. When he opened them again, he narrowed his eyes at Evan. "That wench does know how to please a man's belly. I suspect she can please other parts, too. I plan to find that out soon."

Anger pulsed through Evan, and he gripped his plate tight, so he didn't lunge for the man. Was Gerald trying to bait him? He couldn't sit here and not defend Audrey. He worked to keep his voice level. "She's not a wench. She's a woman worthy of respect. And if she's as smart as I think she is, she won't let you near her."

The man's face morphed back into a scowl. "You act so high-minded, but you're only an English cad. I'll bet you've even imagined yourself with her, too. Well, you won't get her. But I plan to."

That was the last straw. Evan lunged to his feet and closed the two strides between them. A swift blow in the man's cocky jaw would silence him easily enough.

The crack of his fist against bone sent a satisfying shock up his arm.

13

Gerald cried out as his head knocked sideways, but he recovered quicker than Evan would've thought.

With a roar, he lunged to his feet, propelling himself toward Evan with a wild look in his eyes.

Evan was ready for the man, stepping to the side as he gripped Gerald's shoulders and twisted him to land on his back. A quick foot in the blackguard's midsection made him curl around himself.

"You touch her, or even speak of her again without respect, and you'll meet with a great deal more than a fist and a boot." He sucked in air to cool the rage still sluicing through him. Nothing angered him more than a woman or child injured, whether in body or in reputation. Especially when they couldn't fight back.

A scream sounded from the doorway, jerking his attention upward. Audrey stood with the tray in her hands, jaw dropped, and eyes as round as the sausage she served.

Realization sank over him with awful clarity.

He raised his hands to show he had no weapon. "I'm not trying to run. I was only defending —"

"He attacked me." Gerald still lay on the floor but seemed to be trying to uncurl himself. Blood dripped from his mouth, and his words were slurred. Evan had aimed his fist to land cleanly on the jaw, so it may be broken, but the heel in the man's gut hadn't been hard enough to do more than slow him down.

And give him something to help remember the lesson.

Footsteps pounded from the corridor, and Evan's chest tightened enough that he had to work to draw breath. The beating had been foolish. Would they keep him tied again? Stop allowing him time outside? Just when he'd been earning their trust.

Yet he couldn't regret defending Audrey's honor. A few bruises and a broken jaw might not be enough to teach the man a permanent lesson, but at least he hadn't sat and listened to the cad's lecherous dross without defending her. That would've been the worst sin of all.

Audrey glanced behind herself and stepped to the side just as Brielle leapt into the room, hunting knife raised.

She halted abruptly and scanned the room to take in the scene.

Gerald had managed to sit up and was cradling his jaw with one hand. He used the other to point at Evan. "He attacked me." Again, the words were so muddled they were barely understandable. The jaw must be either broken or knocked well out of place.

With another jolt of realization, he realized Audrey might be the one to attend the fiend's injury. That was the last thing she should be forced to endure. This man should be the one held under guard.

"What goes on here?" Brielle directed the words to Evan, her knife still poised to slice into him, her eyes as hard as a warrior's.

He met her stare, keeping his hands away from his body, palms forward. "He said unsuitable things about Audrey. Things no gentleman would voice, much less actually consider doing. I couldn't sit by without acting." He wouldn't tell her the details un-less he absolutely had to. Brielle shouldn't be forced to hear such talk.

If she pushed for more, though, he would at least make sure he told her in private, without Audrey listening.

Brielle shifted her gaze between him and Gerald, then turned to Audrey. "Find the chief and Erik. Have them come here post-haste."

Audrey's face had grown pale, but she nodded and set her tray on the floor just inside the door, then turned and fled the room.

Brielle stayed near the doorway, keeping the partition open. She lowered her knife, although she kept it out and ready.

Gerald lumbered to his feet with a groan. He still pressed one hand against his jaw, smearing blood across his chin. He glanced at Brielle and spoke something, but with his muffled words, it was impossible to make them out. It sounded like he might be speaking French, too.

She shook her head and switched to English. "Stay. When the others come, we'll hear all."

He scowled but then shuffled backward until he could lean against the rock wall — managing to tread on Evan's pallet in the process.

Tense silence settled in the room, broken only by Gerald's heavy breathing. Brielle said nothing, only shifted her gaze around the area, occasionally looking at him or Gerald. She clearly didn't intend to conduct any more business until the others arrived.

At long last, the sound of shuffling echoed from the corridor. Brielle heard it when he did, and she cocked her head to peer through the door.

The two men who stepped into the room were new to him.

A glance at Gerald showed a glare on the man's face. He still supported his jaw with one hand and kept the other fisted at his side.

Brielle spoke to them in quiet rapid-fire French. When she finished, the newcomers turned to Gerald first. The one who seemed to be the eldest stepped near the man. His French was measured enough that Evan could pick out most of what he said. "Why is it you spoke ill about one of our own?"

Gerald's expression sobered into a look of respect. "I said nothing wrong." His face turned into a grimace of pain. "The outsider doesn't understand our language. How could he know what I said?"

A new surge of anger coursed through Evan. Now the man would lie? He'd spoken the lecherous words in perfect English. He clenched his jaw against a rebuttal. If they didn't give him a chance to speak, he'd ask for a moment to set the record straight.

But then the older man turned to him. His eyes studied Evan, and for a second, Evan wondered what they saw. He must look as overgrown as a French trapper by now. He'd been shaving once a week on the trail, for he'd always hated the itch of a beard. But he hadn't supposed they'd allow him use of his razor here. Maybe with Brielle relaxing his guard, he might be admitted that opportunity now.

Or rather, he might have been, before he'd attacked one of their guards.

He pushed that thought aside and focused on the man stepping toward him. The fellow approached and stood right in front of Evan. He didn't maintain the distance the guards did, always leaving enough room so Evan couldn't easily send a blow or kick their way.

But this man's near approach bespoke something of trust. Or at least respect.

The man's gaze held only grave curiosity. And there was something familiar about his features, though Evan couldn't place where he might have seen him.

"And what of you, sir? Did you understand the words Gerald said?"

Evan nodded. "I did. He spoke clear English."

The older man's throat worked, his jaw

hardening. "And what did he say?"

Evan glanced at Brielle. If he asked her to leave, she would protest and insist on staying, he had no doubt. She wasn't the kind of woman to be pushed aside. But maybe this elder would have enough authority to insist.

He looked back at the man. "It's not something suitable to repeat, sir. Especially not in mixed company."

The man turned to Brielle, and apparently only needed to send a single look to elicit obedience. Her face darkened into a scowl, which she sent at every man in the room, but she backed into the hall and closed the door behind her.

The man looked back at Evan, and a sadness seemed to settle over him like a cloak. His voice was lower than before when he spoke. "She is listening on the other side of the door, so you might keep your words quiet."

If the situation hadn't been so dire, Evan might've smiled. This man clearly held sway over his people, and he also knew Brielle well. Evan had a feeling he'd like this fellow, if given the chance to know him.

But as he recalled Gerald's words to repeat them, his smile turned sour. He didn't glance at Gerald as he told the event from start to finish. Then he clamped his mouth shut and awaited their verdict.

The man's gaze held nothing except that same sorrow as he turned back to Gerald. "My son, you have saddened me once again." He started toward the door and waved for Gerald. "Come."

The second man, who'd stayed silent through it all, fell into step behind Gerald. When they opened the door, Brielle stood in the hallway, near enough to hear, just as the older man said she would.

Evan couldn't understand the murmured words she exchanged with the men. Then the trio exited the room, and Brielle stepped inside.

Her face was impossible to read. Maybe a bit wary, but emotions that he couldn't decipher clouded her expression.

She would expect him to sit on his fur as all the guards did. He started toward the pallet so she wouldn't have to command him.

"You're hurt?"

He paused to look at her, then shook his head as he raised a hand. "Just some scraped knuckles." There was a time he might've smiled about that, but inflicting pain held nothing good any longer. The only benefit came in helping Audrey.

Her gaze sharpened on him. "Thank you. For standing up to Gerald. My father said he deserved all you gave him and more."

The older man was her father? No wonder he'd seemed familiar. Now that Evan thought about it, they had the same pointed chin and dark brown gaze. No surprise he liked the father as much as he did the daughter.

Well, almost as much.

He nodded in answer to her thanks. "I couldn't sit by while he said the things he did." He sharpened his gaze on her. "He's different than the other guards." Had she realized the man's nature? It didn't seem she had, the way she'd teased Audrey.

A sadness slipped over her features, similar to the expression on her father's face. "He is different, I suppose, although I've never seen him like this." Her brows dipped. "He lost someone in the massacre — Chrissy, his betrothed. I didn't know him well at the time, but I do remember seeing him smile much more back then. Through the years, he's separated himself more and more. He's not shown interest in any other woman since, not until Audrey." Her face hardened and her eyes narrowed. "I never thought his intentions were so base."

Something inside him yearned to reach

out to her. To soothe away the anger that seemed little more than a cover for deeper emotion. Concern for her friend? Worry? A reminder of her own loss?

"I'm sorry, Brielle." The words slipped out before he could plan something better to say.

She met his gaze, and the pain there nearly stripped him. She'd endured so much. If only he could make things better for her. Bear some of her load.

Instead, he was adding to the weight on her shoulders with his presence alone.

14

Brielle took another step back. "Well." Her voice trembled, so she swallowed and tried again. "I suppose I'll be staying with you for the day."

The awareness sparking between them was already enough to steal her breath. How could she stand a day with him?

Did they really *need* to guard this man? Hadn't he proven himself trustworthy, even to the point that he would defend one of their own? Warmth flowed through her again at the thought of what he'd done for Audrey.

Evan was a good man; she knew it with every part of her being. Even though she didn't know everything about him.

She glanced toward the door. Too bad there wasn't an outside window so she could see how much of the morning had passed. He would love to spend time in the courtyard.

She turned back to him. "We could go skin the elk I brought in this morning. . . . But it might not be best to take you into the courtyard so soon after what just happened with Gerald." The others would just be learning of the incident, and Papa might be in the midst of meting out punishment. Better to keep Evan away until things settled.

Evan motioned to her spot at the wall and gave her a grin that stole away all her angst. "Sit and talk to me." He moved to his fur and sat, settling in.

She did long to learn everything about this man. Not just his intentions toward Laurent or who had sent him, but the things he enjoyed, his childhood stories, every little thing about him. His birthday. She should know when his special day was. She always took effort to make that a pleasant time for her family. How awful if he'd already spent that day locked up in this dark room.

She sank to the stone floor in her usual place against the wall, crossing her legs in front of her as she leaned back against the stone.

"Tell me something I don't know about you." His voice soothed like honey coating a sore throat, and his gaze said he really cared about what she would say.

167

"I have a younger sister and brother. Have I told you that?" That's right, she had mentioned it when she told him of the coming of the Englishmen. She wasn't very good at this game.

He nodded. "But I haven't met them. How old are they?"

"Charlotte is ten and six, and Andre ten and two. Charlotte keeps the house, and Andre spends most of his days with my father and uncle doing metal work. They both want to meet you." She'd commanded in no uncertain terms that her siblings stay far away from this room, but maybe she could bring Evan by the metal shop.

He leaned back and crossed his hands around his knees. "So, you have an uncle here, as well? Any other family? Aunts, cousins, grandparents?"

She shook her head. "We're all family in Laurent, but I don't have any others like you mean."

As good as his interest felt, there was so much she wanted to learn about him. "What of you? You spoke of your brother and your parents. What of other family? Aunts, cousins, grandparents?" She echoed his own words, and it drew a smile from him.

Then a distant look came into his eyes. "I think I have some cousins in Scotland, but I haven't kept correspondence with them." He glanced at her wryly. "I wasn't much for letter writing when I first came to America. I think I may have sent one note to say I arrived safely."

"So, you don't spend your time writing letters. What do you do for pleasure? Other than exploring, that is. Do you play an instrument? Are you a great storyteller?"

He chuckled. "I'm not a great storyteller, although I like to hear a good tale. I remember my father used to sing us songs that told stories." His brow furrowed. "I wish I could remember some of them. There was one about a ship sailing to see a dragon, but I can't recall anything else. Not even the tune." Sadness cloaked his eyes, but then he seemed to make an effort to pull out of his thoughts. "I have a mouth harp, but I'm not very good at playing it."

"You have it with you?" She couldn't deny a yearning to know what was out there in the rest of the world. There must be so much that they didn't know about, being hidden away in Laurent as they were. She loved this village, loved her home and everything about their life — mostly. But . . . what might they be missing out on?

"In one of my packs. Does anyone here play?"

She shook her head. "I've never even heard of such a thing. A mouth harp, I mean, I've seen sketches of other harps. But we don't have anything like that here. How big is your mouth harp?" It couldn't be large. She'd looked through his packs after Papa did but hadn't seen anything that looked like a musical instrument. There were a few items she'd not known, but all were fairly small.

He held up his hand, palm facing up. "A little longer than my fingers. I wasn't lying when I said I'm not good at it, but it would be nice to pass the time with something to do." The corners of his mouth twitched. "The days get long."

She gave him a sad smile. "I hope we can get you outside more. Once things settle down."

The warmth in his eyes soaked all the way through her. "I understand."

His gaze said he didn't blame her for the way she'd treated him. Maybe if he looked at her that way long enough, she could let go of some of her guilt. She didn't regret putting Laurent's safety first, but she did regret treating this man like a criminal and shooting an arrow into his flesh. Not that she would change her past actions if she could . . .

Time to direct the conversation to a lighter topic. "Tell me, when is your special day? The day of your birth."

His brows rose. "My birthday?" The question seemed to flummox him.

She nodded, hooking her teeth on her lip to tether her smile.

"The sixteenth day of February. Why?" He seemed truly confused. Maybe he thought she still harbored animosity toward him. Or maybe they didn't celebrate birthdays where he'd come from.

She gave him a secretive smile. "We try to make special days special around here." No need to say more.

"Hmm." His brows formed a line as he concentrated. "When is your special day?"

"The sixth of May." Would Evan still be here? She couldn't think that far into the future. So many things might happen before then. In truth, she still didn't fully know why he'd come to this area. And the council's vote loomed closer . . .

A needle of warning wove through her chest, but she pushed it away. She would address those concerns later. For now, she wanted to know why he was looking at her with such curiosity.

"So, what does Laurent do to make the sixth of May special for you?" He tipped his head as he waited for her response.

Memories flooded her mind. Her mother had been the chief planner for her youngest birthdays, taking delight in each surprise and plotting gifts Brielle still treasured. Brielle had taken over that planning for Charlotte and Andre, along with Papa's help.

She shrugged but couldn't help a smile. "No more than what we do for everyone." Traditions had grown throughout the years, spreading through most of the families in the village. "Once, on my father's birthday, we made five dozen of Father's favorite fruit pastries and hid them all over our home and his workshop. He ate so much I think he grew sick, but he never said so." The pleasure on his face still sent a warmth through her. Papa wasn't often affectionate, but he'd wrapped her in a warm hug and kissed her forehead. She could still remember the shelter of that hold.

"I can see why he liked that." Evan's eyes lit in a way that made her want to draw closer. Maybe she shouldn't have told him that story. Perhaps she and Audrey could have done the same for him when his day came. He certainly possessed an affinity for Audrey's rolls drizzled with honey.

"Who's the *we*?"

She studied him, trying to make sense of

the question.

He must have read her confusion. "You said *we* made his favorite pastry. You and your sister?"

She nodded. "And Audrey. My baked goods tend to come out scorched, but Audrey can manage them with perfection." Only one of the many things Audrey excelled at. If the woman wasn't such a dear, kind soul, Brielle might struggle to keep her jealousy at bay. But her friend had been a light during some of the Durand family's darkest times.

Evan leaned forward. "That reminds me, I was telling Philip about the cookstoves we have back in America. It's a large metal box that you build a fire inside. The surface on top helps spread the heat more evenly for cooking and baking. If your father does metal work, it shouldn't be hard for him. I could sketch it if you have ink or charcoal and paper. There's a pencil in my pack you can bring me."

She had no idea what a pencil was, probably one of those things she'd not recognized from his supplies. But the idea of building something to help with cooking was an excellent one.

If this cookstove spread the heat evenly enough, perhaps even she could manage a decent meal with it. Not that the thought of bending over a cook fire added to her eagerness in any way. But she did sometimes envy Audrey's abilities. Charlotte had even surpassed Brielle's skill with food long ago.

It just had never seemed to matter whether she could cook. There hadn't been anyone to impress with her abilities. No man had ever sparked her interest enough to wonder what it would be like to cook for him. If she could make rolls as light and fluffy as Audrey's, how would it feel to receive the appreciation he gave her friend?

But she shouldn't think that way. For now, best to focus on Evan's offer. "I'll bring your packs. We have ink and parchment, too." The paper was hard to come by, so she almost never used it. Maybe she should find a flat rock for him to sketch on. As long as they could carry the stone to the place where they would build this creation, which should probably be placed in Audrey's apartment.

A pain pressed her chest. This would be a special gift for Audrey. It seemed like many of Evan's gifts were directed toward her friend. Yet how could she be jealous? Audrey deserved this, and Evan was kind to offer his knowledge. After all, if she had heard what Gerald said of her, she would be hurt.

A footstep sounded in the hallway. That was Audrey's tread, and the soft knock confirmed it. The bar clanged as Audrey lifted it, then her face appeared in the open doorway.

Brielle pushed to her feet and stepped toward her friend, watching for signs of embarrassment or pain from the things Gerald had said.

Audrey's smile held a tinge of sadness as she stepped into the room, but her voice possessed its normal cheeriness. "I came to see if you need anything." Her gaze swung between her and Evan, then returned to Brielle. "I know you weren't exactly planning to be here today."

Maybe this could be her chance to get Evan's packs. The council had commanded he be kept with a guard at all times, so she couldn't leave him alone in the room, even if she felt certain he wouldn't escape. But it would be fine for Audrey to stay with him, just for a few moments.

"I do need to get something. Can you wait until I return?"

Audrey's eyes widened and her words came hesitantly. "Of course."

Brielle worked to hold in her grin as she shot a glance at Evan. "I'll be right back."

The packs were still heaped against the wall in Brielle's family's apartment where she'd left them. She pulled out the two knives and laid them with the musket, then draped the larger satchel over her shoulder and gripped the other in her hand. She scooped up a quill and ink and a flat rock her brother had found, then headed back to the storage room.

When she arrived, Audrey was telling Evan about the clouds that looked like they would bring snow before the day's end. A safe topic, given all that had occurred that morning, but the thought of more snow rarely brought Brielle pleasure.

The winter months would be on them in earnest soon, bringing darkness and a cold so fierce that none of them would be truly warm again until spring came.

Evan's gaze turned on her the moment she stepped into the room, and the smile that played in his eyes washed away thoughts of winter.

"Well." Audrey pressed her hands to her hips. "If there's nothing else you need, I should go check the stew."

Brielle sent her friend a nod. "Thank you. Evan told me about a metal box we can build to make your cooking easier." She motioned to the items she carried. "He's going to sketch an image of it."

Audrey's eyes brightened. "Wonderful." She sent them both a beaming smile, then slipped from the room.

15

Yesterday had been one of the best Brielle could remember. In fact, she couldn't seem to stop recalling every moment now, as she marched through the fresh snow on snow-shoes.

She'd spent most of the day sitting with Evan. For hours, they went through each item in his pack, and he told stories of how he'd obtained them. The mercantile owner who'd sold him the leather-bound journal. The mouth harp given to him by one of their neighbors back in Scotland just before he left for America. And the graphite pencil . . . She'd never heard of such a thing, but it worked like a piece of coal from the fire. Only it was surrounded by wood to keep the charcoal from blackening the writer's hands, and the coal seemed to last forever, barely wearing down when he wrote.

He'd allowed her to write in the book of

blank pages, and she was able to form tiny letters that didn't smudge or blur. For the first time, she had a peek into what her people might be missing by living so secluded from the rest of the world. There was probably a great deal more than what she'd learned. Was keeping their village hidden from danger really worth missing out on such wonders?

He'd also sketched out the cookstove, and with the details he shared about air flow and cooking heat, she could see why the contraption would make preparing food easier. He'd said he would work on more sketches of detailed areas, like the ventilation and warming oven.

But what she enjoyed most about the day was the insight into his life. He didn't seem to have roots grounded anywhere, moving as his work required. When she'd asked where he lived, he shrugged and mentioned he rented quarters when he needed them in a place called Washington. But a bitterness had tinged his tone with the words. Did he wish for a permanent home? Who wouldn't want such?

He'd mentioned his deceased wife a couple times, both in passing. A glimmer of sadness had dimmed his eyes when he spoke of her, but not so much that he still seemed shrouded in grief.

She still didn't have a good understanding of what their marriage had been like. For that matter, she hadn't come to terms with how she *wanted* it to have been.

But that was selfish. Of course, she wanted him to have been happy. Something was growing between the two of them, but she couldn't be so naïve and selfish as to think it was anything close to what he'd had with the woman he'd loved enough to marry.

She had to stop thinking about such things, or it would drive her mad. She'd come out of the village walls this morning to regain the clarity that hiking through the mountains always brought, but every thought seemed to lead back to Evan.

She focused on her surroundings, on the scrawny trees growing along the hillside she was traversing. She strained to hear the cry of a falcon or the throaty call of a grouse.

Where were all the animals?

She froze, then moved closer to a tree as she searched the landscape around her. Something wasn't right, but she had to find out if the threat was animal or man.

Then, over the distant horizon, a form shifted. She squinted to pierce the haze of sun on snow.

Two figures moved, then rose steadily

180

until she could make out the shapes of people treading around the side of the mountain. When they came fully into view, she finally released her breath. Those red feathers were the trademark of Itchka, the leader of the tribe to the west. They were one of the Dinee tribes that lived near enough to come occasionally for trading.

They'd always been friendly, and even now, the approaching figures wore packs on their backs that rose as high as their heads. They must have come to trade one last time before the force of winter made travel impossible.

She stepped away from the tree and raised a hand in peaceful greeting, then waited for them to approach. No need to go to them if she was going to turn around and walk with them back to Laurent.

Itchka greeted her with his usual solemn nod of respect, and she called up the words she'd learned in their tongue. "You come to trade?"

He nodded. "Candles and torches and parchment."

She returned his nod, then shifted and fell into step with them as they retraced her snowshoe tracks. Her people had long ago taught the tribes to make wax candles from animal fat, pitch-covered torches, and the parchment that was so hard to press. Laurent consumed so much of these that it was easier to gain part of their supplies by trading the herbal remedies some of the women made.

When she came within calling distance of the courtyard, Brielle sounded the signal that she was entering with outsiders who approached in peace.

An answering call came from Andre. His was a higher-pitched sound than the signals made by the grown men, but he'd worked hard to perfect the call in every other way. Hopefully, some of the men had also heard her, or at least Andre might go alert one of them.

Another call sounded in her uncle's tone. Good.

The visitors followed her through the gate, and within minutes, women approached from many of the apartments.

After handing over the natives to her father so he could oversee the trading, she headed to their chamber to see what food Charlotte had left warming by the fire for her.

A chunk of roasted caribou sat on the rock where Charlotte left Brielle's meals when she wasn't there to eat with the family, and a basket of dried berries perched beside it.

The usual fare, but the sight of it gave her a craving for one of Audrey's rolls. She scooped up the meat and a handful of berries, then ate them as she made her way down the corridor.

Perhaps she could stop at Audrey's on her way to the storage room. She hadn't been able to talk with her friend since the ordeal with Gerald the day before. Had Audrey heard any rumors about what the man said about her? Papa had refused to tell Brielle what heinous thing he'd spoken, but it must have been bad.

She tapped on the rear door to the quarters where Audrey and her father lived. Her friend's mother had died giving birth to her, so it had always been only the two of them living in this little apartment.

At Audrey's soft "Enter," Brielle pulled the latch string and pushed open the door. The muffled snore sounding from the corner told her Audrey's father's location even before she slid her gaze around the room. He must still be sleeping from his drink the night before.

Audrey was kneeling beside the fire on the opposite wall, laying out dough on the metal rack Papa had built for her baking. She sent a bright smile as Brielle stepped into the room. "Come in. I have tea steeping, and

183

these will be ready soon."

Brielle dropped to her haunches by her friend's side. "I can't stay. I only stopped to tell you that a couple of the Dinee men have come to trade."

Audrey flicked a glance toward the corner where her father's snores still drifted through the bedcurtain. "I'm glad they've come. I don't have need of anything today, though. I traded for our winter supplies the last time they came." She'd probably calculated everything she would need through the winter to the last detail, then tucked each item in places her father wouldn't find them.

Audrey had become adept at running their household seamlessly, despite her father's propensity to overindulge. Strong drink was his main weakness, but when he began to imbibe, he tended to use up other resources, as though each item renewed itself automatically. Audrey had come home more than one afternoon to find a dozen candles lit around their quarters, burnt nearly down to nubs.

After adjusting the twist on a pastry, Audrey reached for a cup hanging from the wall and pulled the kettle from the coals. As she poured the steaming liquid, a rich sweetness wafted through the air. Audrey could tantalize the senses with even a cup of tea.

Brielle took the mug and breathed in the aroma once more, then shifted her focus to her friend while she waited for the drink to cool. How should she ask what Audrey knew of Gerald? A direct question would be easiest, but maybe this was one of those times she needed to find a way to skirt the topic until she'd tested the waters. Audrey's feelings were worth the effort.

"I . . . um, how are Gerald's injuries today?"

Audrey shot her a look hard to decipher. "I don't know. Your father asked Jeanette to tend his injuries." She straightened and released a sigh. "I gather whatever Gerald said spoke ill of me."

As she stared into the fire, Brielle scrambled for what to say. Should she rest a hand on Audrey's shoulder? She finally settled for the truth as best she knew. "Papa wouldn't tell me what he said, but I gather it wasn't a blight on your character. More like something no decent person would say of a woman."

Red crept up Audrey's ears as she grimaced, then met Brielle's gaze. Her eyes were wide and searching. "I don't understand what possesses people to say things

185

like that. I mean, I know Gerald's had a hard life. Especially since Chrissy . . ." Her words died away, but they both knew what she meant. When Gerald's fiancée had been killed in the massacre by the Englishmen, the loss had changed him. Hardened him.

Another sigh slipped from Audrey as she turned back to stare into the fire. "I guess I thought maybe I could help him. He seemed to finally be opening himself up. . . ." She pressed her lips together. "I suppose I wasn't making the difference I'd hoped."

Brielle slid her arm around her friend's shoulders, the act feeling perfectly natural with the moment.

Audrey leaned in and patted her arm. "I'm all right, truly I am. I know there's good inside Gerald. I'll just be more careful in how I seek it out."

Brielle could only chuckle as she pulled back to let Audrey stir her stew. "You possess more good than all of us combined. I don't know how you manage to always focus on the best in people." But as she sipped the rich tea, the memory of Gerald's angry expression slipped in. "I wish you'd be a little more careful, though. And stay away from Gerald. You can't ignore all the vice in looking for the virtue."

Audrey sent her a serene smile. "That's

why we make a good team, you and I. You press the knife blade until you've proven their mettle, then I come in and tend the cut mark."

Brielle nearly groaned as her friend's smile turned to a chuckle. She'd not pressed hard enough with Gerald. On the other hand, those words were too close to the mark concerning Evan. She still cringed at the pain she'd caused him, though she'd only been doing her duty to the village.

Audrey touched her arm. "Take some of these to Evan and Leonard while they're warm, will you? I assume you're going to check on them? Here's one for you."

Brielle nodded. Audrey knew her routine well.

Evan would enjoy coming to the courtyard to watch the trading. Leonard might appreciate a few minutes of break, too.

A knot squeezed in her middle. Was she breaking the council's command in her actions with Evan? She was walking a fine line; she knew that without a doubt.

She believed in her core that Evan didn't intend to hurt her people, but his assertion that he'd only come exploring for the sake of exploring still didn't sit right. As much as she'd learned about him yesterday, he'd remained vague about that particular subject. She'd learned to trust her instincts through the years, and her instincts told her they didn't know all of Evan's reasons for coming to this part of the country.

And the council had to know everything before they would release him.

Maybe she could get a few minutes alone with her father to share how much she was coming to trust Evan. Perhaps he would be willing to speak to the others on Evan's behalf. She'd have to be very careful about how and when she brought it up, though.

For now, as long as one of them stayed with Evan to guard him, allowing him to watch the fun in the courtyard shouldn't violate the order.

After accepting the plate of rolls from Audrey, she left their chamber and turned right toward the storage room. At the door, she gave a warning knock before removing the bar and pushing the panel open.

After her usual quick scan around the room to make sure all was well, she did her best not to let her expression change as she focused on Evan. His face was flushed like he'd been taking exercise, as he did sometimes on the small confines of his fur pallet. The edges of his hair were dark and stood askew, like he'd pushed sweat up from his brow.

Every bit of him possessed the same appeal as the man she'd sat beside the day before.

She lifted the plate. "Audrey sent these for you both." Then she forced her focus to Leonard. "Itchka and another man from his camp are here to trade. I'll take our prisoner for some daylight and to watch the goings-on for a while. You can come with us or take a few minutes to yourself, whichever you prefer."

Leonard pushed away from the wall. "I'll walk out with you, then be thankful for a few minutes alone."

Pleasure slipped through her. She would enjoy a few more moments alone to learn about this man who drew her like no other.

16

Brielle motioned for Evan to stand, and he sprang to his feet with one of those half grins that curled inside her and made her own smile so hard to hold back.

She looked away to lessen her struggle.

After she handed a pastry to each of them, Leonard led the way down the corridor, and she stayed beside Evan, eating her own roll as she walked. The space was only wide enough for two people to travel side-by-side.

As they passed one of the apartment doors, Evan pointed to the metalwork decorating the upper corners. "So much detail here. Who made these? I've noticed each doorway has something different."

She gave a closer look at the decorations he pointed to. "Each family does their own, if they choose. My father made these and several of the others." She couldn't help the pride in her voice. His abilities were well known in the community. His and Uncle

Carter's, too.

As they continued down the rest of the hall, she gave each doorframe more notice than she usually did. Papa's handwork stood out above the others, and not just because he loved to include intricate leaf details on each piece. He used so many layers in his detail; each leaf or scroll or vine stood out from the rest.

Evan looked like he wanted to stop and study some of them, but they kept walking. Better not to allow him special privileges very often.

When Leonard pushed open the outside door, Evan ducked away from the light as he usually did. A fresh twinge of guilt pressed on her. She hated keeping him confined to such a small dark space. Even after they added a fourth torch, the storage room still felt dim and smothering.

Leonard turned to them the moment they stepped outside. "When should I come back for you?"

She glanced toward the milling crowd gathered in the area they used for trading. The exchanges would take a while, as the natives loved to haggle. Even though everyone knew the standard prices her people charged. "An hour or so. Before the noon meal."

191

He raised his brows. "Are you certain?"

She nodded. Evan needed fresh air, and she certainly didn't mind spending time with him. She could work faster at her other duties later.

When Leonard turned toward his home, she slid a glance toward Evan. The corners of his mouth curved up as he met her gaze.

Then he turned his focus to the trading. "What goes on here?"

"One of the tribes come to trade."

He was silent for a moment while they watched Itchka using wide gestures as he spoke with her uncle and Jeanette. He looked to be telling a story, maybe how hard it was for his people to obtain leaves to make the paper he offered. He tended to exaggerate the worth of his goods when haggling.

"What do they trade?" Intense interest covered Evan's face as he watched.

"Our people taught the tribes to make paper, quills, candles, and other things. They also bring food other than meat, which we sometimes lack. Our women make herbal lotions and medicines, and some of the men make weapons, especially metalwork."

He glanced at her, as if seeing her in a different light. Or maybe seeing their village

192

from a new perspective. "Sounds advanta-geous for both groups."

She nodded, her mouth twitching as her body craved to respond to his attention.

Then he tipped his head as his eyes took on curiosity. "So, these are the only outsid-ers who come to Laurent?"

"They are."

"Have you known these tribes many years? Your people seem to trust them."

She gave a little shrug. "As far back as I can remember."

"Does anyone from your village go to their camp? Have you ever been?"

"Sometimes. We usually go in the spring. It's a nice chance to get out of village walls after so many dark days. But sometimes they come to us first, and we have to find another excuse for a trip."

He nodded. "I can imagine. How long does it take to get to their village? Is the land different there than here? I don't sup-pose they also live in caves."

She shook her head. "Not caves. Lodges they make out of skins and poles. They're a lot harder to keep warm and smaller than our caves. It's about a day and a half to walk there in the snow. Less if you don't have to wear snowshoes."

"Are their mountains made of the same

kind of rock as you have here? These seem to be a combination of shale and sandstone."

Perhaps he really had struck out on this journey merely to discover new things. He certainly seemed fascinated with the land and animals, especially those different from what he was accustomed to. She thought back through the land around the Dinee villages. "I think it's similar. I don't remember anything different that I haven't seen here, except maybe a black stone."

Was that disappointment that flashed through his eyes? He gave a nod of acknowledgment, then shifted his focus back to watch the trading again. The smaller man who traveled with Itchka was speaking to Madame Thayer, while two of the other matrons listened in. She had no doubt Madame Thayer would haggle for the rest of the day until the man accepted what she considered a reasonable price. Unfortunately, her cough syrup was the best around, so the visitor would do well to give what she desired.

Even now, she crossed her arms across her substantial bosom and shook her head. The outsider lifted whatever he held and held it out toward her. She shook her head again.

A chuckle drifted from Evan, and the

sound slid all the way through Brielle with a delicious tingle. She glanced sideways at him, then followed his gaze to the native and Madame Thayer.

"She believes in the value of whatever she has to trade." Evan's voice rumbled warm, tightening her chest.

She let her own chuckle slip out. "She makes the best elderberry syrup of anyone. All the tribes know it, too. Keeps their sniffles away, no matter how cold the weather turns."

"Elderberry grows here?" Once again, curiosity marked all his features. She'd never been envious of mountains and plants before, but with as much interest as he showed in them, she was beginning to harbor a bit of jealousy toward God's creation.

She shook her head. "We have an observatory where we grow plants and herbs for medicine. Those who first settled here brought elderberry, echinacea, and a host of other flora that are good for healing. We grow them in a protected area, with a fire that keeps them from freezing."

He turned his entire body to face her, his curiosity turning to intrigue. "You don't say. That must be a lot of work to keep the fire going."

"I can assure you it is. Our young women are tasked with the job." She gave him a wry look. "And there's a substantial punishment if any let the fire go out."

A twinkle slipped into his gaze. "Did *you* ever let the fire go out?"

She raised her jaw. "Of course not."

Smile lines creased the corners of his eyes. "I wouldn't have thought so. But you weren't always such a brave, responsible warrior. Were you ever a young girl at any point in your life?"

A sliver of pain rippled through her. "Not since I've had a brother and sister to raise."

The glimmer fled his eyes, leaving no trace they'd ever brought light to his chiseled face. "They were blessed to have you."

She shrugged. "They were stuck with me, even though my meals were either burned or half raw. I think our father was preparing to take over cooking duties himself when Charlotte finally stepped in. Even at the age of eight, she did a better job than I did. I talked Uncle Carter into taking me hunting with him so I didn't have to spend so much time indoors."

His gaze grew earnest. "You excelled where you were gifted. That's what all people who achieve great things have done. You leaned into your strength and accomplished feats few people would attempt."

She raised her brows at him, trying not to let the warmth of his words stir the parts of her that longed for them to be true. For as long as she could remember, she'd worked so hard to be seen as strong. Her family and close friends knew her weaknesses and vulnerabilities. But among most of the village — especially the other guards — she'd spent most of her life proving her strength and savviness and wisdom as a leader.

But something in her pushed against his praise. "You haven't heard enough to know if that's correct or not."

He motioned toward her shoulder, where she usually kept a quiver of arrows slung. "You're a crack shot with that bow and arrow, a fact I can attest to." His hand moved to the center of his middle. "And you've attained the role of leading this entire band of guards and bringing in meat for who knows how many people. All of this as a woman no older than — what? Two and twenty?"

His praise wove through her, seeping around the raw edges of her confidence and shoring them up, soothing the doubt that always plagued her in moments of weakness.

She tried to summon a modicum of fire

when he mentioned her gender — she hated when men thought she should defer to them and their abilities simply because she was a woman. But there was no sneer in his tone. Nothing but respect shone in his gaze.

Well, not *nothing.*

She didn't dare rely on her ability to read what else shimmered there. Attraction, maybe?

But could there be more? Could anything more exist between them? He came from such a different world. Would he be willing to leave it all for her?

Or would she be willing to leave Laurent for him?

The thought smacked her with a force that made her blink. She'd never considered leaving this place. Not truly. No one left Laurent, not ever. They had everything they needed here. There were enough families within the community to provide matches for those who chose to marry. And those who didn't, like her uncle, simply didn't marry. She'd always thought she would follow in her uncle's steps. But that no longer seemed desirable.

"Brielle?" Evan's voice broke through her churning thoughts. He touched her arm, and only then did she realize she was swaying. She shifted her feet to better brace herself.

"What is it? You've lost three shades of color." Worry lined his brow.

She forced herself to relax and summon a smile to reassure him. "Nothing. I only . . ." She couldn't say what she'd been thinking. In truth, she had no reason to think it.

Sure, Evan had sat beside her and shared bits of his life as they went through his packs. But maybe that had only stemmed from his desire to fill the long, dull hours of sitting on a fur in the dark storage room.

Maybe her attraction to him was simply because Evan was an outsider, not one of the men she'd known since they toddled together in infant gowns.

He was still studying her, waiting for her to finish her statement. She shook her head. "I'm well."

His eyes softened into a look so gentle, she would never have thought a man could manage it. Especially not a man as strong and virile as this one. His thumb on her arm rubbed a soft stroke, and she wanted to drop her hand and let his slide down her arm until their fingers clasped.

But she couldn't do that out here where all could see. In truth, even this simple touch would draw questions if anyone looked their way.

Evan must have realized that, for he pulled his hand back. Then his gaze slid past her to something over her shoulder. His brows knit as he watched, and the sound of young voices told her what he must be seeing. Widow Cameron would be bringing the children to watch the trading.

She turned to watch the procession and grinned at the sight of the little ones straggling across the courtyard. Marcellus must have come to tell them about the trading party, because he led the way with a boy on either side of him. He loved having news to tell, and he seemed to be adding layers of detail to whatever story he was imparting now, enough to enthrall the lads around him.

She'd always known on some level that Marcellus didn't think the way she and the others of their age did. He'd always been fanciful and was not always very grounded. Even when they were youngsters playing Leap the Frog and Steal the Falcon, she would abandon her games and lean in like these lads as he spun a wild tale. She finally realized that only half of his stories were based in reality, but the other half were so fascinating, and the tales lingered in her mind for weeks afterward.

He caught sight of her and Evan and paused in what he was saying to wave at them, a grin stretched wide across his face. He cupped his hands around his mouth and yelled across the courtyard between them. "Evan, come see the trading." He pointed to the cluster of hagglers against the far wall.

Evan's chuckle rumbled through her. He raised his hand to wave, then motioned for Marcellus to go on without him. As the youngsters continued their trek, Evan chuckled again. "If ever you're feeling down, he's a good one to lift the spirits."

She let her grin slip out. "He is that." She'd not grinned half as much before Evan came, which proved he must have that same ability Marcellus possessed to lift spirits. Although in a very different way than Marcellus.

They watched the children scamper across the remainder of the grassy area, two of the youngest ones spinning in circles as they moved forward. Trading days always spread joy through the camp, and the little ones took quickly to the festive atmosphere.

She sent a glance to Evan, and a wistful expression filled his gaze as he watched the children. She'd expected a smile to play at his mouth, not the sadness that turned the corner of his eyes downward.

Did something about the group stir unpleasant memories for him? He'd said he and his wife had no children, but were there some who had been lost? Perhaps he was thinking of his own brother who'd died. Maybe whatever memories these young ones sparked hadn't been unpleasant at the time, but now raised a longing for what had once been. She wanted desperately to ask him, but that felt like pushing too deep. Not unless he invited her into that place.

"Brielle." A familiar voice snatched her from her thoughts, and she spun to see Andre sprinting toward them. From anyone else, running would raise her to alarm, but that boy ran everywhere he went. She'd never seen anyone with more energy than her baby brother.

"Papa says we can have a feast and use the big room. He's invited Itchka and the other man to stay and eat with us." Andre reached them and doubled over, hands on his knees as he worked to catch his breath. He peered up at her with a toothy grin. "Won't that be fun?"

Before she could answer, Andre seemed to realize she wasn't alone. He jerked upright and took a step back, his face sobering as he eyed Evan.

Back when Evan had first arrived and they

knew so little about him, she'd warned Charlotte and Andre to stay far away from him. With the awfulness of their mother's death at the hands of strangers hanging over them all, she had no doubt that both her siblings would heed her direction — at least when it came to a strange Englishman.

Even now, Andre looked like he might turn and dart away. She should ease his angst some. "Andre, this is Evan Mac-Manus, the man I've been guarding in the storage room. Evan, my little brother, Andre." She offered a hint of a smile to show her brother he needn't fear.

Andre's round eyes stayed glued on Evan, his expression a mixture of awe and worry. As much as she wanted to protect her brother, she didn't want him to live in fear. Perhaps they'd placed too much importance on the danger of allowing strangers into Laurent. Of allowing new ideas and new ways of viewing the world into Laurent.

She'd have to ponder that thought later. For now, Evan was reaching a hand in greeting to her brother.

Andre glanced at her for permission to grasp Evan's in return, and she nodded.

The two shook, one hand large and masculine, and the other the gangly fingers of a half-grown lad. The joining of two worlds.

The moment felt momentous, and Andre seemed to grow taller with the act.

When he pulled his hand back, he straightened and notched his chin up. "Are you coming to the feast, too, Monsieur Mac-Manus?"

Evan raised his brows, and they both turned to her for an answer. She sent her gaze toward her father, who stood at the fringes of the trading group. It would be better if he gave permission than if she took it upon herself to bring Evan, even under guard. Maybe this would be her chance to speak to him of her growing trust.

She turned back to Andre and gave a small smile. "Perhaps. We'll see."

17

"I think we can trust him, Papa." Brielle stood with her father in the corner of the courtyard.

She didn't like having a private discussion in the open where others could watch their expressions, but speaking inside presented too much risk that their voices would echo off the stone walls. And besides, the women were back in their homes preparing food for the feast, and most of the men were talking with the visitors, speaking of events from the summer and expectations for the coming winter months.

Leonard had taken Evan back to the storage room, so this was her chance to plead his case with her father.

"What has he told you? How did he know of our village?" Papa wore his Chief of Laurent expression, the one that pondered every aspect before making a decision. He knew whatever command he gave would impact the hundred or so people in his care.

"He says he'd never heard of Laurent before he stumbled upon our wall. I believe that might be true, although I can't be certain. He was born in Scotland but moved to the new states of America after his parents and brother died." She'd told her father before about the changes Evan told of in the East. "He was in the American army for a while, which must be why he had that paper with their insignia marked on it. But after his wife died, he became an explorer. I think he blames himself and regrets not being there for her death and needed to do something different. He went west for a short time, then turned northwest and eventually arrived at our gate."

The lines across her father's forehead bunched as he took in her words, and he clasped his hands in front of him, his thumbs moving back and forth over themselves in the way they always did when he was deep in thought. "For which company does he explore? Who sent him out?"

She shook her head. "None. He merely loaded his saddle packs and set out on his own. He seems very interested in new animals and plants and landmarks that aren't found in his land. I truly think he can be trusted."

206

Her father pondered for several moments longer, pursing his lips as he continued flipping his thumbs back and forth, one over the other. "It seems irresponsible to leave family and friends and country during a time of war, just to set out on a lark. Surely he's come for a reason, maybe to report back to someone what he finds."

She raised her brows. "A lark you call it? He's traveled for three months, eating only what he can find or kill. Sleeping out in the cold." Yet her father's insight didn't sit well in her chest. Was Evan truly as selfish as Father made him sound? If Laurent were being attacked by enemies, she would stay and fight to the death. Nothing would induce her to abandon her friends and family when they needed her most.

But Evan's family had all died. First his parents and brother in Scotland, then his wife from a fever she likely caught caring for injured soldiers. Perhaps he felt he had nothing left to fight for in America.

She met her father's gaze. "I believe he was deep in his grief for his wife when he left their army. I can well imagine he sought to escape into God's creation and the desire to see new lands." Papa could understand that grief, having lived through it himself.

And indeed, her father's gaze softened.

"Perhaps you're right. I trust your judgment, but the council will want to hear several opinions before making a decision. They'd like to vote in three days. I'll come and speak with him myself on the morrow."

She nodded. He would see for himself. Evan's honesty would shine through, she had no doubt.

"In the meantime," Brielle continued, "I would like to bring him under guard to the feast. That way everyone can attend. None of the guards will be forced to stay with him in the storage room. He's not attempted escape even once. Quite the opposite, as you well know."

Papa raised his brows. "Gerald doesn't speak well of Evan. I don't put much stock in what he says, for Gerald seems to have let bitterness poison his thoughts. But you should be aware of his animosity."

She nodded. The council had decided Gerald's punishment should be extra work duty. The people would be watching him. Laurent protected their own. They didn't usually have one of their own turn on another, though.

Lifting her gaze to her father again, she returned his focus to their previous discussion. "So, what of Evan and the feast? It would be good for the people to see him more often. Maybe then they'll feel more comfortable around him."

He studied her a moment longer, and she did her best not to cower under his stare. Papa could see through any mask she tried to construct. She schooled her expression to make sure no hint of soft emotion tugged at her mouth or eagerness showed in her eyes.

"Before you bring him to the assembly room, bind his hands securely and make sure he has nothing on his person that can be used as a weapon."

Pleasure sprung up in her chest. He was agreeing. And his requirements were more than reasonable.

For any man other than Evan, that was. She hated the thought of parading him before the entire village with his hands bound like a criminal's. Maybe Evan's only crime was stumbling upon the walls of Laurent. In truth, if she'd not seen him first, he might not be in this predicament at all.

This was the situation they had to deal with, though, and she was fairly certain he would submit willingly to the requirement. He'd proven himself far more forgiving than most men would be in his position.

Evan paused in his exercises when the outer

bar on the door clanged. He'd finished the additional sketches of the inner workings of a cookstove, then attempted to wear off energy while he waited for news about the feast. With the exertion, he'd not heard Brielle's steps in the hallway.

The door opened, and Brielle stepped inside, her regal beauty sending a surge through him. She had the ability to capture his breath with just the sight of her.

He had to wait for her gaze to do its usual sweep around the room before she really looked at him. He tipped his head in a nod, then she turned her focus on the guard and closed the final steps to reach Philip.

"The chief is permitting me to bring our prisoner to the feast as long as he's bound. So, no one will need to miss the festivities." Her warrior expression softened as she looked at her fellow guard. "Go, attend with your family. Your wife will need help with the little ones."

Philip's solemn expression brightened with her words. He gave one of the first grins Evan had ever seen from him. "Thank you."

With a nod to Evan — which Evan returned — the man strode to the door and slipped out. He was moving so fast, Evan was half surprised he stopped to shut the door.

Brielle finally turned to him and raised her brows. "Looks like you'll get to meet everyone at last." Her mouth tipped in the workings of what might have been a grin.

His heart lurched, maybe from the sparkle in her eyes, or maybe from the thought of seeing the entire village. He'd watched from a distance each day when he was allowed time outside. He'd seen the children playing, the women cooking outdoors when the sun shone, the men stretching hides or skinning game. They'd become real to him, this tight-knit community.

But he'd not had the chance to speak with anyone except his guards. He'd been held at a distance from them all. Would the feast be any different?

He moved a hand up to brush the coarse hair covering his jaw. Too bad they would see an unkempt version of himself.

"What's wrong?" Brielle's voice brought his focus to her. She was watching him with twin lines marring her brow.

He stroked the beard again. "I don't usually let myself get this long." He'd showed her his razor and strap when they were going through his saddle packs, but he hadn't asked if he could use them. Allowing him use of the blade would likely violate the orders she'd been given.

She glanced toward his packs that had been placed against the wall where the guards usually sat. "Would you . . . like to shave?"

His breathing stilled. "Are you certain?"

She looked back at him, her gaze saying she wasn't sure at all. Maybe a bit of levity would help clear the worry from her eyes. "I'll let you do the honors if you'd rather not let me hold the blade." He was only jesting, of course. Mostly.

She shook her head, the certainty clearing all other emotion from her eyes. "You can do it."

A smile spread through him. This offer showed more than anything the trust she was beginning to place in him.

He met her gaze, letting her see his earnestness. He would make himself worthy of her trust. No matter what that required.

Yet how could he prove trustworthy while keeping such a critical secret? Did he dare tell Brielle about the mineral he'd been sent to discover? If anything were to grow between them, he had to be honest with her.

But he couldn't break the secrecy required of his mission. Even for Brielle.

18

Once Evan had settled on the fur with his shaving supplies spread around him, Brielle took her seat against the wall. Silence settled over them as he focused on his work, but the more time passed, the more tension tightened his arms and made his fingers clumsy. The only woman who'd ever watched him shave had been Sophia, but she'd never sat and openly stared at him the way Brielle was doing.

As he paused to wipe the shaving soap from his blade, he sent a smile her way. "I'm not accustomed to an audience."

She raised her brows, and her mouth pressed into a pert line. But she didn't say anything in answer.

He lifted the blade to his jaw again and peered into the metal jar lid he used as a mirror. "Am I doing it wrong?" If he kept prodding, maybe he'd get a word or two out of her.

"I'm usually hunting outside of village walls when my father does his shaving, so I wouldn't know. I think you're doing all right." There was a response. And something in it struck him almost as sassy. As though she'd relaxed around him enough to tease.

He kept working without glancing at her again, pulling a steady swipe across his skin, then wiping the soap off the razor with the cloth. "I've always figured as long as I get the hair off without drawing blood, I've accomplished my goal."

Something was beginning to spark between them. If he were honest, he'd been overly aware of her since the beginning, but she'd treated him differently since the tussle with Gerald. Had he proved something in her mind?

What would it take to prove his innocence completely for her? Would she lay down her defenses enough to give him a chance to win her heart? He had a feeling that winning Brielle would be no easy feat. But she would be worth every bit of effort required.

But what was he saying? This wasn't a mission to find a wife. An entire country — hundreds of thousands of men, women, and children — depended on him to find the mineral needed to win the war. How could he be so selfish as to let them down merely to pursue his own happiness?

As it was, he'd been doing precious little to find pitchblende since he'd been captured. True, he'd been locked in this room for days on end. He'd watched for pitchblende every place they took him, but he'd found no sign of it. Yet he'd definitely seen the orange striations that signaled the presence of pitchblende on the backside of this mountain. He had to find a way to search more in these caves.

He'd have to be watchful during the feast.

He sent a glance toward Brielle. Since they had a few moments, maybe she'd be willing to share a bit more about herself. "I'm curious." Her expression didn't change so he pushed on. "How did you come to be chief of the guards? Was it a dream of yours? Or is it a stepping-stone to more?"

He wasn't sure how many higher positions there could be in a village such as this. Yet she was so capable and still had many years before her. She could accomplish anything she set her mind to, no doubt. But wouldn't she want a family of her own someday?

Brielle's expression shifted — or rather, all hint of her thoughts seemed to fade away. "I've always been a hunter. A provider. I learned archery while most of the other girls were learning to cook. I prefer to be outdoors, outside of village walls." She shrugged, seemingly uncomfortable with speaking of her accomplishments. "I suppose I merely practiced more than the others. Hunted more. I joined the guard so I could help protect and provide for our community. When our last leader of the guards took sick and died, the people voted to select a new leader from among the guards."

He met her gaze and held it. "From everything I've seen, they chose well."

She dropped her focus away. This woman who stood so strong when protecting others didn't seem to know how to accept praise for herself.

To lighten the conversation, he pressed a hand to the arrow wound that had all but healed. "I can attest to your aim with a bow and arrow anyway."

She flicked a look at him, and one corner of her mouth tipped.

Distant voices sounded in the hallway, farther down near the doors leading to the individual homes. Brielle stood, and he hurried to finish the last two razor swipes and clean himself up.

"Sounds like the time has almost come." She opened the door and peered down the corridor, then pulled back and closed it.

Her gaze turned sad as she studied him.

"I've been commanded to tie you, Evan. I have no choice."

He nodded as he quickly rolled the leather strip around his supplies. "I know. It's all right."

When he was finished, she moved his packs back against the wall and knelt before him with a leather cord. The gentleness with which she knotted the binding around his wrists made it easy to imagine her smoothing tears away from her siblings' cheeks.

This fierce lady warrior would make an excellent mother. Caring grew from deep inside her and could take any form the situation required. Whether it be the strength of nerve to slay a caribou to provide meat for her family's sustenance, or the fierceness to shoot an arrow into a stranger's chest to protect the people she loved, or the gentleness to ensure she didn't bring pain, or the loyalty to perform a duty she disliked merely because the people she loved had asked it of her.

When she'd tied the last knot, they both stood, and he followed her through the doorway. Then she slowed for him to come alongside. As they walked down the long corridor, people began to file from the doors that opened into the hallway. Voices chattered all around them, and he recognized several people he'd seen in the courtyard. Audrey emerged from one door ahead of them, baskets piled high in her arms.

An older man stepped out behind her, maybe her father. His arms were equally loaded. How long had the people been planning this feast? Surely she wasn't tasked with bringing *all* the food.

Apparently not, for other men and women bore loads of leather-covered bowls and baskets, and savory aromas wafted all around them.

The door beside him opened, and a lad barreled out, nearly slamming into him. Evan stepped to the side and braced himself just as Brielle's brother pulled to a stop.

"Andre." Brielle's tone held the censure of a mother scolding a wayward child.

And her brother looked properly contrite. "Sorry."

A voice from inside the room called, "He's supposed to help me carry this food."

Evan couldn't see through the barely open doorway, so he glanced at Brielle to catch her reaction. A line formed across her brow as she sent him a weak smile. Then she turned her attention back to her brother. "You know Charlotte needs help."

Andre pushed the door wider, and a young woman appeared. The load she carried hid all but her face, until the boy took two baskets from the top.

"Here, let me take some, too." Evan extended his bound hands for her to place something on his forearms.

Charlotte sent a questioning glance to Brielle and must have received an approving nod. She placed two baskets on his arms. "Now I'll just bring this meat."

Andre shuffled ahead, and Brielle waited for her sister to step out and start down the corridor before they fell into step behind her. Charlotte resembled Brielle in so many ways, especially her dark, almost-black hair that hung in a long braid down her back. The willowy form that gave Charlotte a girlish look would probably fill out into the lithe curves Brielle possessed in a year or so. Yet, she already moved with the same grace Brielle did.

He slid a glance at the woman beside him and caught the look of pride warming her gaze as she watched her siblings. From what he'd seen, she'd done an excellent job as stand-in mother to these two.

They continued past the hallway on the left that led to the outside door, and the murmur of voices grew louder as they approached the wooden double doors propped open. He'd never been this far into the cave before.

When they stepped through the opening, a vast room opened up before them, as large as any ballroom he'd ever seen, larger maybe. The space must be expansive enough to hold every one of the citizens of Laurent. How had they ever hacked it out of stone? But the high domed ceiling felt so natural that maybe this was a cavern that had already been there when the first visitors built these underground homes.

Brielle motioned him forward, and he shifted his focus to what lay inside the space. Rows of tables lined with benches filled most of the area. Torches were mounted around the perimeter and placed on each table. People milled around, some already seated and others in conversation or spreading out food. The atmosphere hummed with energy.

As Brielle led him to a table tucked in the right corner, those they passed turned to watch them. A few stepped back to clear a wide path for him to pass, though there was already plenty of room for him and Brielle to move without brushing anyone.

Yet, for the most part, it didn't seem to be fear marking people's expressions. Simply curiosity. As much as being a spectacle made his neck itch, at least they didn't seem afraid of him.

At the table, Charlotte was already unpacking supplies from the baskets she and her brother had carried, and Audrey stood there also, with the man he'd assumed was her father.

After Brielle took the baskets from his arms and placed them on the table, she motioned to the end of the bench nearest the wall. "We'll sit there." They would have their back to the corner, the perfect position to watch the goings-on without missing anything. Also, it would keep him farthest away from the others. Maybe that would make people feel like he was less of a threat.

Audrey lifted a grin to him. "I hope you're hungry. Today was my usual baking day, so when the feast was announced, I put on extra elk galettes."

He offered a smile even as his stomach growled. "Even if I wasn't hungry, I'd be looking forward to them."

After he settled into his corner seat, Brielle sat beside him. The activity spread around them as people's curiosity about him seemed to wane. She pointed out individuals and families, helping him put faces to the names he'd heard spoken before.

Philip, the guard who stayed most nights, sat at the next table with his wife, who worked hard to keep a young girl contained. The child must be about three. Philip had his own hands full with the chubby-cheeked lad whose blond curls matched his own. The man caught Evan's eye and flashed a ready grin. "Evan. Glad you get to join the feast."

His friendliness soaked through Evan, and he raised a hand in greeting. How long had it been since he'd had a friend? Not a fellow soldier forced to endure the same atrocities of war, but a genuine friend who greeted him out of pleasure? Maybe he and Philip hadn't quite reached friendship yet, but he could imagine it.

Before Evan could form words to respond, Philip's daughter tugged his sleeve and pulled him close to speak into his ear.

A moment later, Leonard stopped by their table, a grin turning his face almost boyish. "Glad you were allowed to come." Then he slid a half-teasing glance at Brielle. "And not just because it means I get to come, too."

Brielle took the banter with a nod and a softening of her mouth. "Leonard, would you mind staying here with Evan for a moment while I speak with Jeanette?" She looked to Evan. "She's Marcellus's mother."

The fact she would take the time to explain sent warmth through him.

Leonard nodded. "Of course."

Brielle rose and strode down the row of tables to an older woman. Or maybe the graying of her hair made her appear older than she was, because on Brielle's approach, her face brightened into a smile that made her appear a decade younger than he'd first thought. Brielle's attention had that same effect on him, but this woman had likely known her all her life. She would know all the flaws and struggles Brielle hadn't shown him. But the affection between them was impossible to miss.

Leonard spoke a few words to Brielle's brother and sister, but Evan couldn't help but watch the exchange a few tables down.

The woman reached for Brielle's hand and held it while they spoke, and at one point, Brielle covered their joined hands with her other. One didn't often see such a connection between women of different generations. He'd never had it himself, even with a fellow his own age. He'd had plenty of acquaintances, colleagues, and even people he called friends. But he'd never shared the warmth that shone between these two.

A man sat beside Jeanette, following the

conversation. Was he Marcellus's father, the man whom Brielle had spoken of when she told of the massacre? She'd said he lost the use of both his legs after that fight. How was he able to come to this room for the feast? Had men carried him? As Evan studied the man's frame, he glimpsed the structure of a chair back behind him. He'd seen a few of these rolling chairs. Maybe they'd built one for him.

Evan shifted his gaze around the room. His focus snagged on a man sitting against one of the long walls, his arms crossed in a sullen posture. Or maybe it was the swelling in his jaw that made Gerald look so brooding.

Either way, Evan didn't let his attention linger on the man. There was too much else to see.

Wesley, one of the other guards who'd taken turns in his cell, was sitting with what looked like his family. The man nodded in greeting when he caught Evan's gaze.

He responded in kind, then continued scanning the room. These were real people. He hadn't set out to invade or investigate them, but somehow he'd ended up in their midst. They were fathers and mothers, daughters and sons, who loved and hurt with the usual trials of life. Their lives might look different than what he'd grown up with or what he'd learned to love in America. But in truth, there wasn't so much difference.

He could imagine them as friends and neighbors. This community, this haven, could be the place he'd sought for so long. Would they allow an outsider to live among them? If by some miracle he found pitchblende somewhere else and fulfilled his mission, could he come back to live among them? Would they ever come to accept him, given the way he'd arrived? Would they ever treat him as one of their own?

After years of living here and working alongside them, the fact that he hadn't grown up among these people might be forgotten. He could see himself one day as one of the gray-haired men leaning over the table to trade stories.

His gaze found Brielle again. His mind formed an image of what she would look like with her own gray hair, the grooves lining her face a testament to happy times, the wisdom gleaned from each year. Perhaps a few of the gray hairs would be brought on by the challenges of raising children to be strong and capable, just like their mother.

A longing rose up inside him with a fierce ache. What would it be like for them to be *his* children?

Brielle turned from Jeanette then, and her gaze found his. Stirring something inside him.

Her head tipped like she was thinking through something. Then someone spoke to her, pulling her attention away. She was so well-loved by these people, such an integral part of her community, she would likely never even consider an outsider.

But as he watched her interact, watched her laugh at something one of the gray-hairs said, he couldn't suppress the longing. Especially when she patted an elderly man's gnarled hand and sent a smile to one of the children scampering by.

He'd recognized her outer beauty from the first time he'd studied her against the cave wall. But this inner beauty was even harder to ignore.

And he wasn't sure he even wanted to anymore.

19

Something was different about Evan.

Brielle watched him from the corner of her gaze as they followed the crowd through the corridor after the feast. He'd seemed to enjoy seeing everyone and watching the festivities. Especially when Monsieur Marley had started up the old French songs. At first, Evan had listened with a smile playing at the corners of his mouth. But partway through the second ditty, his lips had begun to move, as though recalling words from long ago. He'd grown up in Scotland. Maybe he'd even traveled to old France and heard some of the ballads there.

A tiny spike of longing pressed in on her. She'd never thought she wanted to leave Laurent, but a trip like that sounded almost magical. The picture forming in her mind included Evan by her side. Something about him called to her. Made her think there was more to life than what she'd allowed in her tiny existence.

Voices in the corridor quieted after they passed the last of the chamber doors. Soon, they reached the entrance to the storage room. She pushed open the door and motioned for him to step in first. When she closed the partition behind herself, the quiet in the room seeped around them.

He turned to look at her, and it seemed as if he was struggling within himself. A long moment passed before he spoke. "That was very . . . interesting." The way his expression shifted just before the words came out, he might have wanted to say something different.

She lifted her brows as she stepped close and untied his hands. "Food and music are two of the things my people enjoy most. You're lucky Erik didn't bring his mandolin. I should have remembered your mouth harp. You could have joined in."

Evan smiled, his whole face softening. "Not sure I'm good enough to keep up with these musicians." His tone grew almost wistful. "But I liked it. Every part. Your people are special, Brielle. I understand why you treasure them."

The burn of tears rose up her throat and seared her eyes. She never cried, but his words churned so many emotions inside her, she could barely hold the drops back. She loved these people, too. This home she'd committed to protect. How could she reconcile the longing to leave with her intense love for this place?

She turned away from him and pretended to busy herself with the stack of arrows she'd left at her spot against the wall. Maybe he would take the hint and settle himself on his fur. A bit of distance would help her regain composure.

"Brielle?" Evan's voice drifted across the space between them, the hesitance in his tone pulling her back around to face him. The soft light of the torches glimmered in his gaze. "Did I say something wrong?"

The earnestness of his tone nearly broke her. Why did he care so much? Why had she let herself get so close to him? Learn so much about him? See him as more than a stranger, as a potential threat to Laurent? He was a man who cared deeply, who was kind to her people, even the vulnerable. Who stood up for right, even when doing so might make his position more precarious.

Even as she looked at him now, his image blurred with the picture of him grinning as he sang along with the other villagers. He could have been one of them. Did he want to be?

She squeezed her eyes against the image, drawing in breath to still the whirling of her mind, the churning of her emotions. Why couldn't she control herself?

"Brielle." Evan's voice sounded right in front of her, and she jerked her eyes open.

He'd closed the distance between them and now stared down at her with worry furrowing his brow. "What is it?" He touched her arm, and the contact made her freeze.

She stared into his eyes, held there by the warmth. The concern. The . . . attraction. Her breath cut off, stolen by the awareness sparking between them.

This man. He'd proven his goodness through every action. Every restraint. How could she question any longer?

How could she resist what every part of her longed for?

Evan's gaze roamed Brielle's face, cataloging each strong beautiful line. And those lips . . . He'd never had a mouth call to him as strongly as hers did.

He'd not meant to draw so close, but she'd looked so vulnerable, so . . . desperate. His every instinct pushed him to reach out. If he'd caused her pain, he had to fix it. If something else, he had to help.

He forced his gaze upward to her eyes, to a place where desire wouldn't steal away his last bit of good sense.

But her eyes were no safer. Had she been looking vulnerable before? Now her gaze carried heat.

He had to clear the unwise thought of kissing her from his mind, so he struggled for something to say. "Is everything . . . ?" His voice came out breathier than it should, and his traitorous gaze dipped to her mouth again.

Her lips parted. Had he closed the distance between them or had she? He was near enough to touch her face now, and he reached up to cradle her jaw.

Her skin was softer than he'd imagined, and the touch of her sent a tingle all the way up his arm. Her eyes searched his, seeing all the way to his soul. He showed himself to her, the core of him, the part that wanted only good for her and her people. The part that longed to close the final space between them and press his mouth to hers.

Her eyes gave nothing of herself, but her lips . . .

Her lips reached up to his.

His own eyes drifted shut just as her mouth touched his. *Sweet fire.* With as much as this woman liked taking control, the strength in her kiss shouldn't have surprised him. But the vulnerability in her touch swept through him, raising every part of him to life.

He returned the kiss, slipping his hand around her back, drawing her in, letting her feel his protection.

She wove her way into his very being as she responded. How had she become so important to him so quickly?

Yet she had, and with his kiss, he made a promise to her. No matter what happened, he would keep her safe. He would defend this woman who spent her life defending those around her.

Even if that meant protecting her from himself and the mission he was beginning to loathe.

He'd broken through her defenses. And the worst part was, Brielle couldn't bring herself to regret it.

She could barely draw breath by the time Evan pulled back from the kiss. He lowered his forehead to hers, and she let her eyes drift shut again as she soaked in his nearness. She brushed the hair at the nape of his neck with her fingers.

Did she dare draw him back down for

another kiss? She would never have thought she'd have the nerve for the first one. And with the tumult of longing inside her, maybe it was better to step back. She had to regain control.

As if he'd read her thoughts, he groaned and closed the distance between them again, pressing his mouth to hers in a gentle brush.

A brush that reignited the fire within her.

She kissed him back, a give-and-take that strengthened with each breath. She would soon burn to ash if she didn't stop this.

With every bit of strength she possessed, she drew away. And this time, she forced her feet to step back, as well.

His hands slid from around her waist to her elbows, his fingers trailing down until they found her hands.

Her rough, cold-chapped hands. She was no lady. Did he truly know how unfit she was?

But he raised her fingers to his chest, cradling them there, then lifting her left hand to press a kiss on the backs of her fingers.

How could even a gentlemanly kiss like that send a shiver all the way through her?

He focused his gaze on hers as he held both her hands to his chest again. His eyes were so warm, so earnest. "I can't bring myself to apologize for that, although maybe I should."

Another surge of longing slid through her. All he had to do was look at her and she came apart in his hands. "You shouldn't."

Evan lay on his bed pallet as Philip sat against the wall, reading a Bible. Perhaps he should be doing the same, but he couldn't seem to put two thoughts together unless they contained Brielle.

They'd only had a few minutes before Philip had come in for his night shift. For a minute, he'd thought Brielle might send Philip away. But a bit of time away from her would be good for him. Not only to settle every part of him that had sprang to life with her kiss, but he also needed time to sort through how he really felt.

And what he planned to do about it.

He'd never felt anything this strong for another person. His marriage with Sophia had started from mutual respect and need. She needed someone to provide a roof over her head after her father died, and he'd been tired of living his life so alone. They'd become friends, and through their two years of marriage, he'd thought it was love growing between them. It probably *was* love, but

234

this stirring inside him now after two weeks was so much more than that feeling had ever been after two years.

Now, he only had to make sure he didn't disappoint Brielle the way he'd failed Sophia.

He wouldn't dream of asking her to leave her home, her community — her legacy — here in Laurent. Maybe she'd like to travel a little and see the world. He'd take her anywhere she wanted. But he had to be willing to leave all behind to make a life with her.

Who was he fooling? Between Brielle and the people he'd come to know here, he would leave his old life behind in a minute. If he could, he'd gladly head back to the States now and resign his commission, then come back and do whatever he could to woo her.

If she'd have him. Just because attraction sparked between them didn't mean she thought enough of him to accept his courtship.

Besides, he still had a promise to fulfill, and his country depended on him. He was due back by the last day of December, and he had to find pitchblende before he returned.

If he told Brielle everything, would she allow him to leave Laurent and go around to the back side of the mountain to dig into the rock there? She could come with him if they felt the need to keep him under guard. Which they might after he revealed his connection to the army.

He closed his eyes and pictured the striated grooves in the stone there. That was exactly what the old trapper's journals had described. And nearby, he'd find a darker copper.

His chest seized. Copper . . .

Just like . . . he struggled to pull up images from the feast. He'd been so focused on watching Brielle talking and laughing at the feast, the torchlight glinting off the copper in the walls and sparkling in her eyes.

He squeezed his eyes tighter, trying to home in on that wall in his mind's eye. Numerous stripes of various hues, but copper had definitely been among them. The flickering glow of the torch might have distorted the color, though.

A weight pressed hard on his chest. Had he really found it? He couldn't have, not here in the heart of their mountain where all their homes were built.

He dragged in a breath. Just because the rock showed splashes of copper in the light of a torch didn't mean it was pitchblende.

He wouldn't know for sure until he chipped out a piece and tested it.

He fought to keep his breathing even, no matter how fast his heart raced. If he found pitchblende here, that meant it probably would also be in the other mountains around the area. He could still move forward with his mission.

He'd have to tell Brielle he found the mineral here, but he would assure her he planned to keep seeking it in other places. He couldn't lie to her, nor could he keep the truth hidden any longer. Not if he wanted a life with her. A marriage couldn't be built on lies or secrets, not the kind of love he wanted with her.

His thoughts shifted from what he would tell Brielle to imagining how he might get access to this wall to determine for sure if it was pitchblende. She might willingly give him access if he told her right away, but he hated to give weight to her fears in case he was mistaken about the mineral. And maybe when he revealed his mission, she wouldn't believe his words of love. Maybe she would think it was all a ruse to get her to set him free.

His heart squeezed at the thought. Would she doubt him, despite the connection they shared? She would have every reason to distrust him.

He'd do better to find out for sure if what he saw was pitchblende. Even if it risked the growing trust she'd placed in him, it would be easier to sneak out under her relaxed guard.

He had to accomplish this last mission. With the war raging in the east, killing more lives daily, not a minute more could be wasted.

20

Evan forced his breathing to stay steady as he strained to hear every sound that drifted from Philip's sleeping form. Several hours must have passed since midnight. The man should be in his deepest sleep.

The entire village should be asleep after the feast, probably even whichever young woman currently had the task of keeping the fire burning in their solarium. He wasn't sure exactly where that garden was located, but Brielle had pointed toward the far side of the courtyard, so he was fairly sure he wouldn't be in danger of running into the keeper of the fire.

With every part of his body strung as tight as a fiddle, he pulled himself up to sitting. No change in Philip's gentle snores, so he pushed to his hands and feet, then straightened.

He eyed the dark outline of his packs. He kept a knife hidden in the lining of the larger case. Should he pull it out, along with a bit of leather to buffer the sound of his blade on stone, or take the entire satchel? The latter would probably make less noise. And that way, he'd have everything he needed to quickly hack enough pitchblende.

If the job went well, he would take enough for the scientists to not only test the stone but make a single explosion to ensure their plan would work. The army would still have to send hordes of men up to get enough pitchblende to destroy the British troops and end the war for good, but all he'd been tasked with gathering was enough to verify that the plan would work and that an explosion that large was possible.

He used all his stealth training to creep to his packs and lift the larger one to his shoulder without letting the contents inside jingle, then made his way to the door.

He'd studied the bar on the door for a solid hour to determine the best way to lift it without making a clink. Now, he tipped the pin at an angle and eased both the inside and outside bars up. As soon as the door gave, he grabbed the bars and pulled the door just enough to slip through. He had to take the same care to lower the metal, but everything went as he'd planned. Philip's soft snores still drifted from inside the room.

Thank you, Lord, he thought, though the cloud of guilt that hovered around him seemed to stop the prayer from ascending to God's ear. Why did this deception feel so wrong? He was accomplishing the mission his commanders had assigned him. The mission he'd sworn on a Bible to uphold. Surely God wanted him to do everything he could to fulfill his promise.

Yet he was breaking the trust Brielle had begun to show in him.

He moved down the corridor without making more sound than an occasional rustle of his clothing.

Brielle was the one he most worried about hearing him. She seemed to have the senses of a cat. But unless she could sense his presence without actually hearing or seeing him, she shouldn't know he was out here.

But then, when she was in the same room as him, he always knew exactly where she was without seeing or hearing her. As though his body tracked her without his mind telling it to. If she could do the same, he was in trouble.

He finally reached the door to the giant room where they'd held the feast. He'd tried to spot signs of pitchblende in the hallway, but the darkness made variations in the stone impossible to see.

241

The community room would be easier to take samples from anyway. The urge to open the door and slip inside tugged him, but he forced himself to work with the same level of care he'd used on his cell door. Thankfully, this one only had a single bar on the outside. He laid the bar soundlessly on the floor and eased open one of the double doors.

Inside, all was dark. He felt along the wall until he reached the first torch. Better to light this one and move it with him than chance stumbling and making a noise loud enough to draw someone.

He found the Lucifer match in his pack and lit the torch. Light blazed through the room, and he took the first full breath he'd risked since rising from his pallet.

Gathering his pack and the torch, he aimed straight for the place where he'd seen the orange coloring in the stone. Before he started cutting, he needed to check all the walls and see how much was visible on the surface.

He'd have at least an hour, if his sense of timing was accurate. But he had to make sure he was back on his pallet before the earliest risers began their day.

The orange coloring appeared at several different levels in at least five places along that wall. That would be enough for the army to send miners and scientists all the way up here. It may not be as much pitch-blende as they needed, but this much on the surface likely meant a great deal more could be found in the stone.

He started on one of the softer spots, wrapping cloth over the head of his chisel to stop the ring of metal as he struck with the hammer. When he'd shown Brielle the contents of his packs, he'd told her some of the uses for these along the journey, like holding a rope to spread oilcloth over him in the midst of a downpour.

But he'd not told her the main reason he brought them. One more omission he'd have to set straight. As committed as he was to speaking only the truth, so many of his actions lately felt like lies.

The sooner he got away from this busi-ness of being a spy, the better.

The tension in his body stretched tighter with the first blow of his hammer. The muffled *ching* seemed to vibrate in his skull, and he paused to strain for any sound of someone coming.

No cries of alarm, no thud of footsteps. Not even the rustle of fabric reached his ears. He eased out a shaky breath and went back to work.

It only took a few minutes to dislodge the first chunk of orange rock and check the piece the way the army's scientist had shown him.

The stone was, indeed, pitchblende. His worst fears confirmed.

With his chest twisting like a massive hand gripped it, he studied the line of orange rock. He had possibly three quarters of an hour left — not long enough to gather it all, but he couldn't risk more this time. What he'd done would be easy to see if someone came in and studied the wall, but hopefully they didn't use this room very often. At least, not this side of the huge chamber. No matter. He would tell Brielle everything before his work was discovered anyway.

As a fresh wave of bile churned in his middle, he adjusted the leather over the head of his chisel and pounded another blow.

Dark snow clouds rolled in during the night. By the time Brielle stepped out into the partial darkness to begin her morning hunt, an icy wind blew, and the first flakes were beginning to fall. The heavy clouds couldn't press the smile from her face every time she thought of Evan's kiss, nor the lightness inside her. Though the cold definitely seemed determined to freeze every bit of her good sentiment into an icy block.

Their trading friends were wise to leave after the feast the evening before. Snow had been threatening even then, and they'd not wanted to chance staying the night. The two men were likely halfway through their journey by now.

Perhaps she was foolish going out to hunt with snow beginning to fall. But experience had taught her that if she could find a herd of caribou or elk holed up in woods or in the gap between two mountains, that meat would help feed her people even if the snow lasted a week.

She had to at least try.

She found nothing at the first two sections of trees where herds sometimes took shelter. As she set off for the next area, the wind blew heavy flakes in thick swirls around her. She'd not brought snowshoes because a thick ice crust had formed over the previous snow, but this fresh layer was now deep enough to cover her feet as she walked.

When she reached the canopy of barren tree limbs, a reindeer started out of the shelter, moving away from her. It looked like a young buck who'd been separated from the herd. Those animals didn't usually scare so easily when together, but the storm must have it on edge.

The only game left under these trees was a single hare, and she quickly sent a well-placed arrow, then readied the carcass for the trek back to Laurent.

As she pulled her cloak tighter around her shoulders, a long sigh slipped out. Useless hunts didn't usually bother her. In truth, spending quiet hours wandering the mountains renewed her. Perhaps part of the refreshing effect came from the exertion, drawing in deep invigorating breaths as she clambered over rocks and down slopes.

With the majesty of the peaks rising around her, staring out over the vast wilderness of spires stretching to the heavens, it was impossible not to realize the magnificence of God. That the Creator could make all this and still know who she was — it put proper perspective both on how great He was and how much He loved her.

Another frigid gust sent a shiver through her. This would be a bad storm, the first hard snowfall to commence the depths of winter.

As she neared the village walls, she sent the call that she was approaching. Only a faint response sounded through the swirling snow. Even the guards must be taking refuge from the worsening storm. Surely no threat would be out in this swirling gale.

She headed straight for her door, her insides aching for both warmth and food. She probably should have broken her fast with more than a sip of warm water before heading out.

The wind nearly jerked the door out of her hands as she slipped into their apartment. Inside, the blast of warmth soaked around her, stinging her cheeks. Charlotte knelt by the fire, pouring liquid in a cup. She rose with the mug and stepped toward Brielle, offering a smile. "You must be frozen."

"Oui." Her teeth chattered even with that single word. She couldn't yet bring herself to unwrap the layers of furs around her.

She took the cup from Charlotte and lifted the warm brew to her face, letting the steam thaw her for a minute before she attempted to drink.

The burn of the first sip seared all the way down. She let out a long sigh and managed a frozen smile for her sister. "That's good." Charlotte always infused her teas with a bit of echinacea to ward off winter sniffles, and the herb gave the drink a bitter bite that helped when Brielle needed something stiff. Like now.

"Did you bring anything back?" Charlotte

returned to the fire and stirred the pot nestled in the coals.

"Just a hare I left outside. I'll skin it in a minute; just let me get warm first." Brielle took another sip of the drink, and this time the liquid eased its warmth through her without stinging so much. She was finally starting to feel her fingers, but the sting was so sharp, she almost wished they were still numb.

"I can do it." Charlotte's tone held no hint of eagerness.

Brielle shook her head. "I'm already bundled. And I haven't cleaned my knife yet." She'd wiped the tool in the snow but always took time to clean and sharpen the blade after a hunt.

Her sister gave her a sheepish smile. "Thanks."

"Where are Papa and Andre? And Uncle Carter?" The room was empty, and the curtains dividing their sleeping sections were tied back to show no one still abed.

Charlotte rolled her eyes. "They've gone to the workshop. Papa was eager to get back to the new design he's working on. He thought of another idea for it in the night. He's making Andre keep up with his studies while the weather is bad and there's not much else to do."

Brielle would have smiled if her cheeks weren't so frozen. Once the weather turned fair, keeping their brother focused on academic learning became five times harder. Thankfully, Papa had always taken charge of their studies.

"Are you spending the day with Mr. Mac-Manus again?"

Brielle shot a glance at her sister, even as warmth crept up to her ears. Did Charlotte think she was spending too much time with their prisoner? Did she suspect what was growing between them? That kiss . . .

Brielle shifted her focus down to the liquid still steaming in her mug and worked for a nonchalant expression. "I'll check on him as I always do, but Leonard's standing guard today."

"He seemed to like the music at the feast yesterday. I'm glad Papa let him come." Charlotte's voice seemed casual, without a weighty undertone, so Brielle chanced another look at her.

Charlotte stared into the pot she was stirring, but her distant gaze and the tender smile curving her lips must mean she was reliving scenes from the feast.

A memory sprang to Brielle's own mind, a wide grin spreading Evan's face as he clapped along to the music. Even the binding of his wrists hadn't stopped his pleasure as fiddle and voices rang off the stone walls of the great hall. Their music had a way of stirring inside a person and bringing every sense to life. Evan had felt that, too, she was almost certain of it.

Brielle worked to pull herself from the memory and pull the grin off her face. Another glance at Charlotte showed her sister was watching her with a curious expression. Charlotte was old enough now to understand the deeper connection that could grow between a man and woman, but thankfully not quite savvy enough for full understanding.

This would be a good time to step outside. Brielle turned toward the door and set her cup on the small table by the exit. "I'll be back in with the meat soon."

"Brielle."

Charlotte's quiet tone made her pause in the midst of reaching for the handle. "Yes?"

"I like him. He seems like a good man."

She forced herself to turn back to her sister. Though Charlotte's eyes shone with her usual sweet temperament, there was a seriousness about her that didn't line up with the naiveté Brielle had just been grateful for.

Brielle nodded, then forced words. "Good.

I think so, too." Then she turned and fled the apartment.

Crouching outside, she set to work. The air was cold enough a person could freeze within minutes if they didn't keep moving, so she worked quickly to skin the rabbit and cut away the good meat. Although the job only took minutes, she almost wished she'd left the hare and come home empty-handed. At least then she wouldn't be racing against frostbite.

A cry howled on the wind, and she jerked her head up. Maybe the sound came from air sliding between the rocks and crevices of the mountainside.

But a figure hurried across the courtyard toward her. The call sounded again.

Brielle squinted to decipher who it was through the swirling snow. *Jeanette.* Why was she out in this blizzard?

Brielle gathered her tools while she waited for the woman to reach her, then pushed the door open and hurried them both inside, pushing hard to close the partition against the wind.

"Marcellus." Jeanette spoke before she could turn to her. "Have you seen him? Is he here?" Her voice rang with worry. "He hasn't been home all morning."

Brielle glanced at Charlotte. "I just came

back from a hunt." She dropped the soiled things in a pile against the wall, then set the meat on the work surface, where Charlotte could prepare it.

Charlotte stepped nearer Jeanette. "I haven't seen him at all. Not anyone, actually, besides Papa and Andre, and now you both."

Jeanette wrapped her arms around herself. "Marcellus was gone when I awoke this morning, and no one knows where he is. I've looked everywhere. Your father said he hasn't been to the workshop." She turned pleading eyes to Brielle. "I can't think why he would have left the walls, especially with the storm. But maybe he went for a walk before the snowfall grew thick."

Brielle reached for her knife from the soiled pile and grabbed a pair of clean gloves. "I'll go look for him. He can't be far. The snow came quickly; maybe it surprised him and he just hasn't made it back yet." But she'd gone much farther than he would have. He should have come back before her.

"Brielle, take food with you." Charlotte's voice stopped her before she could step outside.

Brielle turned back, and while Charlotte packed several food items into a bag, she

252

used the time to reach for her bow and quiver. As she stood there with all her weapons strapped on, Charlotte was still rolling something in leather to pack in the satchel.

"I only need a bite. I won't be gone long." She marched toward Charlotte to get the bag before she could add in anything else.

"Marcellus will be hungry, too." Charlotte grabbed dried fruit and stuffed it in the bag before handing it to Brielle with an impish smile.

Brielle took the strap and leaned close to slip an arm around her sister's neck. She planted a kiss on Charlotte's smooth hair. "Thank you, *ma soeur*. I'll be back soon."

Slipping the strap over her head, Brielle turned back to Jeanette. "Stay here and visit with Charlotte. I'll bring him back to you here."

But Jeanette shook her head. "Louis is worried, too. Bring him to our home when you return, will you please?"

Brielle placed a hand on her friend's back. "I promise."

21

When Brielle stepped out of her family's apartment, the wind slapped hard. She parted ways with Jeanette on the threshold with a final wave. The thick haze of snow made visibility more challenging, but there were no signs of anyone else around. The large flakes had turned to icy crystals, dusting the air in a thick cloud.

She raised her gloved hands to cup her mouth and aimed her voice toward the gate. "Marcellus!" She kept up a steady march as she listened, but only the howling wind answered.

Her feet sank in the snow halfway up her knee-high moccasins. She really should have taken time to lace on her snowshoes but hadn't thought about it in her hurry. Surely this would be a quick journey. Marcellus must have gotten disoriented as the wind and snow thickened. She knew all the places around where he might've taken refuge, and if he could hear her voice, they would find each other quickly.

After passing through the gate, she shifted under the trees on the left side of the trail, the exact place Evan had taken refuge after she'd shot him on that fateful day. She could still feel the thickness of his arms when she'd pressed him facedown on the ground, pulling his wrists behind him. Even then, she'd been impressed by his strength as he fought the power of the potion on her arrow tip.

What was he doing now? At least he was safe and warm, tucked in the storage room with Leonard to guard him. Maybe he was still eating the food Audrey had brought for his morning meal.

The thought made her own belly grumble, and she reached into the bag Charlotte had packed. As she called again for Marcellus, she pulled out the first bundle and opened it to find roasted caribou. That would give her enough energy to accomplish this mission and get back. She could save the rest for when she was warming by the fire. Just the thought of a warm blaze moved her feet a bit faster.

"Marcellus!" She strained to hear a response as she bit into the meat.

Walking under the trees blocked some of

the buffeting wind, so she should be able to hear him respond.

But no voice called back.

Maybe he'd found refuge in the clutch of cedars tucked against the rocky cliff ahead. There weren't many trees there, but the protection of the stone wall on one side would stop much of the wind, and the branches would keep the worst of the snow off him.

Lord, let him be dressed for the weather. Please.

If he'd not covered every bit of himself with furs, he could be frozen stiff by the time she found him. An awful image flashed through her mind, pressing her faster. That would explain why he'd been gone so long.

But no. Marcellus couldn't be . . . dead.

Lord, please. Let him be safe.

He brought such joy to everyone around him. She hadn't meant the times she became frustrated with him. He always intended kindness.

And Jeanette. What would her sweet friend do if something happened to her boy?

When Brielle left the shelter of the trees and plunged across the open land, the wind nearly bowled her over with its gale-like force. Snow pounded her cheeks, and she pulled her scarf higher to cover every part of her face except her eyes.

Her breaths came harder as she pushed against the wind, and it seemed to take forever to reach the group of cedars beside the cliff wall. If she hadn't traveled this way so many times before, she might not have found the spot. The snow was so thick, she could barely see more than a few strides in front of her.

When she reached the trees, she wove her way through them. Nothing. "Marcellus?" She shook every branch, kicking the lumps of snow to see if he'd been covered.

Still nothing.

Her heart hammered into her throat. Where else would he be? Everyone knew better than to leave the village walls with the threat of snow. Even him.

The knot in her stomach pulled tighter. Maybe he'd seen an elk or other game and thought to bring food home for his mother. Even though they all knew hunting wasn't his forte, if he set his mind to something, it was almost impossible to waylay him.

She stood at the edge of the trees and stared at the white beyond. Should she go south or north? With one mountain at her back and Laurent ahead of her, those were the only two immediate choices. But no matter which direction she chose, a medley of options would soon become available to her. There was no way to track him at this point, not with so much snow covering his prints. Her voice wouldn't carry very far through the howling wind.

Lord, show me. She closed her eyes and let her mind roam over the possible directions. Whether Marcellus knew the trail or not wouldn't matter to him if he'd been focused on whatever he was following. Maybe she should go where an animal would have gone. Most of the near herds grazed to the north, but she'd already checked those areas when she hunted this morning. So perhaps she should head south and search the trails she hadn't yet traveled that day.

Gathering a breath for courage, she started out. At first, she attempted a jog to cover ground faster. But the snow was so deep now and the wind pressed against her so hard, she couldn't maintain the pace.

Dropping back to a walk, she extended her stride as much as she could manage in the soft snow. Every minute or so, she called his name. And in between, she sent up prayers for God to lead her to him.

Worry coursed through her, but it was likely nothing compared to what Jeanette and Louis were feeling. She'd already been gone much longer than she anticipated. At least the gnawing fear kept her from being hungry. With so much unknown, she needed to save the food in case . . .

In case what? Her mind tried to answer with images of Marcellus so cold and weak he couldn't walk on his own. When another picture tried to surface of him mostly buried under snow, she pushed it away. "Marcellus!"

Once again, no answer.

God, where are you? Did He not care about one of the best of His creations? Everything in Marcellus desired to be good and helpful and kind and loving. Surely the Lord would respond the same.

After checking two different places where Marcellus might have sought cover, she was so miserable with cold and fear she wanted to scream. But she didn't waste energy on such a reaction.

Instead, she ate a bit more roasted meat. Her strength was waning, but she had to keep moving.

She wasn't as familiar with this area, as it didn't usually provide much game. There might be places he'd taken refuge that she'd forgotten about, but with the storm swirling around her, she could only move from one known group of trees to another.

The isolation of the blizzard made her feel like night should be coming on, but she probably hadn't been out that long. For a while now, the clouds had covered what little sun there was, casting a pall over the atmosphere that made it feel like the semi-darkness that lasted so much of the winter months.

How long had she been searching by now? Half a day? The storm hadn't let up. If anything, the strength of the wind had worsened.

Should she turn back? She couldn't. Her family would worry, but they would know she wouldn't return without Marcellus.

Had someone told Evan? Was he worried?

But she pushed all those thoughts away. She didn't have the energy to let them fester. She had to find Marcellus. She couldn't return without him.

A dark mound rose up before her, and she staggered toward it. The form took the shape of a scrawny tree standing separate from the others clustered a few steps away. She braced a hand against its trunk and let it bear her weight.

Maybe she should turn back and see if she'd missed him somewhere along the way. If she still didn't find him, she could stop in Laurent and gather supplies, along with one or two others to help search. Then they could go northward and see if she'd missed him in her travels that morning.

The plan sounded as good as anything else her exhausted mind could conjure.

Pushing off from the tree, she turned back the way she'd come and screamed Marcellus's name once more.

Evan eyed the guard as he sat with his paper and charcoal. Leonard had acted more and more worried as the afternoon progressed. The man said a blizzard was raging outside, but did that account for all of his angst?

Leonard stood again and began to pace the short length of the room. Back. Forth. Back again. He glanced at the door each time he turned.

"If there's something you need to go do, I'll be fine here. I won't try to escape. You have my word."

The man jerked his focus to Evan, then shook his head. "There's nothing I can do."

"What is it you're worried about?"

He just grunted and shook his head again.

Evan wanted to pound the pencil point into the stone floor. Anything to vent the frustration building inside him. His own body itched with pent-up nerves, but he couldn't tell if it was merely fear of not knowing what was wrong or an inner sense telling him he needed to take action.

Soft footsteps sounded in the hall, and they both jerked to attention. Leonard strode to the door and lifted the bar with a sharp clang. He pulled the door open to reveal Audrey standing with the tray containing their evening meal.

Her wide eyes stared at the man, then swung to Evan.

"Any news?" Leonard spoke in French, but his voice was loud enough Evan could make out the words without much trouble. He was going to be fluent in that language by the time he left Laurent.

Audrey's lips pressed tight, and even in the shadows he could see the worry lines fanning her face as she shook her head.

Leonard stepped back and motioned for her to enter with the tray. A thick fear hovered in the room, and Evan breathed it in with every breath.

He reached to take the tray from Audrey as she bent to him. "Audrey." His voice made her pause in the process of straightening. She met his gaze, and he searched every nuance of her brown eyes for some sign of what the problem was. "What is it? What's wrong?"

"Brielle." Her mouth barely parted as the

name slipped out.

It sliced through him like a knife blade cutting open a deer carcass. His heart skipped a beat, and his breath grew ragged as the pressure in his chest grew. "Where is she?" He'd wondered why she hadn't come by today but had told himself it couldn't have anything to do with Leonard's worries. Her absence seemed more likely to be from their kiss, a possibility that twisted his belly.

But now this . . . Was she out in the blizzard? She couldn't be. She possessed too much savvy about this land. She wouldn't let herself be surprised by a storm.

He honed his focus on Audrey, willing her to explain, as he didn't have the breath to ask.

"Marcellus is missing. She went to look for him when she came back from her hunt this morning. Neither of them have returned. Brielle's father and uncle went out to look for them."

No. It wasn't possible. Only the urge to help one of her people in danger would make Brielle set aside her good judgment and put herself in so much risk.

"The storm? Is it fading?" He could only pray so. *Lord, let it be dying. Let her be hidden with Marcellus somewhere, protected from the cold and wind. Or better yet, let her be, even now, at the gate, on her way to safety.*

Audrey glanced up at Leonard as she shook her head. "Not yet." The turn in her voice said what she didn't. If anything, the weather was worsening.

He pushed the tray aside and rose to his feet, then looked to Leonard. "I have to go look for Brielle. She needs help. I'll bring her back here, I promise. I won't run away. You can keep my things, I'll sign an oath, whatever you need. I promise I'll be back, but I have to go find her."

The man was shaking his head even before Evan stopped talking. "I can't let you. I have my orders."

Anger sluiced through his veins, and he spun to Audrey. "How long ago did her father go out?"

Audrey's brow lined. "A couple hours, maybe. The storm's really bad, Evan. As worried as I am about Brielle and Marcellus, I don't think the others should've left, either. Now all four are in danger. Unless they found a place out of the cold, they might not make it back." Her voice trembled with her words, and she wrapped her arms around herself.

Desperation threatened to close his throat and he shook his head, turning back to

264

Leonard. "I don't care. If I die looking for her, that just means you won't have to worry about me anymore. I have to try." He spun back to Audrey. "Do they know where she's gone? Which direction?"

Her mouth pressed together. "I'm not certain. Charlotte would know for sure. She and Jeanette were the last to speak with Brielle before she went out."

He stepped forward and gripped Audrey's arm. "Can I talk with them, both of them? His mother might know something that will help us find them."

"No!" Leonard's voice rang off the stone walls, slicing through the thoughts racing in Evan's mind. He spun to face the guard.

Leonard fisted his hands at his side. "I can't let you go. If anyone knows what to do in the storm, it's Brielle. I've been ordered to keep you here no matter what. I can't disregard that, especially with the chief gone, as well."

A fresh wave of anger washed through him, and he had to lock his jaw to keep from charging forward and gripping the man's shoulders to shake some sense into him. "Who's in charge, then? Whose permission do I need?" Everything inside told him she was in danger. He'd promised himself that he would protect her. How could he do that when they wouldn't let him out of this place?

Leonard looked to Audrey, uncertainty marking his features. "I guess one of the council. Maybe Erik."

Evan turned to Audrey and almost dropped to his knees to beg. "Get him, please."

But she was already nodding and backing away. "I'll find him."

"Thank you. And bring Charlotte and Jeanette, too. I'll need to speak with them before I leave."

The moment the door closed behind her, Evan started his own pacing. Leonard didn't seem to mind that he'd left the fur pallet. There was no way he could sit still with his mind churning. He had to make a plan for where to start looking. Every moment could make a difference for Brielle.

It seemed like a lifetime ago that he'd ridden his horse so blindly to the gate of Laurent. He could barely recall the landscape around the rock walls, and his memory of the land he'd traveled earlier that day was even hazier. But it would come back to him when he was outside. It had to.

Give me wisdom, Lord.

22

It must have been an hour before Evan finally heard footsteps again in the corridor. He spun to face the door and barely caught himself from charging forward to jerk it open. At the last minute, he stepped near the fur. Better not to give them any reason to think he was resisting orders.

They had no need to fear he would try to escape. He'd never leave this place with Brielle in danger; he had to make them see that.

Maybe one of the guards would go with him to look for her. Was that wise? Probably not, but he might suggest it anyway. Brielle needed him, and every part of his heart and head ached to go after her.

Two men stepped in, and he recognized one of them as the second man who'd come with Brielle's father to question Gerald. No women accompanied them, not even Audrey. Did that mean she was still gathering Charlotte and Jeanette?

Evan focused on the man he'd seen before. "Brielle is in danger and I have to go help her. I won't escape, you have my word. You can keep my things, and you can send someone with me if you feel it necessary. I'll do whatever I need to find Brielle and Marcellus, then I'll come back with them. After that, you can lock me up or hang me or whatever else you see fit."

The two men looked at each other, and the worry in their eyes was plain. Did they fear for Brielle and others caught out in the storm, or was that look because they were afraid to let him leave? If the latter, they were dimwitted fools.

He took in as deep a breath as he could manage with the adrenaline pulsing through him. He had to remind himself of the reason for their fear of him. Six of their loved ones had been brutally murdered at the hands of outsiders. Though their paranoia wasn't necessary in his case — at least, not the kind of danger they feared — the root of their worry stemmed from desire to protect their people.

That's exactly what he was trying to do. They had the same goal, so maybe he could leverage that fact. If only he wasn't an outsider. If he were part of this community already, there would be no question whether he could help.

God, you've got to do something. Step in here. Please.

He forced himself to manage a reasonable tone. "All I want to do is bring back those who might be lost out in the storm."

The taller man eyed him. "What makes you think you can do that and the others can't? You don't even know the trails and places they might have taken refuge. Unless there's more to your story than you told us."

A new rush of frustration boiled inside him. He shook his head hard. "Everything I told you is true. And I won't stop until I find them. Brielle is in trouble, I can feel it. I have to help."

The other man shook his head. "The storm is awful. You can only see a couple steps ahead and it's bitter cold, especially with the strength of the wind. You'll never survive out there. Our people are accustomed to it."

He curled his hands into fists but stiffened his arms to keep them at his sides. "If I'm going to die out there, then why not let me go? That way you won't have to worry about whatever it is you think I'm hiding."

Both men shook their heads, and the taller one spoke again. "We can't let you go.

269

There's not a good enough reason to over-rule the council's decision."

Not good enough reason? Brielle's life was more than enough reason.

But no matter how he pleaded, neither man budged. At last, the taller man raised an outstretched hand, palm forward. "No more. You will stay under guard. We're all praying for their safe return." The man gave Evan a pointed look. "If you want to help, I suggest you do the same."

As they left the room and the bar clanged into place behind them, Evan sank onto his mat. How could this be happening? Brielle needed him. He knew in the deepest part of him that God meant for him to help her. But he could do nothing while they held him in this cell. *What now, Lord?*

He slid a glance at Leonard. He could overpower the man. Was that what God wanted him to do?

If it be possible, as much as lieth in you, live peaceably with all men. The familiar Scripture from Romans echoed in his mind. He was trying to live peaceably, but Brielle's life was in danger and these people wouldn't listen to reason. In this case, living peace-ably wasn't within his power, was it? Surely that was why the Scripture had added the disclaimer *as much as depends on you.* His own actions *were* within his control, no matter what these people decided.

But, God. Brielle. His heart cried out.

The effectual fervent prayer of a righteous man availeth much. Conviction swept through him with the verse from James. A conviction he did not want to feel.

He raised his face to the heavens and clamped his jaw shut to keep from shouting at God. Brielle was out in the storm, probably dying, and God wanted him to do nothing except pray? *Lord, have you lost your senses?*

Conviction pressed harder. God could take care of Brielle. Evan's mind knew that to be fact.

But his heart . . . his heart screamed that he couldn't leave her safety to anyone else. Especially to an invisible God.

He may have never seen God with his eyes, but he knew beyond a doubt the Lord was real. He created the earth, and even more than that, He knew every man, woman, and child. Had a path mapped out for each person to follow.

A weight pressed so hard on him he had to bow his head, his shoulders drooping under the pressure. Evan had strayed from that path more than once during his life, but since Sophia's death, and then watching

271

all those women and children die in the fire at that Canadian fort, he'd determined he wouldn't take a step without the Lord's guiding.

How quickly he'd forgotten to seek God's will. How easily he strayed.

And though he'd promised himself he would never willingly tell a lie again, so many of his words since he'd come to this place had skirted the truth, even to himself. He had to be honest with these people. Even if he found pitchblende in another mountain around this area, the coming of the miners would still disrupt Laurent.

Lord, forgive me for my deceit. Give me the strength to face even the hard conversations.

A weight lifted from his chest with the words. Not the entire weight, because fear for Brielle still pressed hard. But God's forgiveness had scraped away a layer of tension.

Now, for his next step.

He'd been determined to help look for Brielle, but really . . . what did he bring other than desperation? He had little knowledge of the area and the people here didn't trust him. Yet what he could bring before God — a willing heart and a repenting spirit — is what the Lord was accepting.

God had pressed His instructions clearly

in his mind, and Evan would carry them out with every part of his being.

With his head bowed, he started a fervent beseeching, a prayer that he hoped would affect much to save Brielle.

Brielle had no idea if she was going the right direction.

But she pushed through the numbing cold, forcing one step in front of another. It must be nighttime, but the white swirling around her made it impossible to see the moon and confirm she was going north. She hadn't spotted any landmarks for a while, not since the grove of trees she passed about an hour before.

If someone held a knife to her throat to force her to say whether she was lost or not, she would have to admit she was. But she had to keep moving. She would never find Marcellus if she wasn't looking for him. And if she didn't keep her body heated with activity, she would freeze to death within minutes.

Even now she couldn't feel anything below her knees. She'd stumbled and fallen so many times, snow might have seeped under her furs. She wouldn't know for sure until she took them off, but that wasn't an option out here.

She no longer screamed for Marcellus. Her voice had grown so ragged, the sound didn't carry very far. At least the howling of the wind didn't seem as loud.

A dark mass appeared on her right, and she drew up to catch her breath and squint at it. The form was only a shadow, so she couldn't tell whether it was the sheer face of a cliff or the bushy branches of a cedar.

She stumbled forward, paused to steady her footing, then trudged on again.

The mass took on the shape of stone, and she scanned her memory for where she might be. She knew of no vertical cliffs in the southern area, at least not where she should be. Even so, the rock could provide shelter from the wind.

She reached the stone face and pressed her gloved hands against its smoothness. Ice coated the rock, but the surface was too vertical for any snow to settle.

As she pressed close to its side, the force of the wind eased its pressure on her. Relief made her want to sink to her knees and sleep right there at the base of the stone.

She jerked herself straight. She couldn't stop. Not unless she found a way to make some other form of heat.

Staying as close to the stone as she could manage, she shuffled sideways, hopefully moving northward. She still had no memory of this rock, whether it was simply a big boulder or the side of a mountain. But the farther she went, the more the latter seemed to be the case.

From somewhere in the benumbed recesses of her mind, a psalm crept forward. *From the ends of the earth I call to you, I call as my heart grows faint; lead me to the rock that is higher than I.* She couldn't summon a prayer to accompany the words, but the verse itself was prayer enough, releasing a burst of warm hope within her.

The vertical slope tilted and took on more of a craggy texture with snow piled in the grooves. Still, the rock served as a buffer from the worst of the wind.

She kept moving, and the stone seemed to curve in a gradual arc, like it really might be the base of the mountain. She strained to remember the peaks in this area that didn't have trees near the base. In truth, she had no idea where she might be.

But since she had something solid to follow, she kept moving, ducking low from the wind and staying close to the rock. The stone's incline grew vertical again, for which she was grateful. It warded off more wind that way. This time the surface wasn't smooth, though, jutting out in points and crags. If her mind wasn't so weary, she might stop to ponder what made it different from the other.

But her head had grown numb, even her thinking.

Her stomach cramped, and she reached into the satchel for the bundle of dried berries. She was rationing the food as much as possible, eating only a bite or two every few hours. At this point, she could be out here another day or two. Especially if she couldn't find the way back.

If she survived it all.

So far, she'd not let her mind drift toward the possibility that these might be her last hours. But she had to face reality.

Evan's face filled her thoughts, that intense way he had of looking deep inside her made something twist in her middle. She might never see him again. She should have told him how she felt, no matter whether it was too soon or not. She only knew that her heart had connected with his in a way she'd never thought possible.

If she never returned, maybe Audrey would tell him how Brielle had felt. She and Audrey had never spoken of it, but her friend had given her a look during the feast that said she knew something was growing between them. That look had promised a reckoning, that they would soon have a conversation about the man.

At least her other dear ones knew how much she loved them. After they lost their mother, Papa made sure the four of them never held back words of affection. They all knew how quickly final moments could come without warning. Her last words to Charlotte had been those of love. At least she didn't have that regret.

Her foot caught on something in the snow, and she stumbled forward, dropping to her knees. Pain jolted through her wrists and up her arms. Weakness washed through her, but she worked to push herself upright. She had to keep moving.

She used the rock beside her to keep her balance as she started forward again. Right hand forward. Left foot forward. Right foot forward. Right hand forward.

Except her hand didn't find the rock for placement. It plunged into empty air, and she tipped sideways as she scrambled for a hold.

At last, her palm struck stone, and she leaned into a hollow indention in the mountainside. She forced her fuzzy gaze to focus on the place. Between her exhaustion, the swirling snow, and the darkness, her mind was slow to form the picture of what she saw.

Like a large hand had scooped stone from the mountain, the rock formed an overhang on top and both sides.

There wasn't much snow piled on the ground, but something else lay there amidst the white. An animal? A dead one, from how still it was.

She stepped closer, and the wind no longer blew around her.

The creature was half covered, so she couldn't see its head or legs to determine the species. Whatever it was, maybe she could cover herself with the carcass until the storm ended and morning brought light.

Perhaps the weight would provide enough cover to stay alive.

The creature didn't move as she dropped to her knees by its side. She wiped the snow from one end, trying to dig out legs.

Suddenly, the animal jerked. It came to life, rising up before her.

She screamed and tried to scramble back, but her numb limbs wouldn't do what she told them. She fell on her rear, still trying to scramble backward. Her bow tangled in her right arm, locking it in place and stilling her escape. She screamed again as the creature rose higher.

Then the animal took shape . . . the shape
of a man.

23

Brielle's heart thundered as she tried to make sense of what she was seeing. Snow clung to the fur on its head, but a narrow patch of human skin and eyes peeked through.

Familiar eyes.

The person reached up and tugged part of the fur down, revealing splotched red cheeks.

Marcellus? Had she really found him?

Her mind finally caught up with what her eyes were taking in. She couldn't form words with her face so numb, but she let out another cry and gathered strength to crawl toward him. It took long moments to untangle her arm from her bow. Every movement she attempted was clumsy, as if she moved in slow motion.

But finally she freed herself and crawled to Marcellus. He was still sitting there, watching her. He'd not spoken at all, but she finally managed a stiff, "Marcellus?" He might not have heard her through the fur covering her mouth, but at least her lips and tongue were working again.

She couldn't tell how long he'd been lying there, but he'd created a patch of bare ground the length of his body. Snow rose up on either side of the spot where he'd lain. Likely, he would've been covered completely in a few more hours of snow blowing sideways into the nook.

She turned to face him and worked to form words. "How are you?"

Maybe those weren't the best first words to say, but she wanted to hear him speak.

He stared at her, his eyes barely focused. Had he even heard what she said? She was about to reach out and grab his arm to shake him when a word slipped through the fur covering his mouth.

"Cold." His voice was raspy, but the familiar timbre sent a thread of warmth to her heart.

She reached out and pulled him into a hug. "Marcellus." Tears burned her eyes, but she couldn't let them fall. Moisture like that would only make her colder. Ice had already crusted her eyelashes and probably wasn't helping her ability to talk.

She pulled back and looked him over once

more. His eyes held a little more life than they had moments before. Now she had to make sure they stayed that way.

A glance outside their little miniature cave showed the snow still swirling. They would need to stay here a while. Maybe together, they could keep warm.

She turned back to Marcellus and crawled in beside him. They both wore coats of thick fur. Hers was grizzly, and his looked like it might be the same. Would they be warmer sitting side by side or lying front to back in the place he'd been stretched out before?

Probably the latter. As much as her body craved the chance to rest, she didn't fancy laying out as if she were giving up.

Still, that might be the best they could manage. They had no wood to build a fire and keep it burning, and the only other option was to go out in the wind and snow.

She glanced at Marcellus's legs. Was he able to walk? Would moving in the blizzard be better than lying here, sharing body heat?

In truth, she wasn't sure. Her mind didn't seem to be reasoning well.

Her body told her she wouldn't be able to keep on much longer if she forced herself back into the wind and cold. Staying here together would have to do.

Protect us, Lord. Keep us alive.

Using a combination of motions and the few words she could manage, she had Marcellus lie down on his side. She gave him the two small chunks of meat she had left, then removed her bow and quiver and positioned them with the satchel next to her.

At last, she crawled in to lie in front of Marcellus. He draped his arm over hers, and she could feel the tremble as his body tried desperately to stay warm. Her own limbs wouldn't stop shivering, either.

As she settled in beside him, she finally managed to breathe easier. Was this a good sign or bad? She didn't know anymore. She couldn't think through the fog clouding her mind. Her eyes drooped shut, and she let herself rest for a minute. Just one minute, then she'd keep herself awake — counting snowflakes if she had to.

Evan didn't sleep that night. There were a few times his body tempted him to lie down and rest, just for a few minutes. But his soul wouldn't allow it.

He pleaded with God for Brielle's life. Not just for her *life,* but for every part of her to return whole. Not even a nip of frostbite.

He raised the same prayer for Marcellus and for Brielle's father and uncle. When he asked Philip for full names so he could be precise in his petitions, the man seemed wary about giving those details.

"I only want to tell the Almighty clearly who I'm asking Him to save."

The man nodded understanding. "Her father is Henri Durand and her uncle is Carter Maurier."

Evan raised his brows. "Her mother's brother, then?"

Philip nodded.

Evan turned his focus back to the Lord, praying for God to place angels around each of the four to keep them safe no matter where they went, just as it said in the Psalms. Other Scriptures slipped into his mind through the hours, and he prayed each as they came to him. He'd never felt so close to the Lord as he did now, but the angst in his spirit wouldn't leave.

Please, Lord. That simple cry seemed to say as much as every other word his thoughts could form. Maybe his spirit really did make intercession like Romans said.

Intercede for Brielle. And Marcellus, and Monsieurs Durand and Maurier, too. Bring them back to us whole and healthy and stronger than ever before. Use this time to make yourself real to them. Make your path for them clear, both during the storm, and the plans you've laid out for their future.

He stopped just short of begging God for Brielle's plan to include him. He hadn't yet come to grips with what he should do about the pitchblende.

He knew he had to tell Brielle everything, but beyond that he had no notion. Even when he asked God to show him, the way forward looked fuzzy in his mind. Maybe the conversation with Brielle would give him a vision for how to proceed.

Philip had been sleeping for hours when a step sounded in the hallway. That was Audrey's tread, but it seemed too early for her to bring the morning meal.

Evan scrambled to his feet, and his hands trembled as he waited for her to open the door. She must have news.

When she pushed the partition open, she was carrying a tray. His stomach dropped. That must mean it really was morning. Maybe she had nothing to tell.

Philip awoke with something that sounded like a hiccup and pushed up to his feet as Audrey entered.

She caught Evan's gaze, and the mixture of worry and relief in her eyes worked like a fist to grip his chest and twist hard. "Chief Durand and his brother have returned."

The room seemed to wobble around

Evan, and he took a step forward to steady himself. "Brielle?" They must not have found her. He refused to believe they'd only found her body.

Audrey shook her head. "They didn't find her or Marcellus."

Relief eased through him. At least they hadn't found her dead.

Place your angels around her on every side, Lord. He envisioned shining men with swords, like what the Bible said was placed in front of the Garden of Eden. A powerful foursome like that pressed into a square around Brielle should do well to keep her warm and ward off any animals that might threaten.

"Has the storm stopped?" He'd prayed for that, too, but not as much as he'd prayed for safety and protection.

Audrey hesitated. "The wind has died down. There's still snow falling, but visibility is much better." She moved forward and set the tray on the floor.

Evan gave himself an inward nudge. He should have taken it from her instead of standing like a mindless oaf.

But his thoughts quickly shifted back to Brielle's situation. "Are they going back out to look for her?" As much as he trusted God to bring her back safely, part of him still

286

strained to secure that protection himself.

Audrey nodded. "Two of the other men have already left."

A new thought slipped in, and he straightened. "How are her father and uncle? Do they suffer much from the cold?" He'd been praying for all of them. This might be a chance to learn how God would provide answer.

She shook her head. "They were cold and hungry and tired. I only saw them briefly. I guess it remains to be seen whether they lose fingers or toes from spending so much time in the weather."

He inhaled a cleansing breath. That was a relief, although not conclusive. "Tell me the names of the men who've gone back out. I need to pray for them."

A tiny thread of desperation pulled Brielle from the haze. Everything in her wanted to stay in the cradle of warmth, except that faint worry that wouldn't leave her be.

She forced her eyes open, despite the grainy tug trying to keep them shut. Darkness shrouded her. Not the dusky version that lasted so long during winter days, but the thick black that signaled something covering her eyes. She reached out and felt the underside of the fur over her head.

287

Fingering along the hide, she finally pushed it off to reveal a sliver of brightness. She squinted and struggled for memory.

Like faint rays of dawn, the details slipped back to her.

The storm. Marcellus. Tucking the two of them into the nook under the stone.

The pressure at her back finally penetrated her thoughts, and she twisted her neck even as warm breath fanned her cheek. Marcellus must have covered them completely with the fur. From the regular sound of his breathing, he was still sleeping.

She turned forward again and stared out at the white still falling. The wind had stopped. Mostly. And now the snow fell in large flakes. But at least she could see farther now.

Her cheeks were growing cold, but the rest of her was warm, still covered in the fur and snuggled against Marcellus.

They'd survived.

That fact still didn't seem possible. Against all odds, she'd found Marcellus and they both survived the night and the worst of the storm.

Now she had to figure out where they were and get them back home.

Her gaze dropped to the bit of leather showing under a covering of snow. The food pack. Was there any left?

There might be a little more of something, maybe pastry, but she couldn't remember for sure. She should probably give that to Marcellus, as he'd probably had nothing to eat the day before until she found him.

Jeanette must be so worried. A new pressure sank over Brielle. Her own family would be worried, too. Papa, Charlotte, Andre . . . and Evan. Her heart squeezed. Had anyone told him? What was he doing right now? Worrying over her?

Part of her wished he would come out and find her, but he couldn't do that while under guard. And she didn't want him to risk his own life.

She had to tell her father and the others that he could be trusted. Keeping him guarded at all times until the council vote wasn't necessary. In fact, it was silly. They had much more important things to spend their resources on, like making sure Laurent had enough food through the winter. She would speak with her father as soon as she got Marcellus back.

And now she needed to take action to accomplish that last bit.

As slowly as she could manage, she eased away from Marcellus and out from under the fur, laying it back in place to keep him cocooned in warmth. It looked like he'd used his coat to cover them both. A wise move, and she was surprised she'd not awakened when he moved around to accomplish the task. She must have been half frozen and exhausted.

The frigid air wrapped around her, seeping under her coat at the neck and sleeves, and she pulled the fur tighter. After crawling a little to get out from under the stone ledge above, she pushed up to her feet.

Every part of her ached, and her legs were barely strong enough to hold her. Her feet burned like she was stepping through fire, so she stomped several times to bring them back to life. The pain never eased.

Frostbite would be likely after spending a day and night in the storm. She'd seen dead limbs after people stayed in the cold too long, and they weren't pretty. What would Evan think if her toes or feet turned that otherworldly gray? Or even fell off?

She pushed the thought away. She was grateful to be alive, and that was all she could worry about just now.

Turning her focus to the landscape around, she took in the mountain to her right, the one that had sheltered them. Covered in white, everything looked different. Unfamiliar.

Worry churned in her middle, but she did her best to swallow it down. She would have to start going in the direction she thought Laurent should be and pray she found something she recognized.

She glanced at Marcellus. Should she wake him to tell him where she was going? If she did, he would probably want to go with her. She might have to wander around a while, which would be a waste of his energy. Lord willing, she wouldn't be gone long, so better to let him sleep. She did reach in for her bow and quiver of arrows and lifted the food satchel from under the snow where he would see it.

Then, she started northward. At least . . . she hoped so.

24

Despite the burning in Brielle's feet, she was able to take long strides in the snow. Though what drifted down now was light and fluffy, the cold in the night had hardened much of what fell the day before to an icy crust. Thank the Lord for that blessing at least.

She passed a few single trees, and finally a mountain came into view. The shape of the rocky sides looked familiar, but she strained to place its location in her mind. She studied the cluster of cedars at its base for a few more steps before awareness finally dawned.

Those trees. Those were the very first cedars she'd inspected after leaving Laurent's gate. That peak sat directly opposite the mountain she and her people lived in. She was seeing it from an angle she rarely approached, which was why nothing looked familiar.

She turned and retraced her footprints, already so full of new snow they were mere indentations. When she reached the nook in the mountainside, she bent low to step in, then dropped to her knees beside Marcellus. She pulled back the fur to expose his face to the cold, then shook his shoulder.

His heavy breathing shuddered as his eyes blinked open. His gaze found her face, but his expression held nothing of recognition or awareness. Maybe his mind was as numb as hers had been when she first awoke.

She tugged her fur muff down so she could speak clearly. "Marcellus, it's me, Brielle. We're not far from home. Can you get up and walk?"

He stared at her for several heartbeats, then looked down at the fur covering him as though trying to determine what it was.

She pulled the coat back to let the cold awaken him fully. Then she grabbed his upper arm. "Come. Let's sit you up and put your coat on."

He did as she asked, although he began shivering before they got his second arm in its sleeve. She pulled the fur close around his neck and fastened the straps. "We need to hurry. There'll be a warm fire and good food when we get there."

Maybe she should have left Marcellus and

gone on to the village to bring back help. If he wasn't able to walk, she could still do that. But they were so close . . .

She gave Marcellus the last pastry. But when he sat there eating so slowly, she finally tugged on his arm again. "Stand up and see if you can walk while you eat."

It took several tries, but they finally got him standing. His feet must be either numbed or as painful as hers, for they didn't hold him at first.

She grabbed her bow, quiver, and satchel. "Put your hand on my shoulder to balance while you walk."

He obeyed, then took a step forward at the same time she did. He grunted. "Feet hurt."

"Mine do, too, but we don't have far to go. Let's see if we can make it."

The first dozen steps were slow and painful. Physically painful for Marcellus, and emotionally painful for her. Every part of her wanted to get back to Laurent. The entire village was likely worried about them. They may have even sent someone out this morning after the storm eased.

It seemed to take an hour before she could see the mountain she'd viewed earlier. Marcellus was moving a little faster, but the one time he'd removed his hand from her shoulder, he'd slowed to the speed of a crawl. She gripped his upper arm to keep him moving, and he obediently increased his pace.

"Just a few more minutes and we should be able to see our mountain." Maybe if she kept up a running conversation, his spirits would rise. She'd never seen Marcellus so quiet, not even when his father had been shot by the Englishmen and lost his ability to walk.

Marcellus communicated his emotions through speech. Yet now, he seemed to be locking them in. She would have to worry about that later. For now, she only had the strength for a single focus — getting them both home safely.

"They're back!" Andre's words came even before his face peered through the doorway.

Evan surged toward him. "Brielle found Marcellus? They're both here? Are they hurt?"

Brielle's brother flashed a wide smile. "They both walked in not five minutes ago. I came to tell you first thing, but I'm going back now to see to them again."

Evan reached for the door to pull it open wider. "I'm coming with you." He glanced back at Leonard, who'd stepped up behind him.

With a grin flashing across his face, the man nodded. "Just stay beside me."

Joy flooded through Evan as he jogged behind Andre. If only his legs were longer so they could move faster. But he had to follow, for the lad was the only one who knew where Brielle was.

Andre stopped at a door partway down the corridor, the same one he and Charlotte had been coming from on the way to the feast. Had that only been two days before? It seemed two years.

They all slowed to enter, and Evan's gaze honed on the cluster of people around the hearth on the left side of the room.

Finally, he found the profile he was looking for.

She was barely visible with the fur blanket covering her head and body, but the strong, beautiful lines of her face peeked out, shimmering in the dancing glow of the fire.

He'd covered half the distance between them when she turned to look his way. Maybe someone had mentioned him, or maybe she merely felt the change in the air he always did when she entered the room.

Her eyes were round, more so than usual, and drew him in like they always did. He dropped to his knees by her side and she scooted a little to face him. Maybe he shouldn't appear as if he cared so much, but he was powerless to restrain his need to know how she fared.

He touched the fur that covered her arm and studied her eyes for signs of pain or damage. Red tinted the whites of her eyes, but her gaze looked blessedly whole. And the joy that glimmered there sparked the same emotion in his own chest.

She was alive. Not just alive, but *well*.

He let his focus roam her face, then scan the length of her. But there was nothing to see except the fur covering.

He moved his gaze back to her face. "Are you well? Hurt anywhere?"

She shook her head. "God provided a safe place for us to weather the storm."

He couldn't help the grin that spread across his face. "Indeed." God *had* certainly provided.

She shifted her focus to the others around her, but still spoke to him. "Have you met everyone? You know Audrey and my sister and my father. This is Uncle Carter."

Evan gave a friendly nod to the man who possessed the same strong chin and cheekbones as Brielle.

Carter Maurier had already been scrutinizing him, if his narrowed gaze was a sign. The man offered a responding nod, but his mouth didn't curve into a smile. Any man who sought to court Brielle would likely have to prove himself to the whole family, and Evan would have much to make up for in order to overcome his current status as a stranger and prisoner. He would do his best, though.

Brielle was still making introductions, so he shifted his focus to each as she pointed and offered names. Jeanette was sitting beside Marcellus, her arm wrapped around her son as he sat beneath a heavy fur. The young man didn't seem quite as cheerful as the last time Evan had talked with him, but he still offered Evan a toothy smile that was impossible not to return.

After Brielle finished announcing names, silence fell over the group.

Her father broke it shortly. "Tell us what happened, Brielle."

Evan stayed at her side as she told an incredible story. He'd known the storm was bad, but he'd not realized how strong the wind was, nor how little she'd been able to see. Only God could have led her to that mountain and helped her find the very nook where Marcellus was hiding.

A few times during the telling, she urged

Marcellus to add a comment. But the fellow seemed content to listen and soak in the attention — and the warmth.

When she finished, Evan had to ask once more, "Are you injured anywhere? Perhaps from frostbite?" He slid his gaze from her to Marcellus, then back.

Brielle looked at Audrey, as if for confirmation. "I don't think so."

Audrey offered a shaky grin. "I can't believe it myself, but I don't see signs of permanent damage to fingers or toes."

Evan let his eyes close for a heartbeat while he sent up a prayer of thanks. As God promised in the verse from James, He had used those fervent prayers to avail much in this situation.

"Marcellus." Chief Durand leaned forward slightly as he spoke to the lad. "Can you tell us why you went out?"

Marcellus's eyes widened, and his gaze flitted from face to face. He seemed to shrink back from them all, and his mouth parted, then hung there. His mother wrapped her arm tighter around him and sent the chief a look full of worry.

Chief Durand eased back. "It's all right, son. We can talk later when you've warmed up and feel more like yourself. You've been through a hard time, and we're so glad to have you back safely."

Marcellus's wide eyes eased, but a bit of fear still showed there.

Maybe a change of subject would help. Evan shifted his gaze to Brielle's father. "What of the other two who went out the second time?"

The man gave a solemn nod. "They told us where they planned to look, so two men have gone to bring them back. The storm is mostly over, so we don't fear for their safety."

Evan let his relief show. "Good." But he would add the additional pair to his prayer list until all were safely within the walls of Laurent.

He could understand even more now why these people were so protective of their little community. Their walls were a source of safety. Of protection.

Not just against strangers, but against being lost and frozen in the elements. And being hurt by wild animals. And probably a host of other deadly possibilities. Staying within these walls meant safety. In this land that was more treacherous than any he'd seen, these people had survived, and even thrived, because of the walls.

Would they ever open themselves to correspondence and trade with the rest of the world? For that matter, would they open themselves to an outsider — him — moving in and becoming one of their own . . . maybe married to Brielle? Both remained to be seen.

Another silence settled over the group, and Evan began to receive more than one questioning stare. It was probably time he returned to his cell before they felt the need to force him to. Brielle was safe, and he had some prayers of thanksgiving to send up. Then a nap might be in his near future.

But as he prepared to walk back with Leonard, he leaned close to Brielle once more and kept his voice low. "When you're well enough, I need to speak with you."

Her gaze jerked to his and she studied him, probably wondering what he wanted to discuss.

Alone. He tried to speak that last word with his eyes.

She seemed to understand, for she nodded. "I'll come to check on things soon."

He gave her a smile, but not so big as to draw the attention of the others. "Rest first. Sleep and eat and stay warm. I'll be waiting when you're ready." If the shadows under her eyes were any indication, she hadn't slept much in that time under the cleft of the rock.

Though her mouth didn't speak, her eyes gave him a smile that warmed him all the way down. This woman nurtured his soul, and he had a feeling without her in his life, there would always be a missing piece.

25

As people slowly left their quarters, Brielle could feel the weight of her father watching her. He'd seen everything that passed between her and Evan, she had no doubt. Just the fact that Evan had come to see her, desperation marking all his features, would have been enough to raise Papa's suspicions. She had much to answer for now.

Good thing she'd already planned to tell her father more about why she was certain Evan could be trusted.

All the people who'd come to hear her story had returned to their own homes now, and only the five in their family remained. Papa sent a look to Uncle Carter that her uncle interpreted easily.

He pushed up to his feet and stretched his hands high over his head. "Charlotte, Andre, I have something in my room I've been meaning to show you both. How about now?" His offer was more statement than question. Charlotte might have picked up on that undertone, but Andre scrambled to his feet, simply eager for something to do. Sitting around while the adults talked was not his favorite pastime.

While they shuffled out, Papa refilled Brielle's mug with hot tea, and she cradled the warm cup in her hands. She'd finally heated enough to let the fur hang loosely on her shoulders. Her feet still ached, but it wasn't that fiery sting like before.

As quiet descended over them, she didn't look at her father. He would speak when he was ready, and she didn't have the energy to face his stare that saw all the way to her soul.

"So, I take it you're certain Evan Mac-Manus can be trusted."

She dared a glance at him and nodded. "I said that before."

"I recall you still weren't clear about his purpose for coming here. You merely felt sure of his character. Have you learned more since then?"

How to answer that? The short response would be a simple no, but that wouldn't communicate what she really did know about Evan. Her father would see and understand the way things were, no matter how she hedged or pleaded. And it was probably best that he spent time with Evan to see for himself. That would be the only way he would see the man the way she did. Frank honesty had always been her mien with Papa, and that seemed like the best approach now, too.

She turned her full focus on him. "I've learned much about him. I've learned he's loyal and hardworking, kind and generous. He takes responsibility for his actions and does everything possible to protect those in his care. He's a good man. God-fearing."

Her father studied her, and she willed him to believe her. His brow lined as he mulled through her words. Then he offered her a weak smile. "You've always been a good judge of character, so I wouldn't expect you to give your heart to a man not worthy of it. I suppose the only way I can know for sure is by getting to know this fellow."

Heat flashed up to her cheeks. Just as she'd suspected, Papa had seen all. At least he'd come to the right conclusion on his next step. "Perhaps he can come help you in your workshop. Help you with the cook-stove you're working on from his sketch."

"That's a good plan, and I would like him to join me, but we must have the council's approval first." His look turned pointed. "You know that."

Unfortunately, she did know. And she could feel the loving reprimand in his gaze. She'd been pressing against the bounds of the council's edict.

"You'll speak for him before the vote?" She studied him, looking for any sign of his thoughts.

Papa nodded. "I'll spend some time with this Evan first, then I'll share my thoughts with the council before the vote."

She eased out a breath and took a sip of her tea, trying to untie the knot in her middle. A bit of nerves about Papa's meeting with Evan was normal. She wanted them to like each other.

And they would. Her father was also a good judge of people. And Evan's heart would shine through when they spoke.

"Now, I think it's best you rest. I promised Jeanette I would come check on them and spend a few minutes with Louis. As hard as this was on her, I think he struggled even more, not being able to go out and look for you both." Papa stood and pulled on his coat.

As she nodded her farewell, a yawn overtook her. A few minutes to sleep, then she would go to Evan. As much as she wanted Papa to spend time with him, she wanted the chance first.

So much she had to tell him.

Evan stepped from the Durand quarters with Leonard walking close behind him.

Thank you, Lord. Thank you. With every step he sent up the prayer. Now that the worry had passed, his exhausted mind couldn't seem to manage more than that single thought. Hopefully, Brielle would rest a while, and he could, too. He wanted to be at his sharpest for what he had to tell her.

They'd trudged halfway down the hall when a door behind them opened and footsteps thudded down the corridor.

He spun and saw a young lad — probably not more than ten years old — running toward them. He stopped at the door they'd just passed and paused to turn a wide grin on them. "Papa's back. He and Monsieur Duluth found the two men who went out after Brielle. They're all safe."

The lad opened the door and darted into the apartment before Evan or Leonard could respond.

Leonard glanced at him. "Mind if we stop in and see them a minute? Duluth is my sister's husband. I'd like to make sure they're all right."

Evan nodded. "Of course." The man

307

wasn't exactly asking his permission, but it was still nice he offered the consideration.

They stepped through the doorway the lad had just entered, and Evan glanced around a large room much like the Durands', though the fireplace was set on the opposite wall. These people must have cut chimneys up through the stone, so two dwellings shared the same chimney. A great deal of work had been put into this unique village.

A half-dozen people were clustered around the fire here, too, and Leonard knelt beside one of them. He gave the man a good-natured clap on his back as he murmured words in French, but Evan wasn't close enough to make out what was said.

After a few minutes, Leonard glanced back, as if he'd just realized he had a prisoner he was supposed to be watching. He motioned for Evan to sit. "Make yourself comfortable."

A spot against the wall seemed the best place to stay out of the way. Evan settled there as more people entered through the rear door from the hall — an older man and woman, and two young boys, who looked as though they might be grandchildren.

The volume of noise in the room rose as the adults greeted each other and the boys moved to play with the first lad Evan had seen. It was fun to watch them interact, women doting on the four men who'd just returned and the men plying them with questions.

More people entered the room, until the atmosphere was as festive and the crowd as thick as the feast had been. He kept himself tucked against the wall and seemed to be almost invisible to the others who milled about. At least they no longer seemed as curious about his presence as they'd been during the feast.

Several conversations were happening near enough that Evan couldn't avoid overhearing. By the fire, Leonard was pulling the entire tale of their journey from his brother-in-law, and behind them stood two matrons who were rehashing Brielle's adventure, which they'd heard from Jeanette.

Another conversation drifted to him, but at first, he couldn't find the source. A deep male voice, one that rang with familiarity but raised his hackles. A heartbeat passed before he saw the man and recognition dawned.

Gerald.

He stood near a bedcurtain tied back against the wall. Part of the drape was pulled just enough to conceal whoever Gerald was speaking to.

The hidden man's voice drifted to Evan, and he strained to make out the French words. The partition muffled the sounds, but Brielle's name came through clearly. He worked to keep his interest from showing in his expression in case Gerald looked over and spotted him.

Gerald's face was twisted in an angry mask, clear enough to see even in the dim light. "It's a shame she survived, the little vixen. When I sent the half-wit out, I figured I'd finally taken care of her for good this time. She thinks she's so powerful, just because her papa's the chief. She's not half the warrior I am."

Gerald crossed his arms as the other man spoke again. Evan didn't breathe or move as he strained to catch the words, but the sound was too low and muffled to understand. Did Gerald have something to do with Marcellus going out in the blizzard?

Whatever the unseen man said only heightened Gerald's ire. Deep lines creased the man's forehead and his eyes narrowed. "Someone should have put an arrow through his chest the moment he stepped through the gate. Don't know why we've had to use our good hunters to watch over him. The men who've been sent out to hunt

310

since he arrived are little more than boys. If I were in charge, I'd have taken care of him at the beginning. Matter of fact, this madness has gone on long enough. Think I'll do the job now."

A tingle of apprehension slipped down Evan's spine. Was Gerald speaking of him? He was the one they were using good huntsmen to watch over. He agreed with the man that the use was wasteful, but their way to remedy the situation was as far apart as could be. Did Gerald plan to kill him?

The other man was speaking, and the name *Durand* was the only word Evan could decipher.

The lines across Gerald's brow smoothed and the corners of his mouth curved up. "It's about time someone put her in her place. The wildcat she is, she would probably be a pleasure." His eyes hardened, losing all twinkle. "I know watching her suffer would make me happy. She's given me enough misery, becoming so high and mighty. It's high time the tables were turned."

Evan dared a quick breath as fire raged through his veins. He couldn't risk moving even his chest in case the motion caught Gerald's attention. Was the man serious, or was this merely bluster?

311

If only Evan could see who the cad was talking to. The fellow behind the curtain said something else, and Evan imprinted the cadence and tone in his mind.

Gerald narrowed his eyes again as silence settled between them for a couple heartbeats. "Tonight. I'll put an end to that Englishman while the guard is sleeping. Then when he wakes up and the ruckus starts, I'll grab the wench and have some fun."

The other man spoke, his voice quicker than before, sounding worried. As well he should be, for what Gerald spoke of should be a hanging offense. He might lose his life over such an act, especially with the chief of the council being Brielle's father. And if he'd sent Marcellus out in a blizzard specifically to endanger her . . .

Even if Gerald were punished, what he was speaking of doing to Brielle could never be undone. The scars he would leave on her heart and body were too awful to imagine.

Evan fought with everything in him to keep himself immobile. Gerald was crafty enough to deny saying such treasonous words or to claim that Evan had misunderstood. Then the accusation would make him even more eager to take revenge on Evan and Brielle both.

He had to be wise about this. Had to find a way to stop the man for good. He couldn't risk Brielle's safety on the chance that the fiend was merely boasting.

When Gerald spoke again, Evan pulled his focus back to decipher the words. "Think I'm ready to leave this place anyway. I've never been appreciated here. Chrissy was the only one, and she's gone. You want to come along? We could bring the wildcat with us and take turns with her. I bet she'll tame down pretty quickly."

A new fury roared through him. Take Brielle away? Not for anything in the world. The man would have to kill Evan and every other fellow in this place before he could take her. And Brielle certainly had her own ways to refuse.

Several people crossed the line of vision between him and Gerald.

"I guess we better get back."

Leonard's voice nearly made Evan jump, as close as the man stood. Evan had been so caught up in Gerald's conversation, he'd not seen Leonard come near.

Evan nodded and pushed up to his feet, sneaking a glance in Gerald's direction as he did. Two men had approached and were speaking to him. Distracting him, hopefully. Evan pulled his focus away, so if the man saw him, maybe he wouldn't realize Evan had been close enough to overhear.

The hallway was quiet as they made their way toward his cell at the end. A good thing, for his mind was turning. Should he tell Leonard what he'd heard? The man didn't seem to have enough clout or authority to have Gerald locked up. Leonard would likely have to call someone else. Brielle was his next in command, and it made sense to start with the higher up.

But did he dare tell Brielle what he'd heard? She would be livid and would probably take action herself. And even as capable as she was, he couldn't stand the thought of putting that weight on her shoulders alone. Everyone needed someone to guard their back. He'd committed to be that for Brielle, but in this situation his hands were tied. Almost literally.

So, he needed to confide in someone who could do the job for him.

Her father.

26

The knot in Evan's middle balled tighter as he mulled through what he had to do. Chief Durand was the only person he could think of with enough authority to have Gerald stopped forever. But what would stopping the blackguard consist of? A hanging?

Part of him felt like that was nothing less than the man deserved if he really did plan to carry out his foul plans. The council would have some debate, and Brielle had earned a great deal of respect in the eyes of these people. *Earned,* not inherited, as Gerald had implied. He'd seen the way she protected and provided for even the least of these, often enduring hardship herself, as she'd done in her search for Marcellus. That was more than he'd seen Gerald do for another.

On the other hand, Gerald had shown himself to be a lecherous snake. One who had to be stopped once and for all. Inside his holding room, Evan dropped down to sit on his fur as Leonard took his spot against the wall.

Grit scraped against his eyelids from lack of sleep, but he had far too much to do to waste time with the luxury of rest. How could he speak with Brielle's father? He'd only seen the man a couple of times — right after his fisticuffs with Gerald, and again at the feast. That meant the fellow probably wouldn't just happen to stop by. Evan would have to ask for an audience.

He slid a glance at Leonard, who'd taken up the arrow he'd been whittling. If Gerald stuck to the timing he'd said, Evan only had today to stop him.

Should he ask Leonard to send for him? Or wait until Audrey came and ask her? He trusted her almost as much as he did Brielle, more than any of these other guards.

But Audrey was probably busy tending those who'd returned from the storm. She hadn't brought their morning meal, but she likely wouldn't be able to come until at least midday. Even then, she might send it with someone else. He'd have to make his request through Leonard.

He straightened and turned to face the guard. The man looked up, his brows rising in question.

Evan tried to force the emotion from his voice. "I need to speak with Chief Durand. How can I get an audience with him?"

The man's brows dipped and the confusion on his face seemed to hold a hint of suspicion. "He is busy. If you have something to ask, it's better we take it to Brielle."

Evan's stomach turned at the thought. He should have expected the man to want to bring in Brielle. But he couldn't speak to her of this, not yet. Everything in him said her father was the one to bring it to first.

He did his best to school his expression. "Brielle's still recovering, and, in truth, what I have to tell concerns her father most anyway." Let the man make of that what he would. Maybe his assumptions would induce him to find their chief posthaste.

Leonard studied him, his hands no longer working the arrow. Evan kept his expression blank. For long moments they sat like that.

Did Leonard think he would get in trouble for going straight to the chief? Perhaps. Evan wasn't sure how strict their hierarchy was, but it seemed securely structured. Or maybe Leonard thought he'd be in trouble for stopping by his sister's home instead of coming directly back to this room.

At last, the man tightened his jaw and

pushed to his feet. "Can I trust you to stay here while I walk down the hall and send for him?" His tone had lost the congeniality from moments earlier, but at least he was getting Brielle's father.

Evan nodded. "I won't move."

Leonard left the door ajar, probably so he could hear if Evan shifted around, and his footsteps faded partway down the hall. He called someone, and a young voice answered. After a quick conversation in Italian, Leonard's footsteps sounded, coming back toward the room.

He stepped inside and closed the door, barely sparing Evan a glance. "Jean-Jacques has gone to look for the chief. If he's not too busy, I'm sure he'll be along shortly."

"Thank you."

The man only grunted a response as he moved back to his wall. He didn't sit, just leaned against it with his arms crossed. Probably wanted to be ready when his chief arrived.

Evan should be ready, also. What all should he tell the man? Only what he'd overheard? Durand would probably want to know what existed between Evan and his daughter. He'd been watching closely enough when they were gathered around the fireplace. He must have seen something.

So how much should Evan say about his feelings toward Brielle? And his mission? He'd wanted to tell *her* everything first, then make plans with her about when and how his purpose should be communicated to her father and the others. But if Durand pressed, should he tell him first?

Perhaps revealing his intentions toward Brielle — and likely his mission in the process — was the right thing to do here. Coming clean would draw at least a little respect in the man's eyes. Either that or he'd haul him out to the nearest tree and string him up beside Gerald, so he didn't bring an army of miners to destroy their city.

Lord, show me. He would have to follow the Lord's nudges as the conversation progressed. Wasn't there a verse in one of the Gospels where Jesus said not to plan ahead what one should say when being questioned? In that hour, the Holy Spirit would give the words.

Give me the words, Lord.

Evan's body itched to move, to stand and pace. Or better yet, to go find the man himself. But he'd better settle in and find some patience, for it could be a while before Jean-Jacques even found the chief, much less the time it would take for the man to answer the summons.

But it must have only been minutes after that when the sound of footsteps drew near in the hallway. The bar clanged, and the door opened.

Chief Durand stepped inside. Even without someone accompanying him, the man's presence seemed to fill the room. Maybe that was only the importance Evan had assigned him in his mind. This man had the power to make things very hard between him and Brielle . . . or smooth the way completely.

Lord, give me the words.

Durand looked from the guard to Evan, then back to the guard. "I'd like to talk with him alone."

Leonard's chin jerked up, but then he nodded and stepped toward the door. "Yes, sir."

When the door shut behind him, Durand turned to Evan.

From his position sitting on the fur, the older man towered over him. A feeling he hated. Maybe the fellow wouldn't mind if they found some even ground for the coming conversation. "May I stand, sir?"

The man looked around the area, then moved to the wall nearest Evan, opposite from the spot where the guards usually parked themselves. "Actually, I'd like to sit."

As Durand eased down to settle on the hard floor, his age showed itself in his grunt and the creaking of limbs.

He seemed to be settling himself for a long conversation. A new knot twisted in Evan's middle. He had a feeling he wouldn't get out of this without telling all.

When he was settled with his knees bent in front of him, wrists propped up on both knees, Durand focused on Evan with a thoughtful gaze. "I was coming to speak with you anyway when I received the message you wanted an audience." He nodded at Evan. "You may speak first."

Coming to inquire about his intentions toward Brielle, no doubt. Evan pushed that thought away, lest it tie him up in tighter knots. For now, they had a more important threat to discuss.

He leveled the man with a serious look. "When we left your quarters, the other men were just returning. Leonard wanted to stop there and make sure his brother-in-law was well. He had me sit against the wall near the fire, and there were many other people around." It was important he lay the scene clearly in the man's mind or he might disbelieve what Evan had to tell him.

As Evan recounted what he'd overheard from Gerald, Durand's breathing grew heavier the longer Evan spoke — his only visible reaction. But the air hung thick with enough anger and pent-up emotion; the place might explode if one of them didn't tamp it down.

After Evan stopped speaking, Durand asked, "Is there any more?"

Evan replayed those minutes in his mind, trying to summon anything else that had been said. Maybe he had a few of the men's comments out of order, but he'd given all the details he'd heard.

He shook his head. "My first instinct was to tell Brielle, but I thought you might know better how to stop him. Permanently."

Durand blinked, the only shift in his expression. "I will take care of it."

Evan held his breath for a moment as he tried to find the words for this next part. "I want to help. Brielle's safety is important to me."

Now he'd exposed the next thing they had to speak of. He should let Durand get his own questions off his chest.

The man's gaze shifted, his eyes losing some of their anger as he considered Evan. Long moments passed. Painful moments, but Evan didn't drop his gaze from Durand's.

At long last, the man spoke. "I need to

know more about you before I can give my daughter the blessing she seeks."

Evan let the full meaning of that statement soak through him. Brielle had asked her father to bless a courtship between them? Or maybe to speak on his behalf in front of the council?

But the older man knew there would be more. In truth, the look in his eye said this conversation would determine whether he approved anything — including allowing Evan to take part in protecting Brielle . . . or not.

Give me the right words, Lord.

And with that prayer, he started from the beginning. "I was born in Scotland. When my parents and brother died, I moved to America. I had little money, and the only jobs I could find were small or temporary. So, I enlisted in the United States Army. I worked my way up to captain, and eventually married a woman in the town where I had settled. A marriage of convenience for both of us. She'd lost her family and needed a home, I wanted to settle down, and she was a God-fearing woman of good reputation. Not long after that, the war with Britain started, and I was recruited by the army office to work as a spy." Evan did his best to keep his voice level with that last word, even though Durand's gaze sharpened on him.

"I was sent on various missions to infiltrate British camps and forts. My Scottish accent helped me pretend I was from Europe. While I was gone on one of those assignments, my wife took ill from a sickness she contracted in one of the war hospitals where she volunteered. When I came home on my next leave, I found that she had passed away." Once again, he had to work to stabilize his voice.

"I mourned her death, and I mourned the fact she was alone at the end. I never should have put her in that situation."

He inhaled a breath to steady himself. As difficult as this part had been to tell, the conversation would only become harder.

27

Evan met Durand's gaze and refocused on the next facts. "I had already been assigned to my next mission, which was to go north into Upper Canada and infiltrate a fort there. The place was supposedly occupied by British soldiers and Indians who sided with the British. I was to help bring a wagon of explosives into the fort.

"Then, after I escaped, the wagoner would set off the explosive and get out, too. Everything had to move so quickly, so I ignored my inner warning about a few women and children I saw in the place. But at the end, after the explosion when the people were trying to escape the thick fort walls, the cries of the women and children were unmistakable. There must have been so many more than I thought. I still hear their screams." It was impossible to keep the emotion from his voice.

"I came back to my commander's office

to resign my post. He wouldn't accept my separation from the army and instead offered a mission to scout land in the west. Just to sketch the landmarks for a fort they wanted to build. That sounded harmless enough, and it was. After that journey was successful, he assigned me another mission to go northwest and search for a mineral they thought would be found in the icy mountains that weren't well-known."

Evan paused. "I need to be candid with you, sir. I've been sworn to secrecy, so me telling you all this is direct disobedience to my orders." At Durand's answering nod, Evan continued. "One early explorer who had returned from that land made notes about seeing a substance that was likely this mineral. Pitchblende is what it's called, and on its own it's perfectly harmless. But our chemists have learned it can be used to make a giant explosive compound, large enough to destroy an entire regiment in battle. None of our soldiers would need to die. A few blasts like that, and the British would know there was no way they could withstand. The war would end decisively, and America could keep its lands."

Durand studied him, the look in his eyes showing his mind was spinning with the news. Marking lines from one point to the next, comprehending the extent of Evan's mission. "And have you found this pitch-blende?"

Evan's throat closed up, making it hard to get out the words he had to. "I believe I have. I think I located it in the walls of your large meeting room. After the feast, I snuck out and cut some out, enough to bring back to the army's chemists. When they confirm it truly is the mineral they need, and that its explosive properties will create the blast they expect, they'll want to send miners to cut out as much of the mineral as they require."

The man's expression didn't change much while Evan spoke, but his skin grew paler. A new fear slipped in. Was Durand's heart strong enough to bear up under the weight of this burden?

Thank the Lord this was the extent of the bad news Evan had to impart.

Well . . . unless Durand considered Evan's intentions toward his daughter ill tidings. And he might.

Evan's mouth went dry as he worked for the right words. "Your daughter is a special woman. I didn't know there was anyone out there like her. I haven't spoken to her of this, so I don't know for sure if she would consider me. And I know it's too soon to say what I feel for her is love . . . but it sure does feel that way. If Brielle will have me, I want to return to the States and resign my commission. For good. Then come back here and make a life with her. With you all."

There. He'd said everything. His thoughts and plans and intentions — and even his heart — laid bare. This man had the power to crush them all. To crush his very life. The strength seeped from his limbs as he watched the man's reaction.

Durand still studied him, his thoughts impossible to decipher from his expression. When he spoke, the direction of his conversation didn't ease Evan's angst any. "And what of the mineral your government needs? When you take the pieces back to them, what will they do? You say they'll send miners. Will they destroy our mountain? Our homes? Will they take our land and kill our people? What will be left in Laurent for you to make a life in?" The man's voice held no anger — an admirable feat, for surely the thought of strangers tearing apart his home inspired at least a bit of fury. But his questions were spoken almost casually, as though he was asking what Evan planned to eat for his evening meal.

He swallowed hard at the lump in his throat. "I don't know. The army needs a

328

great deal of the pitchblende. And quickly. So I suspect they would send thirty or forty men. They would cut into the walls as far as necessary to gather what they need. They wouldn't take possession of your land, but I don't know how much they would have to cut away. I don't know what the condition of the homes would be in afterward. When the war is finished, my country may be willing to send people back to help rebuild your homes."

A paltry offering. And he couldn't be sure of even that.

He could only control his own actions. "I'll do everything I can to help put things back together quickly. But one thing I can promise — I'll give my last breath to help bring Laurent back to its former glory." He tried to summon a bit of humor to lighten the weight of the topic. "If there are any changes you've been wanting to make, this would be a good opportunity to carry them out. Perhaps we can incorporate more cookstoves or other modern inventions that might make your lives easier."

The moment the words slipped out, he wanted to pull them back. He certainly wouldn't gain the man's favor by implying that changes were needed in his home or the village for which he was responsible.

Durand sat for another long moment, his eyes glistening with a sadness impossible to miss. Evan tried to prepare himself for the worst.

In truth, there was no good response the man could offer. Evan had asked for his daughter's hand, or at least the chance to ask Brielle. But just before that, he'd told the man he'd been tasked with a mission that would destroy their home and the village they'd invested lifetimes into building and protecting. It was a wonder the man hadn't slapped him in the face or called for a guard to prepare a noose for him.

At last, Durand spoke, and Evan's lungs seized from the moment the man's mouth opened. "If the council votes favorably toward you, then I give you leave to speak with Brielle as you requested. My daughter is wise. She'll make her own way, and I trust her judgment. But if they send you away, that is also my answer regarding my daughter."

Was that a positive answer? At least the man hadn't spoken a vehement no. The tension in the air snaked around Evan's neck and squeezed as he waited for Durand's verdict on the other matter.

"My mind is split about how to respond to your other news. If this pitchblende truly has the ability to end a war and stop so much killing, as you say, how can we keep it to ourselves? I fear, however, the matter is not so easily solved. Is my people's comfort and safety worth allowing such destruction into our homes? And yet, if I say no, how are we to stop such a large nation from taking what they want anyway?"

As the man paused, the gap in his reasoning sprang to the forefront in Evan's mind. They need only kill Evan to stop America from learning that the pitchblende could be found in Laurent's walls. That would protect Laurent and keep its walls intact. Was he not considering this an option any longer?

Durand spoke again. "In truth, it's not wholly my decision. I must bring it before the council." The man's brows formed a V as his expression turned even more troubled. "I will tell them I'm extending my protection to you. That I believe you are a man of honor and will do everything in your power not to hurt our people or our homes. But that is all I can do. The others must make their own decisions."

A wash of emotion flooded through Evan, stealing the strength from his limbs. Yet he wasn't quite sure if the emotion was relief . . . or fear.

A tingle passed over Brielle's body as she straightened her braid and glanced around their quarters. Did she need anything else? What would the council ask of her? And why would they call a sudden meeting on such a busy day as this? The storm had barely subsided outside, yet Andre had woken her from her nap with an urgent summons from Papa and the council.

Perhaps there was damage to some of the homes or the common areas. But why would they want her? She was in charge of the guards, which meant anything that fell under the umbrella of protection or hunting. Maybe part of the outer wall had fallen from the weight of snow? Unlikely.

No matter how she tried to reconcile this unplanned meeting, nothing made sense.

As she moved toward the door, a slight footstep sounded in the hallway, then a tap on the wood. "Brielle?" Audrey's voice was muffled by the barrier.

Brielle closed the final step and pulled open the door. "Yes?"

Audrey raised her brows. "Hello to you, too. I came to check on you. Going somewhere?"

Brielle breathed out the tension in her shoulders and pulled the door wider for Audrey to step in. "My father sent for me. Andre said the council called an emergency meeting."

"About Evan?" Audrey was eyeing her, head tipped and brows lowered.

Brielle shook her head. Her chest locked so tight she could barely breathe. "I don't know. Did something happen while I slept?"

"Not that I've heard." Audrey's gaze grew stronger. "What's going on between the two of you, Brielle? You've not told me a thing, but I'm certainly not blind." A smile softened her words.

Brielle was powerless to stop her own grin, the one that rose every time she thought of the man who'd stolen her heart. Whose kiss still made her mouth tingle. "I . . ." How much should she tell?

Nothing right now. The council waited.

She gripped Audrey's shoulder as she moved toward the doorway. "There is something, but I'll have to tell you more later. Andre said Papa's request was urgent."

Audrey's huff followed her out the door as Brielle turned toward the community room.

When she reached the set of tall doors, she pulled one open and slipped inside the large chamber, then paused to let her eyes adjust. The council members sat in their usual cluster near the front. They only met in this room when the weather didn't allow meetings outside, but that seemed to be half the time. Papa and Erik stood at the front of the group, and he motioned her forward. Had they been waiting for her?

Apprehension knotted in her belly as she approached, but she kept her chin high and her shoulders back. People didn't like to see worry in the one they looked to for protection.

She stopped several paces away from her father and waited for him to speak.

He leveled her with a serious look. "Brielle, a situation has been brought to our attention that must be dealt with quickly. It seems Marcellus's trek into the blizzard might have been intended for his harm and yours. There's also been a threat —" his tiny pause made her chest tighten — "to your well-being. And on the life of Evan Mac-Manus."

The words swam in her mind, not finding solid footing until her father spoke Evan's full name. Then their full meaning slammed into her with savage force.

Questions spun, but she forced her mouth to stay shut. Her father would tell all if she gave him the chance.

"Gerald Arsenault was overheard telling another man that he plans to kill Evan tonight while his guard is sleeping. During the ensuing chaos, he stated he would kidnap you and take you away. He intends to assault you and alluded to killing you later." Father's voice tightened the more he spoke, though it was clear he was trying to keep his words steady. He was doing a better job than she would have managed in his place.

Gerald clearly hadn't learned his lesson from his last punishment. The fiend. How could anyone in Laurent be so malicious? She'd not thought highly of the man, but how had she missed this rebellious streak? This vengeful nature? How long had his hatred been simmering?

Memories flooded through her of his training and all the other times she'd worked with him. She'd been the one to test his skills when he joined on as one of the guards. Had she done something to incite his anger? Or was it merely the fact she was a woman doing a role that typically belonged to a man? She had to push away that line of thought and focus on what should be done with the blackguard.

Her father was speaking again, so she

forced her attention on his words.

". . . be dealt with swiftly. Today. Before he carries out his plot or makes a change we don't anticipate. Do you agree? Or do you feel it's better to assume he'll carry out his intentions as they were overheard, and we should set a trap for him in the storage room tonight?"

Her mind swirled through both options. How likely was it Gerald would change his plans? "Who overheard him speaking? And who was the other man he told this scheme to?" Gerald tended to boast readily, but even *he* had to know such a plot would be swiftly stopped. And punished.

He was a fool to speak it to anyone. Who would he trust so much? Was there a man in Laurent who Gerald thought would keep that kind of secret? She mentally scanned the faces of each male in the village. A few she didn't know well, mostly the youngest men who had just come of age and hadn't yet sought positions as guards and hunters. But she couldn't think of a single person who would go along with such a plan.

"Evan is the one who overheard him. He and Leonard stopped in the Duluth residence when Leonard's brother returned. There were many people in the room, so Gerald must not have seen Evan sitting against the wall. Evan couldn't see the man Gerald was speaking to, but he heard all of what Gerald said."

Father's gaze sharpened as he continued. "I see no reason why Evan would lie about this. I had recently begun to question Gerald's character, even before he spoke such foul words about Audrey. I've long known he wanted to increase his standing among the guards, that he felt he should have been their leader instead of you. Had I thought his opinions were so strongly against Laurent and the safety of our people, I would have taken action before now. But I do believe Gerald is capable of carrying out what he spoke of."

Father paused, but his lips parted as though he wanted to say something more. "Of course, he frequently spouts bluster, so it's possible that's all he meant by this. But even so, the Scripture states, out of the abundance of the heart, the mouth speaketh. We cannot allow such a man free rein in our village. He's already tainting others with his foul heart."

Her heart had caught on Evan's name as her father spoke, but she didn't allow herself to linger there. She couldn't think about what Evan might have felt when he heard this plan.

And though her mind understood why he hadn't brought the news to her — she'd been sleeping, after all — she couldn't help but be hurt.

28

Brielle strained to refocus on the important details as she stood before her father and the council. They had to make a plan, but to do that, she must know all the people involved. "Any thoughts on who the other man is?"

"Evan said Gerald spoke French, but the second man was standing behind the bed-curtain and his voice was too muffled to understand. That makes me wonder if it might have been Hugo Lemaire."

The lad's face sprang to mind, and she could hear his lazy drawl in her ear. She didn't think of Hugo as a man yet. He fell into the group of boys who had just reached the age of majority. His father had been killed in the same attack that took her mother, and his mama had kept to herself through the years. She performed her duties around the village just like the other matrons, but Brielle hadn't had much interaction with her son. He did mumble when he spoke, and from her limited experience with the boy, his approach to life was as lazy as his manner of speech. He tended to take the easiest route to do the least required of him.

Perhaps Gerald had fed the lad his poisonous opinions, and the young man had grabbed onto the attention. Without a strong male presence in his life to teach him the right ways, he might be easily swayed.

She gave a slow nod. "He is a possibility. We would need to question him, but it seems wise to take him and Gerald into custody at the same time." She scanned through the timeline of Gerald's plan once more. His words might only be boasts if he was speaking to Hugo, but if he chose to go through with his plans, he might easily decide to shift timelines. Whether he took action or not, he had to be stopped before his poison leaked further.

She focused her attention on her father and Erik. "I agree we should act before tonight. And neither man must know we're taking the other into custody. Which means we should either take them both at the same time, or one while the other is occupied."

Relief slipped through her father's gaze, and behind him, Erik nodded. She scanned the rest of the group as her mind whirled with possible plans to take the men captive. They needed to have everything lined up perfectly for any of them to succeed.

And they had almost no time to make it happen.

Evan couldn't stop pacing.

Thankfully, Leonard didn't comment on the fact that he'd left his fur pallet. The man just leaned against the wall. Watching. His expression looked half amused, half concerned.

But he wasn't the one worrying Evan. What would the council say about him? Would they act quickly to stop Gerald?

Unless they didn't believe him.

His gut churned as he sent up another petition in a long line of prayers. *Give them wisdom, Lord. Give me wisdom. Help us take the right actions.*

The bar on the door clanged, and he spun to see who was entering. He'd not even heard footsteps in the hall.

Brielle stepped inside, and from the stern expression on her face, she must know something.

Her gaze met his, then she swung her focus to Leonard. "I must speak with you both."

She pulled her hand from her side, and he nearly gasped at the sight of his musket, shot bag, and knives. She set them on the floor by the door, then motioned him and Leonard near as she closed the door behind her.

Apprehension swelled his chest, tightening his breathing. Her father must have told her some of what they'd said. Only the part that concerned Gerald? Or also of his intention to speak to Brielle? Probably about his mission, too.

A pain speared his midsection. He'd wanted to tell her those details himself. In truth, he'd wanted her to be the first to know everything — except maybe Gerald's plan. But it looked like the entire situation was out of his hands now.

I give it to you, Lord. As much as he hated this helpless feeling, God could guide the situation so much better than he could.

In a few short minutes, Brielle shared with Leonard the details of what Evan had overheard. Then she proceeded to tell them both of a plan that sounded riskier than he would have liked. In fact, Brielle seemed to be taking on the greatest risk herself. But she was including Evan as one of the helpers. And for that, a surge of anticipation washed through him.

"You can take your weapons." She motioned toward his gun and knives as she met his gaze. "My father spoke to the council on your behalf, and they moved the vote up to today." Something flickered in her eyes, but it passed so quickly he couldn't decipher it. "They've voted to release you from guard but ask you not to leave Laurent yet."

He straightened. They'd moved up the vote? Maybe this had been a natural result of determining whether he was trustworthy enough for his report about Gerald to be believed. And the vote may have been necessary to free him to help capture Gerald, too.

A wash of relief swept through him. *Thank you, Lord.* He'd not even known to worry while the vote was taking place. God had gone before and prepared the way for his freedom. *Guide us now in this mission, Father.*

Leonard's voice drew him from his prayer. "So, you want me and Wesley to be waiting in the assembly room? Who will you send to summon Hugo?" He didn't seem surprised by Evan's freedom, just focused on the job before them. Good man.

Brielle nodded as she turned to Leonard. "Andre can deliver the summons to him. People are accustomed to him taking messages for my father. He can say that all the men of age and hunting ability are being asked to come. That might even make him eager to be numbered among the men. Evan and I will station ourselves in the shadows of the cave to make sure he doesn't bolt before you and Wesley can tie him."

Evan nodded agreement for his part of the plan. He didn't even know what this young ruffian looked like, but he'd learn quickly enough. It felt good to be numbered among Laurent's protectors.

Within minutes, Leonard was off to gather his weapons and the man who would serve with him. Brielle motioned for Evan to follow her down the corridor. He grabbed his things by the door, then followed her out. They moved softly until they entered the chamber belonging to Brielle's family.

Inside, Andre ran to meet them, full of questions for his elder sister. By the fire, Chief Durand and another man who looked familiar stopped their conversation to watch their entry. A glance around the room showed that Charlotte, Brielle's sister, was the only other person inside.

Brielle motioned for her brother to be quiet. "I have an important task for you. I need you to deliver a summons to Hugo Lemaire. Tell him it's very important." She relayed the message about the hunters

344

gathering. "Say it exactly like that, do you understand?"

Andre tipped his head. "Should I take that same message to Gerald?" The lad must have heard his father speaking of what was happening. Hopefully no one else had overheard.

Brielle speared her brother with her gaze. "No. He is out on a hunt. Speak of this to no one else."

Andre sobered. "Oui."

Brielle patted his shoulder. "Quickly."

As her brother sprinted from the room, Brielle moved into action, striding to a side wall and gathering up her bow and quiver full of arrows. "Charlotte, I need you to use a bit of stealth and find Philip. Tell him to come to our chamber posthaste. Have him wait here until I return to explain what I need him for. He might be sleeping from his night shift but tell him it's important."

He hated standing like a sluggard while Brielle moved from one side of the apartment to the other, gathering weapons and giving instructions. But if he stepped forward, he'd only be in her way.

Instead, he lifted his gaze to Chief Durand and met the man's eyes. Brielle's father gave a firm nod, which Evan could only hope meant all was in order and progressing as it should. Too bad he couldn't pull the fellow aside and ask how much Brielle knew.

No matter. He'd ask Brielle that question when Gerald was safely locked away. Brielle had said he would need to be tried by the council to determine his fate.

At last, Brielle spun and marched toward him and the doorway he was blocking. He reached for the handle and prepared to step aside but didn't open the door yet.

When she stopped beside him, he murmured, "Where do you plan for us to watch from?"

He had no doubt she had places in mind. Better he know her intentions before they stepped out so he could be a help, not bumble loudly in the darkness.

"I'll blow out the torch across from our door. Then we can tuck inside each of these last two doorways. There will be enough darkness Hugo shouldn't spot us unless we make noise." She was near enough he could hear her exhale when she finished speaking, and his body longed to close the tiny gap between them and wrap his arm around her. But this wasn't the time, nor the audience to take such an action in front of. Later, Lord willing.

Brielle stepped into the hallway first, a

346

good thing, for someone down the corridor greeted her. Audrey, from the sound of the voice. But he couldn't quite make out the words, muffled as they were, and probably in French.

Brielle responded with a pleasantry also in French, then a few seconds later she opened the door wider and motioned him out.

While he eased the handle shut behind him, she stepped across the hallway and snuffed out the torch. Only their immediate area fell into murky darkness. Two doors down, another torch flickered brightly. The lights seemed to be stationed every two doors. Most people would think the light had simply gone out from the torch burning low, or maybe blown out by a soft breeze. There was certainly enough wind outside that a draft could've come in when someone opened the outer door.

In the opposite direction, a torch was mounted at the corner where the short hallway to the exterior door split off to the left. Hugo would come in that door from outside, then turn left at the crossroads, moving away from them on his way to the assembly room.

Brielle motioned for him to stay tucked into her family's doorframe, and she moved down to the one closest to the corner.

Of course she would put herself at the most risk.

He tightened his grip on his gun and made sure his knife was positioned for easy access. No telling which one he would need if he and Brielle had to step in and halt Hugo's escape. Aiming the gun at the man should stop him quickly, as long as there was enough light for the youngster to see the weapon.

He worked hard to school his breathing as they waited in silence. His heartbeat pounded in his ears, and he could only pray his breaths didn't sound as loud to anyone else as they did to him. For her part, Brielle was so silent he would have never known she was there.

Only a few minutes passed before the scrape of wood and rush of wind signaled the outer door being opened.

He froze, straining to hear every sound. A voice murmured from that direction, then a shuffling footstep echoed down the hall.

As the sounds drew closer, he could make out two sets of footsteps. The shuffle might belong to Hugo, and the crisper tread sounded like Andre's.

He flicked his gaze to the place where Brielle was hiding. He couldn't even make out her outline in the darkness. Had she realized her brother would accompany the man? Did she worry he would be caught in whatever ruckus ensued? Even with four armed guards — counting himself — they couldn't know for sure Andre would be safe.

He gripped his gun tighter. He would have to make sure nothing happened, both for Andre's safety and for Brielle's.

Soon enough, two figures came into view. For about two seconds, he could see both outlines before they turned the opposite corner and faded into darkness again. Hugo was only a head taller than twelve-year-old Andre, and not much stouter. Surely the barely grown man couldn't put up much of a fight.

Down the hallway, Andre's voice drifted to them as he told Hugo in French that everyone else was likely already in the assembly room.

The swishing sound must be the door opening, then closing.

Evan prepared his body to sprint forward but held every part of himself still so he could hear the first sounds of alarm.

Andre's footsteps coming toward them were the only sound through the corridor. "I think he believed me, Brielle." The lad's whisper could probably be heard all the way down to the storage room, and Evan had to fight both a cringe and a chuckle.

Brielle's silhouette appeared against the light filtering around the corner as she stepped from her hiding place.

Evan did the same.

"Go to our chamber. Wait there." Brielle's voice barely carried loud enough for Evan to hear, especially since she was already striding toward her brother and the assembly room.

Evan pushed forward to catch up to her but had to step out of Andre's way so the lad didn't run into him in the dark.

Outside the double doors, Brielle pressed her ear to the crack between them. Evan held his breath so she could hear better.

The murmur of deep voices drifted from inside, but not loud enough to make out distinct sounds.

Brielle whispered, "It doesn't sound like he's struggling."

A thread of relief stole over Evan. Maybe they could take both men into custody without trouble. Then he would only need to ensure Gerald's punishment would stop him from ever being a threat to Brielle again. That might be harder to accomplish than the capture.

Brielle pulled open the door and slipped

inside before Evan could request to go first.

So, he followed her. Just following this woman kept him on his toes.

Leonard and Wesley had Hugo lying facedown on the floor, with one man on either side of him. It looked like Wesley was tying Hugo's wrists.

Leonard stood as Brielle approached. "He's ready to go to the holding room."

"He gave you no trouble?" Brielle spoke English, but in a low voice.

"I've done nothing wrong." With his cheek pressed against the stone floor, Hugo's lazy French was a challenge to decipher.

"That will be up to the council to determine." Brielle's French was much crisper. She stepped back and motioned for the men to lift Hugo and lead him toward the door.

As the group passed by Evan, Hugo shot him a curious gaze. "What's he doing out?"

No one answered, and they moved into the hallway. Evan fell into step beside Brielle as they followed the prisoner and the other two guards. Thankfully, no one else entered the corridor during the walk to the cell at the far end. The fewer people who knew what was happening, the better.

29

Evan stayed out of the way while the two men secured Hugo on the fur pallet, binding his legs at the ankles, then tying the straps at his wrists and feet together. Evan didn't envy the man who would be tasked with guarding this mouthy lad. The more they trussed Hugo, the louder he denied his guilt.

No one wasted their breath to argue with him. Hugo may be guilty of nothing more than letting a fiend drip poison into his ear, but that would be up to the council to determine.

When they were done, Brielle motioned for Wesley to stay and guard Hugo, then waved Evan and Leonard with her as they left the room. She didn't speak again until they reached the Durand chambers, where Philip paced by the fire.

He spun to face them as they entered. The room held no sign of Brielle's father or anyone else. Had the senior Durand taken his younger children away to allow them privacy to plan?

Brielle motioned the three of them around her and quickly brought Philip up to speed on Evan's release and Hugo's capture. She skimmed over the reason why Hugo and Gerald needed to be apprehended. "Now it's time to ready things to take in Gerald. He's out hunting now, and one of the elders is watching for his return. He's not expected until dusk, but he may come back early to ready things for his plot tonight."

Packing for his escape, no doubt.

Brielle's gaze shifted between them as she spoke, but it seemed to hover on him more than either of the others. As much as he tried to push aside his feelings and focus on the work at hand, he was having trouble making his body obey.

"There are several ways we could take him into custody, but I'd like a vote. It's critical we're all of the same mind for this to succeed." She looked at each of them in turn. "We could have a lookout posted outside the gate or in the gatehouse to alert us when he's coming. Then the four of us can take him there at the gate." She narrowed her gaze as she spoke. "Or we could wait in his chamber and capture him there."

That sounded like the safer option of the two, giving Gerald less of a chance to escape. If he made it out of his chamber, he'd still have to flee to the outer walls to be free. Not likely he could accomplish that with the four of them giving chase and others watching. But if Gerald did get away, could he survive out in the cold on his own? He would have his hunting gear and winter clothing, so he might manage it.

But they wouldn't let him get away. Evan would have his gun and could stop the man with a well-placed bullet. Not that he relished shooting anyone, but he would do what he had to for Brielle's safety.

"A third option would be to wait for his return and have him summoned, as we did with Hugo." Brielle's mouth settled into a firm line as she waited for input. He couldn't read in her manner whether she preferred any of the suggestions over another.

"Do you think Gerald is likely to obey a summons? Or will he be suspicious?" Evan asked. From what he'd seen of the man, Gerald seemed the suspicious type, especially if he was in the middle of carrying out a traitorous plot.

Brielle raised her brows. "I suspect he'd try to avoid it, even if the command came from the council. He'd have little reason to pacify our leadership."

Just as Evan had thought. It felt good to be of the same mind as her.

"Your second plan seems like the best way to ensure he doesn't escape." Maybe Evan should give one of the others the chance to offer an opinion, but neither man seemed eager to speak up. He turned to them. "Do you think it likely someone else could be injured if we took him captive in his chamber?"

Philip still seemed to be absorbing the entire situation, but Leonard drew his brows low. "Gerald lives in the smaller homes, where some of the unmarried men reside. I doubt any of them would get in the way. There's a slight chance he would try to sway some of them to help him. I can't imagine any would, once they saw he was resisting arrest. Most people see through Gerald's bluster."

Evan nodded. Leonard spoke like he knew the young men, possibly better than Brielle, which made sense. "So, there's a good chance of success with that plan?"

Leonard's nod came slowly. "That seems the best approach to me."

Brielle turned to Philip. "What say you?" The man gave a single nod. "I agree. The whole situation is unfortunate, but I think that's the best way to do what has to be done."

Brielle cast her gaze around the group. "We're agreed? Any opposed?"

After receiving an affirming nod from each of them, Brielle laid out the specifics that she must have already plotted in her mind. He couldn't help but admire her leadership skills. No wonder these men submitted to her authority so well. She gave each person a voice, even when she probably had already planned every detail. Her methods had likely been successful in the past, or they wouldn't agree as easily as they did now.

When they'd discussed everything Evan could imagine needing to know, Brielle stood and moved to the door, then peered through a slot. "Dusk will be on us soon. We should take our places."

Brielle was glad she'd assigned Evan to wait with her inside Gerald's apartment. A few quiet moments to talk were certainly in order.

Yet they couldn't do more than whisper, for they had to make sure Gerald didn't hear anything until he entered the room. Philip was hidden outside, and Leonard in the chamber next door where he could watch for Gerald through a crack in that room's door, then signal the man's approach.

It would be up to her and Evan to capture Gerald while surprise still gave them the upper hand. Philip and Leonard would come behind as reinforcements, if needed.

She glanced at Evan, who stood on the other side of the entry door. He met her gaze, his eyes searching. The room was too dim to see if he found what he was looking for on her face.

She wanted to ask why he hadn't come to her when he first overheard Gerald's plot, but such a question shouldn't be whispered across the space of the doorway. She needed the full volume of her voice to make her feelings clear on the topic. She wanted to see the truth in his eyes.

Yet she couldn't let him see her hurt. He hadn't trusted her with the truth, but she had to put this behind her. Or at least make sure she could keep her thoughts hidden. Hurt feelings didn't belong in the mind of a warrior, especially not when she needed all her senses and instincts for the mission at hand.

She pulled her gaze from Evan, casting her focus around the small room. Gerald's housekeeping skills were worse than she'd expected, with bits of clothing and weaponry scattered across the floor. The walls contained a host of nails that were likely intended for organization, but not one of them was being used as such.

Her little brother had left his garments and toys in haphazard piles like this in his younger years, but he'd finally started listening to her and Charlotte's nagging. Now, he did a better job of hanging things up. It seemed Gerald's habits had suffered from his lack of older sisters.

"Can we talk?" Evan's voice drew her focus back to him. "After this is over?"

Yes. They desperately needed to talk. She had to know what he was thinking. Wanted to hear in his own words that he'd kept the secret from her for her good, and not because he didn't trust her. Wanted to know there was nothing else he was hiding from her.

She worked hard to keep the desperate yearning from showing on her face as she nodded. "Yes."

He returned the nod, and his Adam's apple bobbed like he was preparing to say more. His mouth parted, but he didn't speak. Did his heart ache as much as hers did?

A cough sounded from the chamber beside them, then another. Philip's signal.

She crouched against the wall, knife poised. While keeping her gaze honed on the crack between the door and frame, the edge of her vision registered Evan with his gun at the ready. Hopefully he wouldn't have to use that weapon, but it would stop Gerald if nothing else did.

The latch string raised the bar on the door, and the crack widened to reveal a sliver of dusky light.

Gerald's body stepped in to block most of the light as he pushed the door open.

His gaze locked on her before he'd placed more than a single foot inside, and he reacted instantly, even before his face registered surprise.

He stepped backward, pulling the door with him, but she grabbed the wood before he could slam it shut.

A shout came from outside. Leonard's voice.

Gerald reversed directions, pushing the door open with the force of his shoulder. She released the wood and raised her blade high. "*Arrêtez!* Halt! You're under arrest."

Gerald didn't stop, just plunged into the room, ducking away from her blade. She gathered herself, preparing to fling the blade into the fleshy part of his arm.

In the split second she took aim, her gaze registered Evan standing right behind Gerald. The possibility that she might hit him froze her.

She focused her aim tighter. The shift took only half a heartbeat, but it was enough.

Gerald swung around with speed she wouldn't have credited him with. He reached a beefy arm around her neck, positioning himself behind her, and gripped her knife with his other hand.

Her instincts took over and she stomped hard on the inside of the man's foot, then plunged a fist upward to strike his nose.

Men's yells sounded around them, but her world narrowed to only the man whose thick muscle was cutting off all breath. He was so big, and he had her arms pinned so she couldn't get a good angle on his face. She tried to use her elbows in his side or gut, but he had her strapped too tightly to his body. With her moccasined feet, she didn't seem to be causing any pain to his knees or feet. Probably the thicker leggings he'd worn on the hunt gave too much protection.

With his greater strength, he jerked the knife from her hand and strapped both arms to her side. Then the sharp cold of a perfectly honed blade pressed into her neck.

Lord! Brielle froze as the pain registered in her mind. The man's arm no longer locked off her breathing, but her lungs still wouldn't expand as fear held them constricted. This couldn't be the end. Not after everything she'd already been through.

She scanned for the others, and relief eased her body at a glimpse of Evan with his gun aimed at Gerald. The dark hole of the barrel peered at her too, but she didn't let herself linger in the fear. Evan's aim was likely good enough that he could hit Gerald instead of her at such close range.

Through the open doorway, Philip and Leonard stood frozen, Philip with his knife raised, and Leonard's hatchet poised to strike.

She soaked in a bit of renewed bravery but had to be careful not to draw much breath, or Gerald would slice her neck without even trying. "You're outnumbered, Gerald. Let me go. There's no use fighting more."

His humorless chuckle vibrated through her back, and his breath burned her ear. "But I have captured the queen, and that makes me greater than all of you."

The pompous cad. "Slice my neck open if you want, but these three will still arrest you. And you'll hang for sure, then."

"For killing the chief's daughter? Of that you're right. But I have a feeling these men would do almost anything to save your pretty little head . . . and the rest of you." His thumb caressed a line down her side, pressing parts no man had touched. The motion probably wasn't visible to any of the others, but she had to work hard to hold in a shudder.

"The only way to save your life is to let her go." Evan's voice rang strong.

"You think I'm a fool? You're the fool, you foreigner. There's not a doubt in my mind that her papa will string me up now that I've taken arms against Laurent's favorite." Another huff of hot air blew across her ear, and the pressure at her neck tightened, burning the skin there. A drip of something slid down her neck, itching as it went. She had to bite her lip to keep from jerking with the sensation.

"The only way I'll go free is if the three of you escort me to the gate yourselves. And I'll be taking the wench with me to make sure you don't follow after me. If you're lucky, I'll let her go in a day or two."

She caught the flare of Evan's eyes, but with her attention distracted by the increasing pain at her throat, she couldn't tell if it was fear or anger that drew his reaction.

Don't worry about me. She tried to send Evan the message with her eyes, but his attention was split also, shifting between the knife at her neck and a spot above her head. Gerald's face, no doubt.

She had to get away. If Evan did something foolish in an effort to save her, they might lose Gerald completely. Or worse, someone else could be hurt.

"You all stay put while I get a few things, then we'll be off." Gerald tugged her backward, clamping even tighter around her chest as he hauled her back a step with him. "Don't even think of moving."

The knife pulled away from her neck as he reached for something behind him. She tried to suck in a deep breath, but the solid band around her chest wouldn't allow much air to pass.

Before she could form a plan to use this reprieve for escape, Gerald had grabbed whatever he needed and pressed the knife against her neck again. The man could move far quicker than she'd ever thought his bulk could muster. This time, the knife blade pressed farther to her left, even closer to an important artery. Her neck would look like a cutting board once they were through this.

If she made it through.

30

Gerald twisted Brielle to the side as he bent to pick up something from the ground, the knife once more leaving her throat for only the space of two breaths. If he did that again, she had to be ready to act.

She worked to keep her body from stiffening, both so he wouldn't suspect she was devising a plan and also so he didn't press the knife any harder into her neck.

He stepped backward once more, dragging her with him, and Brielle prepared to make her move.

Help me, Lord.

This time, Gerald didn't pull the knife away to use that hand. Instead, he twisted Brielle down so she was suspended an arm's length above the floor. Then he used the fingers on the hand wrapping her middle to reach for the item he needed.

Although his beefy arm still pressed against her belly, the looser hold of his hand let her pull her right arm free.

With the new freedom, she grabbed his wrist holding the knife at her throat and pulled her right foot up to kick as close to his groin as she could manage.

With Gerald bent down, her sudden actions threw him off balance, knocking him backward.

His arm tightened around her chest, but this time she had her right hand free and a firm grip on his wrist holding the knife.

He landed on his back, and the strength in his right arm tried to force the knife to her neck again. But she had desperation on her side, and the burning reminder of the damage that blade had already done.

She braced hard against his wrist, barely keeping the blade away from her. She wouldn't be able to hold off his greater strength much longer.

Yet, what he possessed in muscle, she could match in agility. With a hard thrust, she twisted her body within his hold so her front was facing him. Then she tucked her head low to duck out of the path of the knife.

As she twisted, she lost her hold on his knife arm, and her left arm was pinned between their two bodies. But she still had her right arm free and she was powered by a growing hatred for this man as she stared into his malicious gaze.

Suddenly, a body appeared from her left. A knife blade flashed, and the evil on Gerald's face twisted into pain as a hand plunged the blade into the man's shoulder. His arm around her loosened, and she scrambled backward, crawling on her hands and knees until she was free of him.

Evan stood over the fiend, and Leonard charged in the moment she cleared out.

"Philip, get my gun." With one hand holding Gerald down, Evan reached out to accept the weapon.

Philip scrambled for the musket, then handed it to Evan.

"Philip, you take my spot while I step back and aim this bullet at him. Then you and Leonard flip him over and tie him up." Evan's breaths were coming hard, and his hands shook a little as he exchanged places with Philip and pointed the gun at their prisoner.

For her part, Brielle was shaking, too. She needed to stand up and be helpful but had to grab the door handle to pull herself up to standing. Good thing the men were too occupied to see her unsteady legs.

She inhaled a deep, settling breath. *Thank you, Lord.* That could've gone so many other ways. Though she'd not let her thoughts dwell on the likely outcome, she'd known that could have been her final moments of life.

Life on this earth anyway. As much as she looked forward to eternity around God's throne, there was more here she wanted to do.

Her gaze honed on Evan. Much more.

As if he felt her focus, Evan looked back at her, his expression as raw as she'd ever seen it. "Are you hurt? Your throat's bleeding. Press something to it."

She shook her head, the skin of her neck pulling tight with the motion. But she wasn't gushing blood. And nothing seemed broken. "It's not bad." She forced her attention down to Gerald. He had to be their focus until he was fully secured in the storage room. Then, once she was in the safety of her home, she could let her quivering knees give out.

Her gaze slid back to Evan, who'd also returned his focus to Gerald. How good it would feel to be wrapped in his strong arms when she finally succumbed to this weakness. She should abhor a thought like that. Shouldn't want anyone to see her so fragile. Especially not this man she loved, the man she wanted so desperately to think well of her.

But even if he only loved her half as much as she did him, she needed to let him see every part of her. Even the vulnerable parts. Somehow, she didn't think Evan would think less of her for the weakness.

Evan's arms ached as he followed Gerald and the guards down the long corridor. Philip gripped the man's arm, while Leonard and Brielle walked a few steps behind them, weapons poised in case the man made a sudden move.

His own arms didn't strain from the weight of the gun in his hands, but from the intense desire to wrap them around Brielle. To touch her and feel for himself she was unharmed.

The image of her in that fiend's hold, the knife blade pressed to her neck, blood oozing down her smooth skin . . . he couldn't clear it from his mind.

He'd known the moment the look in her eyes changed that she was planning to resist. She'd found a course of action she thought would free her.

Everything inside him had wanted to scream for her to stop. Not do anything that might force the man's hand — literally —

and cause him to slice the blade deeper into her throat.

All Evan had been able to do was pray. Just like the last time Brielle's life had been in danger from the blizzard. In both situations, God had given him the sacred task to pray for the woman he loved.

The effectual fervent prayer of a righteous man availeth much.

And God had granted her safety both times. Only the Almighty could have knocked Gerald backward and loosened his hold enough for Brielle to twist in the man's arms.

The distraction had been enough.

With Brielle's head lowered, Gerald's full shoulder had been exposed. Evan hadn't wasted a heartbeat dropping his gun, raising his knife, and plunging the blade into the man's flesh.

It wasn't a mortal wound, but Gerald would be tender in that spot for weeks.

And now they'd finished. Accomplished their mission.

Once Gerald was safely tied in the cell anyway.

All praise, glory, and honor to you, Father.

At last, they had Gerald secured in the cell, on the opposite side of the room from Hugo. The young lad was shooting foul looks at Gerald, clearly disabused of any hero worship — or even a kind thought.

Philip and Leonard offered to stay with Wesley to watch the two prisoners. Perhaps Evan should have volunteered also, but Brielle was his priority now. Both for his own peace of mind, and hopefully to be of help to her. And maybe once all the reports had been given to her father and the council, the two of them could find a quiet place to talk.

When he and Brielle entered her home, Brielle's family waited with Audrey and her father, Martin.

Audrey gasped at the blood streaked across Brielle's neck, but Brielle motioned her away. "I'm not hurt. Just need water to wash it off."

Charlotte offered Brielle one of the seats by the fire, and Evan stood near the outskirts of the gathering as the woman he loved relayed the events for her father and the others.

Thankfully, Audrey found a bowl of water and a cloth, and used them to clean Brielle's neck while she talked.

Brielle gave her friend a long-suffering look as her tending got in Brielle's way a few times. Audrey's lips only curved as she kept her focus on her task.

For his part, Evan couldn't seem to pull his gaze from Brielle. When Audrey's efforts at her neck exposed bright red gashes, even though they were clearly surface wounds, his stomach twisted. The bile in his gut tried to infuse a fresh round of anger into his veins, but he forced his focus to lift to her face.

The battle was over. That blackguard was being held and would be tried for his actions. There was nothing Evan could do to change the past.

Brielle's features came alive as she told the tale, drawing his focus to her beauty. The intelligence in her wide eyes, the strong angle of her cheeks, the point of her chin, the sweeping curve of her lips. He needed another taste of those lips.

With effort, he pulled his gaze away from her to keep his blood from boiling for a very different reason this time.

At last, she finished the story, and her father eased out a long breath. His brows had dipped through most of the telling, no doubt from worry for his daughter. Though the man may be responsible for leading Laurent and trusted his daughter's ability for the protection of their community, he couldn't be immune to worry for his own child.

371

"The council plans to meet in the morning to discuss what should be done next. You've done well, Brielle." Then the man's gaze shifted to Evan. "You too."

A hard knot formed in Evan's throat. Something in the man's gaze felt fatherly. A look he'd not seen in many years. He'd almost forgotten what it was like for a man to look at him with pride in his eyes. "Thank you, sir." The words choked as he forced them out.

Durand's gaze hovered on him a moment longer, then shifted to Brielle, then back to Evan. "I suppose that's all we need to do for tonight. I'll call the council to meet in the morning to plan our next steps. You two might want to stretch your legs to settle from all the excitement."

Evan barely kept from raising his brows at the obvious opportunity for them to talk. Instead, he managed a nod. "Good idea."

A look at Brielle showed a bit of extra color in her cheeks. A sight that nearly made him chuckle. Maybe she wasn't as tough as she seemed.

But as they gathered furs and stepped out into the cold, he knew the thought was at the same time very wrong and very right. Brielle's strength, both inner and outer, was greater than any person he'd known. But she was vulnerable, too — how could anyone with her passion not be?

And he wanted to be there to protect her when necessary. He wanted to be the one to petition the Lord for everything she needed. Especially when her life was on the line.

Which brought up a point he had to get off his chest. He turned to her as they strolled through the courtyard in the general direction of the gate. "I've never prayed so much for one person as I have for you these past three days, Brielle. And while it's certainly brought me closer to the Lord, I prefer you not put yourself in mortal danger quite so often if you can help it."

She slid a sideways glance at him but kept walking. Her mouth formed a pert smile. "I'll see what I can do, but I make no promises."

Strolling along with the fur of her hood framing her beautiful face, sassy expression and all, Evan could barely keep himself from pulling her into his arms. That should wait until they were outside the gate, where there weren't so many prying eyes.

Maybe that was her thought as well, for she led him straight to the opening. Memory returned to him just before he stepped through, and he stopped.

Brielle turned to look at him, her brows

raised in question.

He nodded toward the gate. "I'm not supposed to leave Laurent, am I?" No matter how much he wanted time alone with Brielle, he wouldn't compromise the trust these people had placed in him.

She glanced at the stone wall beside her, then turned back to him with a twinkle. "Consider yourself under guard while we're outside of village walls." Then she reached for his hand.

His heart picked up speed as he placed his hand in hers and they stepped forward together.

Outside the wall, she turned to him again, the sass falling away from her expression. Every part of her seemed fragile, and when he opened his arms, she stepped into him. She seemed to sink into his hold, and he wrapped himself around her, cradling her. *Be her strength, Father. Renew her.*

She stayed in his arms for long minutes, and he breathed in her scent, relishing the solid feel of her.

Whole. Alive.

She fit perfectly in his arms, her height exactly right for her cheek to rest on his shoulder. Her breath warmed his neck, tempting him.

But that would come later. For now, hav-

ing Brielle in his arms was more than
enough.

31

Brielle had never imagined being held by a man would make her feel so secure. So renewed.

The Lord had brought her through more hazards than she cared to remember, both these last few days and in the past. He was her Sustainer, the One who completed her. And now He'd sent this man to fill the place she'd not even known was void.

She drew one more deep breath of Evan, then pulled back. She managed a smile for him, and the way he was looking at her made her heart beat faster. The earnestness in his gaze showed his concern for her, but the love in his eyes was what really stirred her insides.

She slid her hands up the front of his coat and cradled his cheeks. Even though the weather was much warmer than yesterday's blizzard, his cheeks still bore chilly pink circles, and his skin was cold to the touch.

They would both be warm in a minute.

He met her kiss with the same fire he had before, yet with a tenderness that nearly stole the strength from her legs. His arms wrapped around her waist, seeming to know she might need extra support.

They still had much to talk about, but she'd seen the strength of this man's character in all his actions for weeks now. If she had anything to say about it, she'd love to continue at his side for the rest of their days.

Far too soon, Evan eased back. But with one hand holding her close and the other brushing her jaw, he didn't let her go far. Instead, he rested his forehead on hers, warming her face with their mingled breaths. Soothing her soul with his nearness.

"I love you, Brielle. You've taken root in my heart. I didn't think it was possible that another person could be such a perfect match. Could make me so much better." He pulled back a little, enough to study her. His gaze turned troubled. "There's much I need to tell you."

He glanced around, then led her to a fallen tree. She almost smiled at the fact that this was the exact place where they'd tussled that first day, after she shot him with the arrow.

But the swirl of emotions churning inside kept her from speaking. She'd wanted him to tell all, but now that he was about to, what if he shared something she didn't want to hear?

He kicked snow off a log, then motioned for her to sit. After settling beside her, he took her hand in his, and the warmth of his touch seeped through their gloves. His gaze grew earnest. "You know some of this, but I'd better start at the beginning so I don't miss anything."

She prepared herself not to react to whatever he would say. But as he poured out the details of his life since coming to America, her heart ached for the troubled story.

He'd been seeking for so long, although maybe he didn't realize what he was trying to find. She couldn't help comparing his story to her own. He lost his family in Scotland and had been trying to re-create that belonging ever since. First in the army, then with his wife.

And then he'd given up.

She knew what it was to lose a parent — that heartrending pain. But she'd never lost her belonging, her family, her people. With everything in her, she wanted to pull Evan to her. To share her people with him. To give him the home and family he needed.

But as he told of the mission where he was assigned to find pitchblende, a new thread of fear wove through her.

She leaned closer, worry and frustration twisting inside her. "Why didn't you just tell us that was the reason you'd come?" So much could have been different between them. Her people would have been reasonable, surely. Maybe some of them had even seen the mineral he sought on nearby mountains.

Pain seemed to consume him. "I wanted to, but I'd promised my superiors I would keep the mission secret. They didn't want the British to learn of it. But by the time I realized you seemed to share the same . . . attraction that consumes me . . ." His eyes softened into a look so full of love it made her throat burn. "I decided I had to tell you everything. If you and your people agreed, I would leave Laurent and hurry through the rest of my mission, hopefully finding pitchblende farther north. Then get the mineral back to the States, resign my commission, and come back to you here."

Hearing his intentions to come back to her sent a warmth through her that raised gooseflesh on her arms. Yet the knot of dread only tightened in her belly. She pulled her hand back from his. "You said that was once your intention. What changed?"

Misery slipped over his features, coiling the knot in her belly tighter. "During the feast, I discovered what looked to be pitch-blende in the walls of the assembly room."

Her entire body gripped tight, and she couldn't draw breath. She could only sit now, immobile as he continued to speak.

"You have no idea how much I struggled, Brielle. I knew I had to tell you everything. You already owned my heart, and I couldn't keep this from you any longer. My struggle was whether I should find out for sure if what I saw was pitchblende or tell you first. I didn't want to make things harder on you without knowing for sure." His eyes pleaded with her to believe him, and the desperation in them could never have been feigned.

She'd believed in her heart she could trust him, but knowing and actually doing were a world apart. Especially when he'd been so secretive. If he planned to destroy her peoples' homes, how could she give her heart to him?

Evan let out a shaky breath. "I decided it was better not to worry you without know-ing for certain. So, that night while Philip was sleeping, I sneaked down to the as-sembly room and cut samples of the rock from the wall."

She jerked her gaze to his face. He'd deceived her?

Apology shone in his eyes, mixed with that pain from before. "It was wrong. I shouldn't have sneaked. I wish I had told you first. I can't tell you how many times that choice has haunted me. Especially since the next morning was when you went out in the blizzard to find Marcellus. The fear of losing you tore me apart, especially when I hadn't told you how much I love you."

Confusion churned inside her. Part of her wanted to jump to her feet, to step away from him until she knew for sure what he planned. But just as she'd trained herself not to react in front of the council, to wait and learn all the details before responding, she held herself still now.

"I hated that the last thing I'd done was an act that broke the trust you'd placed in me." His voice cracked and the sheen in his eyes illuminated the red lacing them. "I'm sorry, Brielle. Can you forgive me? I won't ever lie to you again, not for any reason. It's so —" his voice cracked again, but he continued, even as his words wobbled — "important that you trust me." He pressed his free hand to his chest as though it hurt as much as hers did.

Her own heart ached with the emotions

381

swirling. Could she accept his apology? Had he really told everything now?

She stood and walked a few steps away to give herself space to think. If they were to move forward, they would both have to commit to full truth. They would have to focus on rebuilding trust.

She spun to face him, working for the right words. He slowly stood, watching her, looking as if he were trying to decide what she wanted from him.

She met his gaze. "What did you find about the rock in the assembly room?"

His face turned grim. "It is pitchblende."

Her chest tightened. They were facing the worst, then. She lifted her chin and braced herself for him to continue his story. "What next? What happened after you found the mineral?"

"When I learned you were out in the blizzard, I did everything I could to be allowed to go look for you."

Audrey had said he was worried, but she'd not heard details. In truth, there'd not been much time to talk between her return and learning of Gerald's plot.

Evan nodded. "Audrey brought two men from the council for me to plead my case to. One was the taller man who'd come with your father the first time Gerald and I brawled."

"Erik?" Erik was responsible for maintaining the lawbook, and he tended to follow rules and edicts to the letter. He would not be likely to change a command the council had issued.

"I guess. He wouldn't be swayed."

She bit back a smile. "He usually can't be."

Evan's gaze grew earnest. "God showed me that my role in helping you was prayer. I spent the night interceding on your behalf. And Marcellus's. Then for your father and uncle and the other men who went out."

Again, his gaze shimmered, and the emotion in his words softened her fears a little. If he was focused on seeking God's will, on obeying Him even when it was hard, maybe she could trust his actions.

"God answered those prayers." Emotion caught in his voice. He eased out a long breath as he worked to gather himself.

Then a slight chuckle slipped out, and he shook his head as if he couldn't believe how the story was about to turn. "I was determined to tell you everything as soon as you came to my cell. But when Leonard and I were on our way back to that room, we stopped for him to see his brother-in-law, who had just returned from looking for you.

That was where I overheard Gerald's plan."

His shoulders sagged and his chin dipped, so he had to look at her through his upper lashes. "Again, I didn't know what to do. I was afraid if I told you what I'd heard, you would try to handle Gerald yourself . . . without help."

He straightened and leaned in with that same earnestness as before. "I'd sworn to myself I would be your protector, Brielle. You're so strong and brave and capable. But everyone needs someone standing at their back, shoring up the vulnerable parts. I want to be that person for you. I want to support you and be there when you need me."

The burn of tears stung her eyes, and it was all she could do to press the moisture back. How could he understand her better than she understood herself? The picture he painted called to her.

He inhaled a deep breath. "So, I turned to the only other man I could trust with your safety. Your father." He eased out a breath, finally finished speaking. After all, she knew the rest.

Her mind spun as she thought through everything he'd said. She refocused on him as he studied her. He seemed to be waiting for her to speak.

She took a deep breath and worked to sort through her churning thoughts. "It hurt that you didn't come to me first about Gerald. But I understand now why you didn't. I need you to trust me, though. Just like I want to trust you." She swallowed as she prepared for the next part. Was she really going to say this? She had to. For both of them.

"I love you, too, Evan. Even though saying that scares me. I want you to know you can tell me anything and not fear my reaction. I suppose that means the opposite has to be true, as well. Which is why I need to ask what you plan to do next."

She held her breath as she waited.

Evan's brow still furrowed, his expression a mixture of earnestness and tenderness. He took a step toward her, then stopped. "The selfish part of me still wants to do the same thing. Go find another mountain that contains pitchblende, then take some back and sign off on my mission, resign from the army, and return to you. If you'll have me."

Her breath caught at the words. Would she have him? Could she trust him? She pressed her eyes shut. *Lord, is this right? Is this your will?* The angst in her spirit eased, and a peace settled over her, almost like the Lord's arms wrapping around her in a hug.

She breathed in the sweet scent of His presence, then opened her eyes. A haze clouded her vision, but in the midst of it stood the man whose presence made her heart leap.

He stood a few steps away, hands by his sides, fingers spread, as though open to her. The look on his face caught her breath. His expression so vulnerable, his eyes revealing hope . . . and love.

She took a step forward. Then another. When her feet brought her within arm's reach, she stopped. "No more secrets?"

He shook his head. "No secrets. Ask me anything."

A new swarm of emotions welled inside her. This time love overrode everything else. If they could both commit to truth and seek the Lord's guidance for each step of their path, this love between them could grow into something wonderful.

She took the final step forward and he wrapped his arms around her, cradling her tight against him. She breathed in the rich scent of him. Breathed in the love surrounding her.

If only she could sit and soak in his love for hours, but they needed to make a plan. His country needed him. With her cheek still pressed to his shoulder, she asked a question that no longer scared her like before. "What would happen if you told your superiors about the pitchblende in our caves?"

His arms tensed and his voice grew tighter. "They would send miners and scientists. They'll need a great deal of the mineral. My guess is they would destroy the comfortable homes you've developed. But when the war is won, I'll request they send people back to help rebuild. I don't know if they will or not, but I promised your father that no matter what, I would work as long as I had to in order to return Laurent to its former glory."

His words sent a sliver of shock through her, and she straightened, pulling away far enough to look in his face. "My father? You spoke of this to him?"

Evan nodded, his eyes pleading for forgiveness. "I told him everything when I shared Gerald's plan. I knew he wouldn't believe me unless I gave all the details."

Relief slid through her. Now she didn't have to be the one to break the hard news.

"I also asked for his permission to speak to you of my love."

Another shock rippled through her as she lifted her gaze back to his. The grin on his face was almost boyish and a little shy. She couldn't help a smile herself. "You're full of surprises."

From the light dancing in his eyes, Papa's response must have been encouraging. A surge of warmth for her father slid through her.

"Don't you want to know what he said?"

She pressed her lips together to rein in her smile. "I hope he said to ask me yourself. God blessed me with a good mind and sound judgment, and He expects me to use them."

A chuckle slipped out from the man she loved. "Those were almost exactly his words."

She nodded. "My father's a wise man." She paused for effect before adding, "I expect the same from the man I marry."

Evan's gaze slid over her, his eyes darkening to a delicious look that warmed her blood. "I'll do my very best, my lady warrior."

Then he leaned close and captured her mouth with his. This man she'd never thought she'd find . . . this love she'd never dared hope for . . . both were better than she'd ever imagined possible.

32

Evan sent a final glance around the small living quarters to make sure he was leaving the place in decent order. Brielle's Uncle Carter had been kind to share his chambers during Evan's first night as a free man in Laurent. It wouldn't have been proper for him to stay with Brielle's immediate family.

Uncle Carter seemed amiable, much more than when Evan had first seen the man after Brielle returned from the blizzard. Perhaps the events since then — or maybe a word from Chief Durand — had softened his concerns about Evan.

Even with his friendliness now, the man still didn't seem to require many words. They'd spent most of the evening in Brielle's home, then Evan and Uncle Carter had followed the dim hallway, weaving their way through the metal shop to Carter's small room in the back. When morning light filtered through the window to awaken

Evan, the man had already left for the council's meeting.

As Evan walked through the metalwork shop now, he took the opportunity to see the place in better lighting. An assortment of metal pieces hung around the room, most with intricate scrollwork and leaf patterns. Even serving ladles and pots contained Durand's signature marks.

The man created nothing commonplace . . . only the exquisite.

Evan couldn't help a grin as that line of thought progressed. Durand had achieved the same level of perfection in his oldest daughter.

A work area against one wall caught Evan's eye, and he stepped nearer. The sketch he'd made of the cookstove lay on a small table, and large metal panels leaned against the wall. These must be the side panels for the unit.

The man had made excellent progress, and his notes on Evan's simple sketch showed a level of detail that shouldn't surprise him by now. A few of the scribbled comments mentioned ornamentations he planned in certain spots.

No wonder Brielle was so talented and had achieved so much in her field. Being raised by such an equally talented father must have taught her the work ethic and passion to pursue her dreams with excellence.

The sound of a footstep in the hallway grabbed Evan's focus, and he spun that direction as Andre pushed the door open.

The lad paused to suck in a breath and flashed a wide grin. "The council just finished meeting. Papa said you should come hear the news."

Though a bit of apprehension knotted Evan's stomach, Andre's grin was too infectious not to return. He strode toward the lad. "Lead the way."

They passed a woman and toddler on the way to the Durand home, and she greeted the two of them with a pleasant nod. No hint of suspicion or fear in her eyes. How wonderful it would be to live as part of this tight-knit community. To be fully accepted as one of them.

When Andre charged through the rear entry of his quarters, the rest of Brielle's family was already waiting there, sitting in casual conversation around the cook fire. Even Uncle Carter had joined the group.

Brielle greeted him with a sweet smile, her eyes saying all the things that stirred his heart into a faster rhythm. As he settled into the seat beside her, she reached to take his hand. The gesture wasn't showy, but neither did she attempt to hide the tender touch.

A glance at her father showed the man watching them. His mouth held a firm line, but his eyes glimmered with an amused twinkle. When Evan and Brielle had returned from their walk the evening before, they'd shared with her family that — if the council allowed him to return to the states for a short time to settle his affairs — he would return to Laurent and court her.

They'd made no mention of his mission or pitchblende, but Evan had found a quick moment to pull Chief Durand to the side and ask for permission to speak with him and Brielle together today. He intended to ask the two of them what they would like him to do regarding the pitchblende. He couldn't bring himself to initiate the destruction of their homes.

Now, the chief straightened and cast his glance around the group. "The council decided much this morning. Because we were in agreement — for once — on the main topics, the discussion moved quickly."

Durand's voice grew stronger. "Because Gerald was raised in Laurent, and his treasonous actions were against our own people, we agreed the entire community should determine his fate. A vote will be cast among all men and women of age. The people will choose whether he receives severe punishment, exile, or death."

Evan tightened his hand around Brielle's. Even exile seemed much too risky. Already, Gerald's actions had proven him vindictive. Brielle spent so much time outside the village walls, he would have an easy time of attacking her in the wilderness.

Evan met Durand's gaze. "Sir, do you feel the people will make a wise judgment? A decision that will keep Brielle safe?" Maybe he shouldn't have called out her name specifically, and the glare Brielle sent him showed exactly how she felt about his doing so. But he couldn't take her protection lightly.

Her father's nod came slowly as he thought through his answer. "Gerald has few friends in Laurent. Probably none who will stand by his side after his heinous actions. Our people have always worked together as a united group to ensure our safety. I trust my neighbors in this." His final words came with strength and surety.

Evan inhaled a deep breath, then eased it out. If he was to become part of Laurent, he would have to learn to trust these people, too. And if the outcome of the vote left him any concern for Brielle's safety, the two of them would have to work through precautions together.

"We also discussed Hugo." Durand's voice broke through Evan's thoughts. "We'll be assigning him a mandatory apprenticeship to learn a trade. We've asked Monsieur Trivet to take him under his wing and teach him a skill where he can contribute to the good of Laurent. They'll also be taking part in daily Bible studies. And each of the council members will be spending time with the lad each month. We feel Hugo is not so set in his slothful ways that renewed focus and purpose can't guide him into a better path. The path the Lord has planned for him."

Evan nodded. A wise choice, probably. Every boy needed a man of strong character to guide him, and it sounded like this community who cared so deeply for their own would unite to help guide Hugo.

Durand's gaze settled on Evan again, and his intensity deepened. "We also discussed the pitchblende America needs to end the war with England."

Evan's body stiffened. Durand told the entire council? Evan hadn't asked the man to keep it to himself, but he'd told him of his own oath of secrecy.

The older man's gaze softened. "We have

an idea about how to help the Americans while lessening the effects on our homes. You take the pitchblende samples back to your government and tell them what you found. Have them gather their men and come to us.

"In the meantime, we'll begin making some long-planned additions to our homes within the mountain. We had already intended to cut deeper into the mountain, and this winter will be a good time to do that. Show us exactly what this mineral looks like, and we'll gather as much of it as we can find during our labors."

A smile slipped into the man's gaze. "As our families continue to grow, we need more rooms. Some of our newlyweds would like their own space, I'm sure."

Evan couldn't help a grin at the insinuation, and he squeezed Brielle's hand as he glanced at her. A pretty blush had spread into her cheeks, and if they'd been alone, he would've leaned over and kissed that pinking.

But then the full import of Durand's words slammed into him. Laurent was offering to do some of the hard work themselves. "Are you certain? That will require a great deal of effort."

Durand gave a single decisive nod. "It's

the best way to ensure the safety of our people and homes. And we wish to help this America that managed to gain its freedom from the English. We feel something of a kinship with your people." The corners of his mouth tipped with his words.

"When your people come, we can help them cut whatever more of the mineral is needed to ensure their victory. That way, we can also ensure our homes are protected. Since the winter months are quiet, with the days short and dark, our young men grow restless. This will give them a way to use their energies and keep their bodies strong."

Evan's mind worked through each of his arguments. He'd never imagined Laurent would have a plan to ensure the safety of their village while yet helping him accomplish his mission. He'd never expected they'd be willing to offer of themselves. This truly was an amazing community. Only God could have orchestrated their plans to expand deeper into the mountain during this exact time when the mineral would need to be harvested. He sent up another prayer of thanks.

At last, he raised his gaze back to the chief of Laurent. "I can't find anything more to question. All I can say is thank you."

With their help, he could complete his

mission and return to Brielle so much more quickly. His throat clogged with the depth of joy washing through him. He honed his focus on her father's face, letting him see the earnestness in Evan's next words. "I thank you a great deal. For everything."

As he spoke, he stroked the top of Brielle's hand with his thumb, letting her know that by *everything*, he meant *her*.

EPILOGUE

Brielle's heart was fuller than seemed possible. How could it be that less than a month before, she'd first laid eyes on this man in nearly this exact spot? It felt as though she'd known him her entire life.

She was a different person now, better for knowing him and his love. Stronger standing beside him, with his strength shoring up her weak places. His prayers gave her more understanding of their heavenly Father.

Evan paused as they walked side by side, hand in hand down the path outside Laurent's gate. As he turned to her, a weight of emotion clogged her chest.

Not yet. It couldn't be time to say goodbye yet.

His eyes shone with as much emotion as she felt. He cleared his throat. "I wish I didn't have to leave so soon, but my superiors expect me back by the end of the year. I'll return as soon as I can. Four months at the most, less if I can manage it."

She nodded, but the burn rising up her throat and stinging her eyes wouldn't let her speak.

He lifted her hands and pressed a kiss to first one glove, then the other. Then his eyes found hers again. "Is there anything you'd like me to bring you back?"

You. Only you. Her heart cried the words, but if she tried to speak them aloud, she would lose the fingernail grip she had on her emotions. Instead, she shook her head. She wanted nothing to slow down his return. Things didn't matter. Only this man.

Evan pressed her hands flat on his chest and lowered his forehead to hers. "I love you. More than I can say." His voice roughened, but he pushed on. "I *will* come back to you. Wait for me. Please."

He didn't even have to ask. She would never stop waiting for him until he returned, even if that was until her very last breath.

He lowered his mouth to hers, a kiss so achingly sweet it shattered the last of her defenses. Tears streamed down her cheeks as she kissed him back, her hands gripping his shoulders. How could she let him go?

Lord, protect him. So many things might harm him on the journey, and she had control over none of it.

Only their Father did. Before, God had charged Evan with praying her to safety. Now would be her turn. *Prepare the way for him, Father. Station angels on every side to protect him. Bring him back safely to me.*

With the peace that settled over her, she eased back from the kiss and took Evan's face in her hands, so he would have no choice but to see her heart in her gaze. "I love you, too. And I'll be praying without ceasing for your safe return. There is one thing I'd like you to bring back, but please make sure it doesn't slow your return."

A tear glimmered in one of his eyes to match those still flowing down her face. "Anything." The husky timbre of his voice nearly made her lose control again.

She swallowed down the new surge of emotion and smiled. "A wedding ring."

His grin was slow in coming, but the joy spread across his face like a spring sunrise after a long cold winter.

He dove in for another kiss, this one not the tender caress of moments before, but a heart-throbbing, blood-rushing promise of much more to come.

When he pulled back, he was laughing. A laugh that bubbled inside her to form an image she would cling to in the months to come.

He locked her gaze with his, his eyes making a solemn vow. "I will. No matter what. And I have a feeling my life with you, Lady Warrior, will never lack adventure." He leaned in and brushed his lips against the tip of her nose. "And I can't wait for it to start."

ABOUT THE AUTHOR

USA Today bestselling author **Misty M. Beller** writes romantic mountain stories set on the 1800s frontier and woven with the truth of God's love. She was raised on a farm in South Carolina, so her Southern roots run deep. Growing up, her family was close, and they continue to maintain those ties today. Her husband and children now add another dimension to her life, keeping her both grounded and crazy. God has placed a desire in Misty's heart to combine her love for Christian fiction and the simpler ranch life, writing historical novels that display God's abundant love through the twists and turns in the lives of her characters. Learn more and see Misty's other books at www.MistyMBeller.com.

The employees of Thorndike Press hope you have enjoyed this Large Print book. All our Thorndike, Wheeler, and Kennebec Large Print titles are designed for easy reading, and all our books are made to last. Other Thorndike Press Large Print books are available at your library, through selected bookstores, or directly from us.

For information about titles, please call:
(800) 223-1244

or visit our website at:
gale.com/thorndike

To share your comments, please write:
Publisher
Thorndike Press
10 Water St., Suite 310
Waterville, ME 04901